PRAISE FOR THE 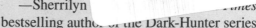 SERIES

"Dark and clever full moon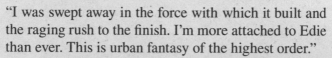
blood, crawl under your ski
—Sherrilyn ...mes
bestselling autho. of the Dark-Hunter series

"I was swept away in the force with which it built and the raging rush to the finish. I'm more attached to Edie than ever. This is urban fantasy of the highest order."
—Angie-ville

"An innovative read that offers a whole new look at paranormal creatures and the humans who happen to live in their world. Readers are sure to enjoy this book, and will be eager to see what awaits Edie next."
—*RT Book Reviews*

"I enjoyed every bit of this book. The Edie Spence series is for sure one of the best UF books around."
—Under the Covers

"Immense fun with incredible world building. Alexander adds wonderful new facets to old myths and legends and a completely new spin on everything."
—Fangs for the Fantasy

"Steamy and entertaining . . . Edie's growing personality—and the cliffhanger ending—will keep fans hooked."
—*Publishers Weekly*

"Full of action, fantastic characters, and situations that will make you want to kick some bad guys where it counts."
—Urban Fantasy Investigations

"The story is richly detailed, the plot is complex, and Edie Spence is absolutely delightful. A winning blend that's not to be missed."   —Rabid Reads

"*Moonshifted* is even better than the first. There was more action, more snarkiness, and even more sexiness. I can't wait to read more from Alexander and more about Edie Spence."   —Book Sake

"The best debut I've read all year. *Nightshifted* is simply amazing!"

> —Kat Richardson, bestselling author
> of the Greywalker series

"Edie Spence has a distinctive, appealing, and no-nonsense style that you won't quickly forget. Add to that a paranormal population that needs medical care for some very odd reasons, and you have a winner of a debut novel."

> —Kate Elliott, author of the Cold Magic series

"Fresh, exciting, dark, and sexy, *Nightshifted* is excellent urban fantasy that grabs you by the throat and pulls you along for a wild ride. Cassie Alexander is an author to watch!"

> —Diana Rowland, author of *Mark of the Demon*

"A fast, sexy return to the utterly unique world of Edie Spence. *Moonshifted* takes the world Cassie Alexander presented in *Nightshifted* and adds a whole new level of danger and intrigue. Absolutely recommended."

> —Seanan McGuire, award-winning
> author of *Ashes of Honor*

"Alexander's first novel launches a new series that should appeal to fans of medical thrillers as well as urban fantasy." —*Library Journal*

"*Nightshifted* is like a dark and twisted version of *Grey's Anatomy* with vampires, zombies, and werewolves taking up residence in County Hospital's Y4 wing . . . The story moves at a similar pace to a hospital setting where there are small lulls in action and sudden, even frantic, bursts of action. That sort of pacing made *Nightshifted* an exciting read as I was constantly on edge, waiting to see what was going to happen next." —All Things Urban Fantasy

"I loved this book. What a breath of fresh air! A very strong start to what promises to be a wonderful new series!" —My Bookish Ways

"*Nightshifted* brought me back to *ER* with the added fun of paranormal creatures . . . Because it is a fresh voice and premise among the crowded shelves of Urban Fantasy, I eagerly anticipate what's in store next for Edie and her colleagues."
—Clear Eyes, Full Shelves

"Alexander has created a wonderful world of paranormal that we don't usually get to see. Edie Spence is so wonderfully human in a world of ghost CD players, vampires, zombies, weres, shifters, and crappy paychecks. Read this book and you will be swooning (I promise), yelling, and laughing, all at the same time. A must-read indeed!"
—Bodice Rippers, Femme Fatales and Fantasy

Also by
Cassie Alexander

Nightshifted
Moonshifted
Shapeshifted
Deadshifted

BLOODSHIFTED

CASSIE ALEXANDER

St. Martin's Paperbacks

NOTE: If you purchased this book without a cover you should be aware that this book is stolen property. It was reported as "unsold and destroyed" to the publisher, and neither the author nor the publisher has received any payment for this "stripped book."

This is a work of fiction. All of the characters, organizations, and events portrayed in this novel are either products of the author's imagination or are used fictitiously.

BLOODSHIFTED

Copyright © 2014 by Erin Cashier.

All rights reserved.

For information address St. Martin's Press, 175 Fifth Avenue, New York, NY 10010.

ISBN: 978-1-250-03795-4

Printed in the United States of America

St. Martin's Paperbacks edition / July 2014

St. Martin's Paperbacks are published by St. Martin's Press, 175 Fifth Avenue, New York, NY 10010.

10 9 8 7 6 5 4 3 2 1

In honor of Elin S. Miller

ACKNOWLEDGMENTS

It's been a long ride, hasn't it? And yet there's still a little further left to go. I need to acknowledge, as always, my husband Paul, whose support means more to me each passing day—I could not have written this book without him. And my alpha reader, Daniel, whose encouragement has always kept me on my toes and pressing on. I'd like to thank Rose Hilliard, my editor, who makes all of my books vastly better than they would have been otherwise, and Michelle Brower, my agent, without whom I would have no books out at all.

Other people I owe a debt of gratitude for being patient with me while I paced, stared off into space, or who listened to me figure things out on GChat or Twitter are: Rachel Swirsky, Barry Deutsch, Cory Skerry, Sam Schreiber, Deirdre Saoirse Moen, and Brittany Maresh.

After five books, my real-life friends deserve another round: Violet, Char, Jocelyn, Marra, Melissa, Corinna, thanks for listening and caring and giving me a life to have outside of books and writing.

And last but in no way least—the girls on my shift deserve one last shout-out. Nightshift rules, dayshift drools. I love you all.

CHAPTER ONE

We were alive.

It didn't matter that I was blindfolded and being kidnapped by vampires, as long as my child and I were still alive.

Right?

We just have to get through the next eight months, baby. The car I was sitting in shifted gears. I felt it speed up and knew each mile was carrying me farther away from everything I knew and everyone I loved. My past was spooling out behind me like a ribbon and I didn't know if I'd be able to catch the end of it before it ran out.

If Anna was smart, she'd made Asher go back with her on the next flight home. I imagined him looking out a plane window at the same blackness I saw inside my blindfold, wondering if he'd done all he could, if there'd been another way. I wanted to touch him again so badly I ached.

I reached up for the necklace he'd given me instead. The vampire sitting beside me growled in warning, and I carefully set my hand back down.

Eight months was longer than Asher and I'd even been dating. But when I'd found out I was pregnant everything felt right—up until the cruise ship we'd been on had been taken over by a madman who'd released a parasite designed to ensure the death of everyone on board.

We'd had to fight for our lives, and I'd gotten infected. By the time our life raft was found, I was dying. Asher and I had already watched the parasite take down an entire ship, so we knew there was no cure. Except for vampire blood, the supernatural cure-all. Anna had called in a long-distance favor to save me and the other survivors when she realized she'd never make it across country in time. Unfortunately, the vampire blood came with an actual vampire, Raven, and had the side effect of binding me to him forever afterward, completely under his control, like a chained dog.

Which was why I was currently racing away from Asher and the dream of our future life—because now, not that long after treating daytimers back at floor Y4, I'd been forced to become one.

My job was to get through my pregnancy in one piece. Once I had the baby it would be safe for Anna to change me into a vampire too. Then I'd be free of Raven, and back with Asher. I just had to make it eight more months. I didn't know how I would manage to be a wife or a mother as a vampire afterward, but I'd be free, and it would be enough. When I was back with Asher, we could work everything else out somehow. I had to believe we could—because eight months being enslaved to a strange vampire without thinking I had a semblance of a life to go back to would kill me.

I slid my arms across my stomach to hug myself, and my right hand found the cool metal of the seat-belt buckle.

"You can't escape." A fact, stated by my now-Master, Raven. He was driving, and his accomplice Wolf was sitting beside me in the backseat. I kept my hand on the buckle in a small act of defiance. But the truth was that if he ordered me to let go of it, I'd have to. Or if he told me to open the door and throw myself out onto the open road, I'd have to do that too. I'd survive it—Anna had told me I'd be almost invulnerable for a time, as Raven had given me so much blood to heal me that he'd taken me to the edge of turning me himself, enough to give me the beginnings of fangs—but it would still probably hurt.

I'd been hurting for so long that being well now was strange. My last days on the *Maraschino* had been punctuated by pain—morning sickness, a black eye, a dislocated shoulder, the parasitic infection that'd taken most of the other cruise passengers' lives, then being stranded on a life raft for days with no water or food. It was ironic to finally feel whole just as everything in my life was becoming irrevocably fucked.

By now my family would know that the *Maraschino* had sunk with everyone on board. There'd never be any safe way to explain what had happened and how I'd survived, much less the vampire blood thing. It would be kinder to just let them think I was dead, and that was an ache not even blood could fix.

Thinking about my mom, that she wouldn't ever get to meet her grandson—the velvet bag Wolf had blindfolded me with suddenly felt too tight. My heartbeat sped up before I could control it and I knew the vampires would know—

Cold fingers pressed against mine on the buckle. Apparently my captors weren't convinced I wouldn't try something stupid. Maybe they knew me better than I did. Wolf chuckled as he pried my fingers off. He ran his hand underneath the sash across my chest, yanking it tight, touching far too much of me along the way. "Safety first," he warned sarcastically.

I stayed absolutely still, like a rabbit when a hawk passes overhead. He noticed that too, and I could feel the contour of the seat beside me shift as he leaned even nearer.

"Stay scared," he whispered. "Servants last longer when they're scared."

I twisted my head away from him and toward the window. He laughed as though he'd just made the most amazing joke—and I realized he was laughing at me. The ice of my fear dissipated, thawed by my rising anger, and my heartbeat slowed, becoming deliberate.

If I died, it would kill Asher. I'd promised him I'd survive—that we both would. *Anything we have to do, baby, we'll do it.*

"Fear makes servants more eager to please, doesn't it, Wolf?" Raven chided from the front seat. His voice rumbled over both of us with power, giving me a chill.

"Yes, Sire," Wolf agreed, returning to his own side of the seat. I felt the car downshift and take a left-hand turn. I didn't know where were going but I knew for sure we'd be there by dawn.

* * *

Raven raced the night. I could feel us swoop around other cars on the road, taking turns at speed. I'd started off trying to memorize things, as if I could bread-crumb trail my way back to my old life, when I realized we were going in circles, probably more to make sure that we weren't being followed than to trick me. But we were slowing now, making turns more frequently—we'd reached civilization, wherever that was.

Then the car slowed drastically and descended, and I realized a parking garage belowground made sense for vampires. We wheeled sharply to the left and came to a precise stop as Raven hit the brakes and shifted into PARK.

"Home sweet home," Raven said. He got out of the car, slamming the door behind himself.

Wolf exited the vehicle as well. I sat still, waiting, until I was startled by a knock at the window to my right. "You can open up your own door."

I felt blindly for the door handle and opened it. I'd been sitting next to an unlocked door this whole time. Had they'd been hoping I'd run? How foolish had I been to not even try? But there was nowhere I could go that Raven couldn't find me—another one of the perks of being his daytimer. I fought not to grind my teeth.

You'd better grow up to be a really awesome person, baby. I got out of the car and stood beside it, and the blindfold was snatched off me.

Lank pieces of my own hair slapped my face. Being turned into a daytimer hadn't magically fixed my personal hygiene. I stank of sweat, and my clothes were crusted with salt water from my time at sea. I took in the dim room at a glance and saw I was right: we were in a subterranean garage. There were several expensively exotic cars in a row, and Raven was nowhere to be seen.

"He has business to attend to," Wolf informed me. I didn't know if I should grunt or nod—but I did know I didn't want to be alone here with him. I figured Raven wanted me alive to curry favor with Anna but I didn't know how much safety, if any, that personally guaranteed me.

"Are you sure?" He angled his head toward the hill we'd driven down, where I supposed the entrance to the garage was. "It's not too late for you to run."

And if I did, it wasn't too late for him to chase me down and hurt me. "You're not the first vampire to tell me that."

Years ago, right after I'd started working on Y4, a vampire named Dren had encouraged me to run so he could chase and kill me. I hadn't run then either. My life would have been much different—and probably a lot shorter—if I had. Wolf snorted when it became clear I wouldn't play his game, then turned and walked deeper into the garage. I curled my hands into fists at my sides and felt my short nails bruise my palms as I followed him in.

Wolf led us through a series of unmarked tunnels but I felt sure I'd be able to remember my way back to the garage. It was easy now as a daytimer to spot the subtle differences between the walls, things I might not have noticed before as a human—a small chunk of cement missing here, a chip in the unrelenting gray paint there.

The last leg of the hall opened wide like an entryway, ending in a half-open oak door with ancient-looking iron fastenings, and I could hear a quiet conversation taking place inside the room ahead of us.

"Is she a spy?" a feminine voice asked.

"She's no concern of yours, only mine," I heard Raven say with a note of warning. The conversation immediately stilled as Wolf led me in.

Raven was in the center of the room, lounging on a backless couch covered in folds of deep purple satin. With his shining black clothing and black hair, the only parts of him that were easy to see were his elegant white hands and his pale face. His lips were pulled into a sneer, but there were dark circles around his closed eyes. Saving me had pained him. Good.

The room itself was huge and carved from stone with no paint. I couldn't see the ceiling above; the light from the naked bulbs strung up on the walls didn't travel that far. Given the cathedral-like nature of the room, and the presumable age of its occupants, I wouldn't have been surprised if there'd been torches illuminating us instead—and I realized that without Raven's vampire blood in me, I probably wouldn't have been able to see.

I took in the rest of the room at a glance. With the exception of one daytimer kneeling beside Raven's couch, everyone else remained standing. The vampires—two men and one woman—were spaced equidistant to one another as though they didn't trust anyone within arm's length. Wolf I'd already met; he looked like an old-school biker, with muttonchops and a beard, his face as grizzled as his leather vest. The other male vampire looked like an action hero, buff with a blond buzz cut, and the female vampire was dressed in night blue, with smooth waves of long copper hair giving her an old Hollywood look. There were two daytimers in a circle outside of that, ready to attend, a man and a woman, him in a vest and her in a dress, and they appeared to match their owners. I wondered if that was on purpose, or just how things worked out. It was easy to tell the vampires and their daytimers apart, as the vampires only looked at me once, taking all of me in, making up their minds about me in milliseconds, content to ignore me—or to pretend to ignore me—after that. But the daytimers weren't as good at hiding their surprise at having another person suddenly join their ranks. Two of them in particular wouldn't stop looking at me—the one whose vest matched Wolf's, and the one kneeling at Raven's side, who looked up at me with complete venom.

Everyone else in the room was wearing dark colors. In the last outfit I'd worn aboard the *Maraschino* before she sank, light T-shirt and jeans, I matched no one and stuck out like a sore thumb. And I realized none of the other people I'd last seen getting into a lifeboat on the *Maraschino* were here either. "Where are the rest of them?"

All of the vampires turned to eye me as one, and I gathered I'd spoken out of turn.

"The rest of the survivors. There were others. I heard you mention them." When I'd been leaving Asher and Anna, only hours ago.

A smile tickled the corners of Raven's mouth as though my concern were droll. "Other Houses. Not ours.

Anna wasn't incredibly particular about who saved you, only that you must be saved."

"Oh," I said, because it seemed like he was waiting for a response.

"Oh," he repeated, mocking me. Without taking his eyes off me, he addressed someone else. "Jackson, teach her manners, will you?"

The daytimer in a leather vest bowed deeply. "Of course, Master."

"Now then," Raven went on, addressing the kneeling man at the bottom of his couch. "With everyone come down here to gawk, who's minding upstairs, Lars?"

The kneeling daytimer's head dropped even lower. Would Raven expect me to grovel like that for him? I couldn't imagine myself doing it now, much less six months from now with a pregnant belly. "We closed early, Master," the kneeling man informed him. Raven's face fell into a look of profound disappointment as Lars went on. "I took the liberty of procuring a meal for you, Sire."

Raven reached down to pat Lars's head as though he were a particularly obedient dog, and I watched the man's shoulders tense. "Lars, when I need your help hunting, I'll ask for it—or I'll just drain you."

I could see the panic on the face of Raven's daytimer—his other daytimer, if you counted me. Raven's hand wound through Lars's hair as though considering options. The female vampire smirked to see such obvious fear, and then looked at Raven, one impish eyebrow quirked. "I'll eat your dessert if you don't want it, Sire." She had a slight French accent, which made her seem even more exotic.

Raven released Lars and stood. "As it turns out, I'm not in the mood to share tonight." He turned to pierce Lars with one last look of disappointment.

"I apologize, Master," Lars said, nodding eagerly now that he was free.

"Is there anything else of concern?" Raven asked, looking around. One by one, the rest of his vampires shook their heads. "Then we'll reconvene tomorrow night." He stood up fluidly and stalked out of the room via its only other door. The other vampires followed suit, and then it was just me and the rest of the daytimers left inside.

They stared at me, and I stared at them. I swallowed. *Eight months, baby. We can do this.* "Hi. My name is Edie."

CHAPTER TWO

Lars rocked up to his feet, turned, and left, after one more nasty look in my direction. The man next to me in the leather vest that matched Wolf's laughed. "I'm Jackson. Don't take that personally—" He jerked a thumb toward the slamming door. "He's just jealous of you is all. Getting so much blood."

Jackson had dark hair, a thick mustache, and soulful eyes. He looked like the poster of a young Burt Reynolds from the 1970s that my mom had had on the inside of her closet door when I was a child.

The woman in the room crossed her arms. "He's not the only one." She was beautiful, and she would have been without being a daytimer. She had honey-blond hair wrapped up in an expert chignon and was wearing a short black dress, with bright red lipstick—she could have been a girl in the background out of twenty different music videos from the 1980s. "Who the hell are you, and why did Raven save your life?"

That was a very good question. I didn't know his game yet, but I was sure there was one. He hadn't saved me out of the goodness of his heart—vampires didn't have hearts. Except for maybe Anna.

The female daytimer took two quick steps to cross the distance between us and stood in my way. "You know something. Tell us," she demanded. I had two inches on her, even though she was in her heels, but she probably had decades of being violent on me.

"Because Anna told him to?" It was the only answer I had. I didn't know if Anna's name would mean anything to them.

The female daytimer blinked, as if she hadn't heard me right. "Anna—the Beast? The Ravenous One?"

I nodded slowly. Anna's last words to me were a warning not to believe all the stories I'd hear about her. "Yeah."

Jackson let out a low whistle, and the woman looked aghast. It was hard not to feel a little worried—I was an entire continent away from her almost, and these people still knew her by name. By many names, apparently. What exactly had Anna been up to while I'd been out of her life?

"So—you're what to her, then?" The woman's head tilted, showing me the angle of her jaw.

This, I was smarter about sharing. "I don't know."

"You're a shitty liar, Edie," Jackson said. His tone wasn't unkind. In fact beneath his mustache he had the beginnings of a grin.

"I've been told that before," I said, giving him a hesitant smile back before looking around the room. "Where are we?"

Jackson answered me. "You're in the Catacombs.

The actual catacombs beneath the Catacombs, because we believe strongly in ironic names."

"And where is that, precisely?" I asked.

"You mean you don't know?" the female daytimer said.

"I was wearing a hood when they brought me here."

"The City of Angels. Los Angeles, California," Jackson said, drawing it out dramatically the same way that TV announcers on game shows said it, as if just by being here you'd already won a prize. I realized we weren't all that far from the docks where the *Maraschino* had taken off less than a week before.

Baby, I so hope Anna got your dad onto a plane.

"It's a popular nightclub—running it's an easy way to get fresh blood and money and other things, as our Masters desire," Jackson continued.

I assumed all the vampires had gone to bed for the day—I had a strange feeling in my gut that the sun was shining now outside. I took another look around the room. I'd had a lot of vampire blood, more recently than either of them—

Jackson shook his head as if he was reading my mind. "No use running. He'd only catch you when he woke up in the evening, and you can't even imagine what he'd do to you then."

Because of where I'd worked before, as a nurse for supernatural creatures on Y4 back home in Port Cavell, it actually wasn't so hard for me. That, plus I'd heard Raven say he technically only needed me to be alive to return to Anna after having my child.

Technically, to have a baby, you didn't need arms. Or legs.

I inhaled deeply and swallowed. "What do you all do during the daytime?" was the only potentially safe question I could think to ask.

Jackson gestured in a circle to include all of us. "What do *we* do, is the question you should be asking."

The woman checked a very expensive watch on her wrist. "I've got to get upstairs where there's reception. One of my girls is going to check in."

"Celine runs a prostitution ring," Jackson explained. I tensed before I could hide it.

Her lips pursed and she snorted. "Don't worry, it's high-class. By which I mean you wouldn't last a day." She turned and stalked out the door Lars had taken, deeper into the building. Jackson jerked his head at her, to indicate that we should follow.

"Lars, the daytimer from earlier, keeps the books and is a dealer," Jackson explained, holding the door open so we could pass into another tunnel set with more weak lights.

"Of?" I asked, because I honestly hoped it was something like cars, or blackjack.

Jackson chuckled, and it echoed. "Drugs. Have to keep the cattle happy, and it's easier when they're high."

I felt like I'd just walked onto the set of some impossibly strange film. Los Angeles after all. "And what do you do?" I asked him.

Jackson paused at the entrance to a side tunnel and gave me a mocking bow before walking up it. "I'm the handyman. Like my Master. Which is why it's my job to show you around."

* * *

Despite the fact that I could find my way back, I still felt lost trailing after Jackson. The farther we walked into the catacombs, the more distant the world I'd left felt.

"You'll learn the lay of the place. We've got the run of it during the day," he explained. "There's some places you don't want to go, though—I wouldn't go exploring solo if I were you." He stopped and shouted up the hall, "Hey, Celine!"

"What?" her irritated voice echoed back.

"I'm putting Edie in your room."

"No!"

"No choice. Otherwise she'll be sleeping in the hall."

"Put her with Natasha."

"If I put her with Natasha, she won't wake up again. She's with you."

If Celine was the lesser of two evils, I didn't want to know the greater one. Was he bunking me with her as punishment for her, or as a kindness to me? I probably wouldn't know for a while. I wanted to trust him, but I knew that was only because I was scared.

We went down another hall, and then reached an inset door, which he pushed open with one hand.

"This is it. Welcome home," he said, and stepped in.

Celine's room was about as big as Asher's living room, and done in a lot of dated black lacquer and chrome. I suspected she'd been turned into a daytimer sometime in the 1980s, back when this style was in vogue, and it'd frozen her sense of interior design along with the rest of her. A massive vanity stood along one wall, the lights around its edge the only illumination in the room. It was covered in makeup and bottles of perfume, and framed head shots of Celine, a testament to her past. Being a daytimer didn't completely suspend you in time the way becoming a vampire did, but it came close.

A Nagel painting, or forty, would not have been out of place in here, only it would have been hard to hang since all the walls were black-painted stone. The only thing on the wall was a bell contraption near the door.

"Sorry, she doesn't have much taste." Jackson looked out of place against her charmless décor, with his brown hair and leather vest over a black T-shirt. He started pushing a coffee table aside.

"Let me help." I moved over to pick up the opposite side of the table.

It was a thick wood piece—quality, even if ugly—and I easily hefted it. Almost into my own face. I yelped and nearly dropped it, then caught it in time. Fast. Too fast. I carefully set my end back on the ground, staring at my hands as if they belonged to someone else.

Jackson set his side down and grinned over at me. "It's pretty great, eh?"

I didn't know what to say to that. I didn't want to admit that it was. "Is this what being a daytimer is like? Being super-strong?" I thought I knew the rules, but I wanted to hear him say them, just in case.

He waved his hand indeterminately in front of him. "Yeah, for a while. Until the blood runs thin. You'll be strong, and quick, and able to hear quiet things, and you'll heal fast. You feel better, don't you? After as much blood as you got, you must."

I nodded slowly. My tongue touched the tiny pointed ends of my canines inside my mouth.

"The downside is now you're attached. Think of it like a psychic umbilical cord between you and him."

I pulled back. The image hit too close to home. Jackson went on, "You'll want what Raven wants, for at least as long as you're around him. You'll do what he tells you to do. He'll always be able to find you when he's awake at night." His smile faded into more of a grimace. "From here on out, it's his way or the highway, as they say. And if you do try the highway, well, God help you."

It wasn't hard to imagine Raven running me to ground. "How long does it last?"

"As much blood as I heard you got? You'll probably feel like Superman for a month."

"And after that?" I pressed.

He shrugged. "If you don't get more blood, you'll start to feel sick soon. You won't like it when your humanity comes back, with all its aches and pains. You'll start to age, and you wouldn't be supercharged anymore. But you'd still have to obey him, even after the good parts wear off. It's a devil's bargain—you make it once and you make it for life, either your lifetime or his. After a while without blood you'll feel like you took a drug, missed the high, and got only the shitty side effects."

I tried not to frown, but Jackson easily read my face.

"You're new. Everything'll take a while to get used to. Let's move this over there." He jerked his head toward a zebra-print rug on the floor. We picked up the coffee table together again, and I realized as we neared the rug it really was the skin of a zebra.

"Wow." I knelt down to pet it after we set the coffee table down.

"She can be a bit exotic."

I made a show of looking around the rest of the room. Her bed occupied most of it, looking like a four-poster throne, and I noticed the vanity mirror pointed toward it. Shining chrome bars joined all the posts at top, and curtains hung off these, along with several sets of handcuffs.

"You think?" I said, trying to sound as ironic as I could. If becoming a daytimer had stranded Celine in the 1980s, did that mean I was going to be frozen circa 2014?

Jackson clapped my back. "I think we're going to get along just fine, Edie."

It took all my strength not to nod in hope. He looked down at the floor where the coffee table had been. "Okay then. Let me go get you a cot," he said, and left the room.

I had that urge you get when you're alone at a stranger's place to go through all their stuff. But I didn't know when Celine would be back—and I noticed there weren't any locks on the door, which seemed odd. Jackson returned momentarily, carrying a cot, and unfolded it for me. It was covered in unfortunately placed stains.

"Sorry about that. There's sheets somewhere too, I'll find them. It's been a while since we had company."

"Thanks." I looked down at myself. I was still encrusted with sweat and salt from the sea. "Is there any clothing here?" I knew Celine and I weren't the same size since she was a foot shorter than I was.

"Yeah. You want to take a shower first?"

I did. If—and it was a big if—it was safe.

Jackson grunted at my hesitance. "You just got a pint or two of vampire blood. No one's going to be able to hurt you for a while, unless they manage to physically pull off your limbs."

All too easy to imagine—at least while the vampires were up. "Somehow that image doesn't help."

He snorted. "Sorry. I guess not. But you'll need to know where the bathroom is anyhow; you'll need to pee eventually. Come on, it's just down the hall."

The door to the bathroom looked just like the door to Celine's room, only I could smell the water behind it.

It was half prison bathroom, half horror movie. The toilets were inside stalls, all missing doors. Across from the toilets there was one long countertop with five sinks, and three showerheads at the far end, without any curtains. A row of lockers was tucked in between the showers and the sinks, but none of them had locks. The tile floor had divots leading to multiple drains—the easier to clean up bloodstains, I presumed.

"Classy," I said after taking it all in.

"Yep," Jackson agreed. "I'll go work on sheets and clothing. Everyone's busy now—it's a good time for you to shower, if you're going to. You can use my stuff—" He popped open a locker, revealing a shaving kit and a few bottles of toiletries. "If you go back to Celine's room smelling like her shampoo, she'll kill you in your sleep. We get decent water pressure, but it takes a while for the water to get hot," he said, and left.

I stared at the showers once I was alone. I was disgusting, the salt embedded in my clothing rasped at me, and I stank. But it was hard to feel comfortable showering anyplace it looked like a slasher film was about to break out in.

Then again—I stretched my hands out in front of me, remembering the strength I'd had when I'd lifted the coffee table. I'd never be safer here than I was right now, with Raven's blood fresh inside me.

Okay. Let's do this, baby.

I quickly stripped off all my clothing and cranked the water on.

Everything from Jackson's locker seemed to have a slight manly scent—and I wondered if that was true, or if it was just me now being more sensitive. In an effort not to wind up smelling like he was my boyfriend, I borrowed just a bar of soap, swiping it over myself and lathering it into my hair, trying to take the fastest shower I'd ever taken in my life.

I wasn't quite fast enough. Jackson came back in the room and walked past me, a stack of fabric in his arms.

I slammed the water off and picked up my clothes to cover myself with, quickly shoving my feet back into my tennis shoes.

"I thought you might need a towel," he said, coming back to me, holding one out. I took it from him and made an indelicate transfer while he looked away. The towel was a short one, and I was nervous when he looked back. I didn't care if he saw me, but I didn't want him to see my stomach, just in case. I knew I still had meat on my bones despite my recent starvation, and there was no way I was showing yet. But if Raven hadn't told anyone else about the baby and my subsequent ticket out of here in eight months, courtesy of Anna, I wouldn't volunteer it. Just thinking about it made me want to shelter my stomach with my hand.

"Do you all usually bring in your own curtains?" I stepped out of the shower and slunk over to the clothing he'd put by the sink.

"They aren't big on giving us any privacy." I could tell he said *They* with a capital *T.*

I folded the towel under my armpit and picked up the shirt he'd brought me. It looked two sizes too small. "I don't think this'll fit me."

"It will. It's mostly spandex," he said, and seeing my mouth open he cut me off. "Don't ask where it came from."

"Okay." I held it up in front of me and waited for him to go away.

He made a show of turning around, arms crossed. "We aren't big on privacy with each other either, just so you know."

"Duly noted." I pulled the shirt on quickly, over the towel, then held up the skirt. More spandex, ugh.

"Now's as good a time as any for me to tell you the house rules. First off, never speak to one of them until they ask you to. And then address them as *Sire* or *Madam.* Their names are not for you," he said, talking to the wall before him. I held the skirt open, stepped into it with my shoes on, and wrestled it up.

"Only tell them what they ask you to. They don't want to hear your stories, they don't care. Don't make excuses, and don't lie. Generally, they'll know, and then it's bad for you. Don't assume they can't hear you because when they're up, it's just safer to assume they can. Don't ask about where they sleep, you don't want to know. If you ever make one of them mad, bow and beg immediately for forgiveness. Pride will only get you killed."

I had my underwear in one hand, the towel in the other. I didn't want to put my old underwear back on, but I didn't want to ask him for a "new" set, not when I suspected they were off other people and I didn't have access to malathion. I tried to nonchalantly shove my current pair underneath my towel as he turned back around.

He took me in, black spandex much closer to Spanx, and pointed at the corner of my underwear peeking out with a head shake. "You'll learn not to have any shame soon enough. Shame only gives other people power over you."

I tucked my underwear in. "Does your Zen vampire philosophy come with a side of detergent?"

He snorted. "Nope. We use a laundry service." He walked toward the door and stopped to look back. "Any other questions?"

A thousand—and none. Where in LA were we? What would I do here? Celine had a phone—could I have one? Could I call home? Who paid for things? How?

But I didn't really need to know the answer to any of those yet. Without context the answers would be frustrating or overwhelming. I decided to ask the only easy one that I was genuinely curious about. "How often have you given this talk?"

"Too many times." He gave me a sad smile and opened up the door. "You've had a long few days, I'm sure. We get the news upstairs, the *Maraschino*'s sinking has been all over it. Why don't you take the rest of the day off and rest? I can finish the tour this evening. I'm sure you can find your way back to Celine's room."

I nodded, and he stepped outside.

I washed my underwear as best I could in the sink, and then wrung it out before folding it up in the towel and taking it and all my old clothes back to Celine's room. When I got there the door was open, and the room was empty. The lights were on, and I didn't see a light switch, but that was fine; I didn't want anyone sneaking up on me in the dark.

I walked across the room over to the mirrored vanity. Despite feeling healthy, I still looked wan—not even vampire blood could "fix" depression, I supposed. I hesitantly lifted my upper lip in a semblance of a smile. I didn't have the full vampire fang jack-o'-lantern thing yet, but my teeth were on their way. I frowned at myself and turned back to the rest of the room.

Jackson had stacked sheets on the cot, in a faded forest green. I folded them out carefully, so that only one side ever touched the old stains on the cot and I could lie on the cleaner opposite side.

I'd have to figure out how to get new clothes before I did start to show—I was bustier than my top's original owner, so there was a band of naked skin between shirt and the skirt, and the skirt was so tight it would probably show off the outline of whatever I ate next, like I was in an old-fashioned cartoon.

I looked around for someplace safe to set my underwear to dry, and thought for a dark moment about using the bars on Celine's bed like a clothesline. Staring at her bed, imagining her horror if she did come in to see my muted blue-floral cotton panties strung up by handcuffs, I crossed the room.

Her bed, the wood it was made out of, plus the chrome playset, had to weigh several hundred pounds. I listened carefully to determine whether I could hear anyone in the hall, and then bent down. I knew about body mechanics from moving patients at the hospital. I squatted, braced my back, set my shoulders into their sockets, put my hands underneath the bed frame, and—

"What are you doing?"

I let go and whirled. I'd been concentrating too hard—and I'd just gotten a lesson in how quiet another daytimer could be.

Celine was standing in the doorway, lips pulled into a frown, her dragon-red lipstick the only bright color on her.

"I—I was just looking around."

"Don't ever touch my things." She stalked over to the vanity to survey her belongings, in case I'd stolen some. Where would I have hidden them in this awful stupid outfit? I imagined her looking for her favorite bottle of perfume in my vagina. When she was done with her circuit she looked back at me critically. "You'd better lose that weight soon. If you're not careful, you'll get stuck with a muffin top for eternity."

"Thanks for the advice," I said drily. She didn't know I was pregnant, at least. Maybe if I ate a lot while I was here I could pretend to just be gaining weight, like those people on TV who didn't find out they were pregnant till they were hovering over a toilet.

Despite my shirt's high collar, the necklace Asher'd

given me popped out, its amethyst stone like the first volley from a Roman candle. Her eyes leapt on it like a cat. "Pretty."

I quickly tucked it back inside. "Thanks."

I stared at her, and she stared at me. I wasn't physically tired—or sore, or hungry, or thirsty, or any of the other thousand feelings I should have a right to be—but I was emotionally exhausted. So far, being a daytimer was like walking on knives. If couldn't be alone, then at least I'd like to close my eyes and keep to myself and pretend, even if that meant sleeping on a grungy cot without a pillow.

She kept staring. Daytimers must always win at the staring game—unless they were playing against vampires.

"I think this is the part where if we were in a Western the harmonica would start playing really fast," I said.

Her frown lessened by point zero zero zero one degree, and she snorted. "I'm going to get ready for bed now. Stay on your cot. I'll know if you get up, so don't, not even to pee. And if you snore I'll smother you in your sleep."

I nodded and, always keeping one eye on me, Celine walked to a black lacquer panel ornamented with carved fans and stepped behind it. Once she was hidden, she started taking her own clothing off.

I crawled into my bed, such as it was, my stupid skirt hitching up around my waist. I didn't want to keep watching for her, because I felt like some kind of voyeur, but not watching her felt dangerous, like turning your back on a dog known to bite. She must have felt the same way because she kept watching me, her eyes peeking over the panels until she took off her heels and bobbed down four inches, emerging immediately afterward in a simple black slip.

She crawled into her bed-palace, drew all of its curtains, and with a remote turned off the lights. I could tell she was still awake by the sound of her breathing—had vampire blood made my ears better too, taken them back to the pre-bass time of my youth? Or had it changed my brain somehow? How did it work? Now that I was a daytimer—and because the only daytimers we'd ever treated in Y4 had been ones who weren't getting enough vampire blood on their own, the sick ones on their way out who hadn't been chosen to change—I realized how much I didn't know about vampire physiology.

Her breathing was still distracted, and I heard the sound of her skin rubbing on her silk sheets as she turned, waiting for me to sleep first.

Maybe you can sleep for the both of us, baby, because I don't know how I'm going to.

It was going to be a really long eight months. I didn't have to enjoy it or make any friends—it would be like biding my time at any other shitty job, and it wouldn't be the first one I'd had. But I could do it. For the baby, and for Asher.

I concentrated on the thought of seeing him, trying to conjure him up out of the darkness in my mind. I thought about the house we shared and how my things seemed to fit just right after I moved in, and how much happier Minnie was with all the windowsills and sun.

If I thought hard enough on it I could imagine walking up to the door knowing Asher was already home, the fireplace roaring, see him sitting on the couch, reading a book, looking up as I walked in—

CHAPTER THREE

"Edie?"

He put the book down and stood up like he always did when I came home. I stopped in the doorway and covered my mouth with one hand.

Was this a dream? Or had everything that happened before just been a nightmare?

"Is it you?" I whispered, scared I'd break the bubble of this fragile reality.

A familiar smile creased his lips. "Who else would it be?"

I ran across the room to hug him, almost tackling him in the process.

"Hey now—" he began, defending himself while hugging me back.

I knew it couldn't be all the way real. But it was real enough. I could feel the muscles of his back, the heat of his body, smell the scent of his skin.

My hands ran up into his hair, pulling his face down so I could see him more clearly. He beamed down at me. If I wished and hoped and clicked my heels three times—I leaned up to kiss him and closed my eyes and—

Maybe if I hadn't had Raven's blood I wouldn't have noticed it. But the moment before our lips touched, after my eyes shut, when I was already replaying what was about to happen in my own mind to milk its full sweetness, because knowing what's about to come is almost as good as when it actually happens—I realized his eyes weren't right.

I pulled my head back, still holding his in place with my hands. He was beaming down at me, and the fireplace was reflected in his eyes, but there wasn't any of Asher's own light.

I shoved him away, and the thing that looked like Asher but wasn't released me. "Who are you?"

He tilted his head to the side. The gesture was still Asher's, but the longer I looked into the eyes the more wrong they became.

"How did you know?" he asked, taking a step toward me.

"Stop that." I gestured wildly at him, and around the room we were in. "Stop all of this. If it isn't real—or at least really from me—stop pretending."

"I thought you would appreciate the familiar surroundings."

I did. Oh, God, I did. "This place is mine. You have no right to be here. Stop it."

Asher's living room shimmered and blurred, as if I were looking at it from a great height. "What would you like to see instead?" he asked.

I shook my head strongly. "Nothing. No more games. Who are you? And why did you try to trick me?"

"I thought it would be easier to talk to you if I appeared like this." He gestured to himself, Asher's form that he wore like a suit.

My eyes narrowed, even in my dream. "What are you?"

"A vampire."

"How are you awake during the day?"

"I'm not awake. When I sleep, I can walk from dream to dream."

"Which one of them are you?"

"No one that you've met yet." He took a step toward me. "I am a prisoner here, just like you."

"Why?" I demanded.

He grinned just like Asher did, a little rogue. "Why were you imprisoned here? Bad luck, cruel whimsy? It doesn't matter why—only that we both long to be free." He reached a hand out. "If you can find me, I can free us both."

I crossed my arms. Whatever he was, he was dangerous. I already had a plan; all I had to do was stay alive.

"Do you really think it will be that simple?" he asked, which was when I realized he was in my head. It made sense, all the familiarity and the dreams, but it made his intrusion more violating. I took another step away from him, nearer the blurry glow of the fireplace. "I can only read surface thoughts—only what you're thinking now."

"I'm thinking I don't need your help—"

"But you do. And I need you—to find me and free me," he said, with Asher's face, even as his voice was changing to someone else's. "I'm the only one who can get you out of here alive."

I shook my head, refusing him—whatever *he* was—when his face became stern and frightening. A shock of cold fear raced through me as he lunged in and I screamed, diving backward into the fireplace's imaginary flames.

I went rolling across the cold rugless ground in Celine's room. Only we weren't alone anymore and there was a sharp metallic sound as something hard hit the cot I'd been sleeping on. I heard the metal of the cot's frame bend and break, and even in the dark I had no doubt if I'd still been in it, I would have died.

CHAPTER FOUR

Celine had to know she'd missed. I crouched down, trying to make myself a smaller target, reacting on instinct. Everything in my body narrowed, condensing, focused—maybe the blackness helped—and I calmed down until I couldn't even hear myself breathe.

I heard Celine take a step and there was no time for thought. If I waited, I might lose her in the darkness. I took a hunched leap to where I'd heard her and then swept up to standing, hopefully inside the range of any weapon she had. I grabbed her bodily and took her to the floor, and heard her weapon clatter away, part of my mind registering where it landed for later—when I realized I wasn't fighting a she; there were huge muscles underneath the cotton in my hands. The man I was wrestling with took advantage of my half second of surprise and grabbed me, whirling me down, and I knew he was trying to hold me against the stone while reaching out for the weapon he'd dropped.

I punched him with my free hand, in the chest exposed below his reaching arm, and was horrified to feel ribs break. The man groaned but didn't stop reaching. I knew I couldn't take the chance of him grabbing it, whatever it was—I punched again, and the same ribs that I'd just broken cracked fresh under my fist.

I wasn't the only one who was at least a little invulnerable. I punched again, and again in the same spot, remembering when I'd watched Lucas's hand pierce a werewolf's chest with his own supernatural strength. With each blow I could feel the man shudder over me as if he'd been shot, but he didn't let go of me or guard himself; he just kept straining out. It made me even more afraid of him reaching the weapon—whatever it was had to be bad.

Our stalemate couldn't last forever—and I'd rather it ended on my terms than his. I used the force of one more punch and the leveraging of a leg to get him up and hurl him away from me, and from the thing he was reaching for, and then I went for it. I grabbed a handle, snatched it up, and fell into another soundless crouch. My feet were on top of the zebra skin now. I instantly knew where in the room I was, and from the feel of the handle and the weight of one end, the thing I was holding was a hammer.

My eyes widened in the dark. A hammer wasn't a joke. Whoever I was fighting had meant to kill me. And if I died, so would my baby. My first instinct was to scream, and I bit my lips to keep it back. I was supposed to have eight months and then get home safe, not be murdered on my first day here. It wasn't fair—but nothing had been fair for a while now, had it? My baby and I still weren't safe.

Something cold and angry flowed through my veins. I felt as though a tap had been turned on inside myself;

it had that feeling you get after certain shots or drugs, where your body knows that what is entering isn't right. It felt like liquid death—like I imagined embalming fluid would feel if someone held me down and plugged it into my carotids. I forced myself to breathe in and out silently and listened with ears that were eerily good for my attacker. I was standing between him and the door, and he had to know that I had the hammer—he was probably trying to figure out if I was willing to use it.

Half of me was. I could see myself cracking his skull like an eggshell, and while the thought of his brains spilling out made part of me recoil in disgust, this new dark part of me was completely fine with him getting what he deserved. I shivered in the darkness, trying not to listen to it.

A true daytimer wouldn't think twice about mayhem, and neither did this new part of me. I could feel muscles bunching up without thought, as half of me readied like a hunting cat.

But I wasn't one of them yet, and I didn't even want to be one. I hadn't gotten a choice in being changed—and I didn't want anyone's brains on my hands. Maybe I'd feel differently later, or I'd invest in gloves, but not today.

I took the hammer in both hands and snapped the head of it off at the top of the handle before I could do anything else.

The man ran past me at the sound, rushing for the door. I swung the shaft of the hammer up like a club, catching him in his chest and taking him down to the ground on instinct, and then, holding the head of the hammer in my hand like a roll of quarters, I knelt down and punched his stomach, hard. I felt the infirmity of flesh as he gasped, all the air knocked out of him.

Just because I didn't want to kill him didn't mean I wanted him to escape.

I knew whatever advantage I had could be temporary, so I didn't stop. I was scared to set him free until I found out who he was and why he'd attacked me. He tried to leverage his legs up, and I swung the shaft out to the side, punching at this new target as hard as I could without thought, catching him simultaneously hearing and feeling his nearest femur snap. Oh, God—

He exhaled in a rush of pain, and then gasped, "Mercy!"

A ploy to gain time to heal? I didn't want to hit him a second time—but would he fight me again if I didn't keep breaking things? He'd tried to kill me—and my baby. I let the darkness do what it wanted to in me and swatted the hammer's handle down again, smashing the same spot on his leg between the hard wood and the stone floor, hearing a fresh crack.

"Mercy!" he grunted.

The obvious pain in his voice brought me back from the brink. This wasn't me. I couldn't torture someone who'd already surrendered. Taking in a shuddering breath, I lowered the handle to the ground. "Jackson!" I howled—hoping that the person I was using as a punching bag wasn't him.

The light came on in the room, momentarily blinding me. My opponent was blinded too, lying in front of me, leg mangled but healing. It was Lars. Celine—present for the whole fight, ensconced on her bed—finally intervened.

"Why did you attack me?" I shouted down at him. I could see his loose leg pulling into place, the bone resetting. "Why?" I shouted at the top of my lungs. Soon he'd be better and I'd have to make a horrible choice—

"Edie!" came a new voice. I whirled, and Jackson was in the doorway. "Calm down. You're safe."

"No I'm not! He attacked me!" I clutched the fist with the hammerhead in it to my chest.

"You're winning. You've won." Jackson patted the air between us to calm me as if I were a wild horse.

"But he tried to kill me! Why?"

Jackson spared Lars a dark look. "He fought you because he thought he had to. Because he's a fool."

Time slowed back down as I did, and I realized my entire fight with Lars had taken thirty seconds. A minute, tops. I looked down at Lars, his leg slowly becoming whole, and looked at Jackson to watch his face when he answered me.

"Will he attack me again?"

"Probably not tonight." He frowned, but I didn't get the sense he was lying.

And now that I could see I was kicking and breaking someone already down on the floor—I shook my head and quickly stood up.

"Mercy, mercy," Celine taunted Lars, from the safety of her bed. Now that he wasn't in mortal peril, Lars scrabbled backward. It seemed like it was taking him longer to heal each time. Maybe injuries were cumulative? I already knew from Y4 that the healing properties of vampire blood were finite, one of many reasons why daytimers stayed close to their Masters.

"You and Lars and Natasha share the same Master.

There's not always enough blood to go around—and blood is power," Jackson explained, as Lars transformed from someone who looked like he'd lost a fight back to the man I'd seen earlier this morning, minus his torn clothes.

"I was here before you," Lars growled. "Never forget that." He brushed by me on purpose on his way out of the room. I stood my ground as his shoulder hit mine.

"So he thought he'd get the drop on me? By attacking me my first night out?"

"He was hoping the blood hadn't taken yet. Apparently, it has." Jackson shrugged. "Plus, he's not much for long-term planning. He's not the lull-you-into-a-sense-of-comfortable-security type."

I stared at him, trying to keep my thoughts off my face.

"Like me," he added, with a wolfish grin. My fist tightened around the added weight of the hammerhead. "Oh, come on, you knew we were both thinking it," he went on.

Despite my horror, it was hard not to crack a smile. I tossed the hammer handle up and down in my left hand. It was old wood, solid. "The only thing I know for sure now is the next person who tries to wake me is going to get hurt."

Jackson, still grinning, gave me a short bow. "Then I believe I'll leave you two ladies to sort things out."

I watched him head out the door—and realized what the bell I'd seen earlier was for. Daytimers might not be allowed to lock their doors, but they could make sure guests wouldn't arrived unannounced. Celine had come in last, and she hadn't set the bell. She'd known Lars would come for me tonight.

Which meant she was conniving, or she didn't like to dirty her own hands—or she knew she was too weak to fight me herself. I turned toward her, where she sat on her black bed in her black slip—given the whiteness of her limbs, she looked like a porcelain doll—and I kept my eyes on her as I stalked across the floor and set the bell's hinge out, so we wouldn't get any other unannounced company. Her lips tightened at this. She knew she'd been caught. Then I walked over to the destroyed cot.

The frame was bowlegged from the violence of Lars's blow. And the stone that'd weathered the hammer's first hit was chipped. Exactly where my brainpan would have been if I'd still been lying down at the time. No wonder everything in here was black—it made it easier to hide the blood.

I swept my sheets up and turned back toward her, staring her down while wearing my ridiculous clothing, my spandex skirt only fractionally below my crotch, with the hammer handle in one hand like a knife, and my fist still around the hammerhead brass knuckles I'd made at my side.

I'd won. I could ask for the bed now, and get it. I could make her sleep not on a cot, but on the floor, in the hall. Or in her bed with me, doing whatever I liked.

Or I could be kind to her and manage to live with myself for another day.

The thing was, if I did that, she'd think I was weak. She'd tried to have me killed—and showing her mercy would earn myself nothing in return. I'd had too many sociopaths before as patients at work; I knew how they worked. No matter how kind you were to them, some dogs would always bite.

But I didn't want to be one of *them*. Yet.

"Give me all your pillows except one."

She threw them at me like an insolent preteen, and I kicked them over to the zebra rug. Between it, the pillows, and the sheets, I could make a tolerable bed. I did so, and then sat down in it, like a bird in a strange black nest. I set the hammer handle down and said, "And throw me the remote for the lights." That she threw more carefully. I caught it, and she angrily drew her curtains closed.

I thought I'd probably weathered all the attacks on my life there would be tonight. I decided to dare kicking off my shoes, but set them carefully beside me so that I could easily find them again—and in doing so saw a splash of black roll like mercury inside the right one, to stay hidden. I frowned instantly—I had a sinking feeling I knew precisely what that was, although I couldn't investigate with Celine in the room. The last conversation I'd had with the Shadows had been on the life raft before coming here. I didn't know why I'd assumed they'd have left me alone, but it'd been foolish of me.

Were they responsible for my dream of Asher? It didn't seem like them to taunt by proxy when I would be so much more depressed knowing they were here themselves. Hopefully I'd get the chance to ask them tomorrow.

"Can you turn the light off?" Celine asked petulantly from behind her curtains, having decided I was unlikely to wreak revenge.

"Don't get out of your bed without telling me," I warned, and then with a sigh that I hoped that the Shadows could hear, I clicked off the light and lay down in the dark.

CHAPTER FIVE

We don't have eight months anymore, baby.

Lars's attack had broken whatever illusions I had about biding my time here safely. I'd been lucky, that was all. If Raven couldn't give me any more blood without turning me, then my powers, limited as they were, were already on the wane. And the longer I waited to escape the more cumbersome I'd be as my stomach swelled, and the more dangerous it would become for both of us.

But how could I escape when Raven would always be able to find me? The only way out was to kill him—but that would bring all his followers and their daytimers after me, and there was no way I could kill all of them at once. I hadn't even managed to talk myself into killing one just now, when I'd had a good reason to.

I turned over on my side—facing Celine still, just in case—and brought my fist still holding the hammerhead up to my chin. I wished she hadn't turned on the light: the image of Lars as he begged for mercy was scarring. Some vampire I'd make, even if I did manage to live that long.

Did it have to be like this? I didn't think so, but who knew? I'd always thought daytimers were craven before—but if this was what it was like to be one, what choice did they have? All the nice ones got brained. I frowned in the dark.

I strongly doubted whoever ruled the roost next would be willing to sleep on the ground, and I was sure Lars was already planning his next attempt, and Celine was probably still willing to help him, and who knew what stake Jackson actually had in things. And that was all before I even dared to guess whatever longer game Raven was playing with Anna.

I reached out for my shoe and held it like a conch shell to my ear, hoping that the Shadows would be willing to whisper to me. When they'd last talked to me on the life raft, they'd said they wanted to meet my son, so maybe—a moonshot of a maybe—they would be willing to help me out. But either they were gone or my current level of panic was too delicious for them to interrupt.

That left the man pretending to be Asher in my dreams. Which meant I'd have to sleep again, somehow.

Fat chance.

Eventually I did sleep, but I didn't dream again, or if I did I didn't remember it. Celine's voice pulled me back into the real world.

"I'm getting up now," she said, and I heard her slide her curtains back. Without any visual cues, being in our room was like being in an abyss. I had no idea what day or what time it was. It was hard to pretend I was somewhere else, though, when I was still holding on to a hammerhead and a stake. "Did you hear me? Are you going to turn the lights on?"

I sat up and found the remote where I'd put it, right beside my shoes, and clicked the largest switch. When the lights came on I found her staring down at me out of her bed like a vulture. "What time is it?"

"Time for some of us to go to work. Assuming I have your permission, of course," she said, giving me an insincere smile.

"Sure," I said. She hopped off her bed, swept some clothing out of her black lacquer wardrobe, and gave me a look before heading out the door. The bell hanging over it jingled merrily.

I was suddenly glad I'd taken that fast shower yesterday. I picked up my right shoe and tilted it, trying to see into its depths. "Shadows?"

There was a movement in the toe—something scampered, like a beetle or baby rat.

"Are you still here?"

"Are you trying to kill what's left of us?" the contents of my shoe protested with a hiss, and I quickly tilted it back, moving to block it with my body from the light.

"Sorry, sorry!" I ducked down, trying to keep an ear out for anyone moving in the hall, or Celine's return, while cradling the shoe against me to protect it from the light as I cast enough of a shadow to get them to come out and talk. I felt a flood of relief, and then shame—to think that I was so desperate to have a piece of home that I was happy to see the Shadows. "Have you been in there this whole time?"

"Unfortunately."

My eyes narrowed, thinking back to the talk I'd had with them on the raft—and I remembered that they'd escaped the *Maraschino*'s sinking by hitching a ride on me. "You all owe me. Get me out of here. Now."

The disembodied voice inside the darkness of my shoe cackled aloud.

"It's not funny—" I could easily tuck one of the vanity's lightbulbs in my shoe and kill them.

"It pains us to admit this, but here we're almost as powerless as you. We left the vast bulk of ourselves behind in Port Cavell when this small piece went with you in your luggage. And not all of us agreed as to the wisdom of hiding on you in the morgue on the doomed ship, so we became even more divided. Those fools went down with the *Maraschino,* and met our more difficult cousin. The portion of us that remains, you could hold easily inside your palm."

"But—" The Shadows back home were able to heal people, and make them forget things and do things they didn't want to do—

"But nothing. We've been trying to escape since your helicopter landed. *We* want to go back to the rest of *us,* where *we* belong. Only there was no dark opportunity to hitch a ride safely on your shapeshifter or Anna, and so now we're trapped here. Again. With you." They sounded indignant, as if they were the ones getting the worse end of the bargain. "We went scouting last night, but all the hallways here are lit, and most of the construction is solid stone. There's a lot of food here at least, not counting you, although we do enjoy your generally high levels of paranoia."

The Shadows fed on emotions—that was why back

home they lived underneath the hospital. My elation at discovering them was fading fast. "Don't feed on me—"

"We could hardly help it after the attack last night," they tsked. "We are what we are." And what they were was self-serving. I frowned again, as they went on. "But we do want to go home, and we would be willing to pool our efforts with you toward that end."

By which they meant they'd help me as long as I helped them . . . but if they found their own way back, they'd ditch me without a second thought. Still, it was more than I'd had last night. *As far as deals with the devil go, baby—well, at least it's a devil we know.*

There was a knock at the door. "Edie? You still alive?" Jackson's voice. I dropped the shoe and stood up to shimmy down my skirt, which had become a belt on me the second I'd turned in my sleep. Then I swooped up the hammerhead and makeshift stake, just in case.

"Still breathing," I said as he pressed the door open and came inside.

"Glad to hear it." He gave me a genuine smile, then shook his head after looking at my hands. "We're not allowed to have weapons here."

I set the hammerhead back onto the post left in the hammer and held the whole thing with one hand. "Look, now it's back to being just a tool!" I said in my best magician's-assistant voice.

Jackson snorted. "Points for trying. I figured I could make an exception for you last night, but you can't walk around with it—I can't have you killing anyone by accident. Give the stake to me to dispose of." I handed it over reluctantly. "You can hide the hammerhead somewhere in here for now. No promises it'll be there when you get back, but it might, if you make it hard enough to find. I'll wait outside."

I knew he was probably right outside the door, which given his hearing meant I wasn't all that private. And the hammer wasn't the only thing I wanted to ditch—I didn't like the idea of the Shadows hanging out with me all day. I looked around the room trying to find a place for both things, and my eyes lit on Celine's mattress.

She was shorter than me—and she wasn't a princess. I didn't think she'd feel something if I jammed it into the end of her bed. I pulled up the lip of the fitted black satin sheets and used my unreal strength to shove the hammer head inside, after making a hole. Then I picked up my shoe. "You guys too," I whispered, shaking it.

For all their blustering, in a lit room they were really at my mercy. I thought I saw something scurry from my shoe to the mattress, but I couldn't be entirely sure. Maybe they were dividing up again, splitting their chances. I squinted into the depths of the hole I'd made in the mattress, and then into the toe of my shoe, where I didn't see any abnormal darkness, then I pulled the sheets back down and tucked them into place.

I pulled on my shoes, and rescued my vaguely clean underwear from the corpse of the cot to pull them on too, then went out to join Jackson in the hall.

"What now?"

"Now I finish showing you around and make you useful," he explained as he started walking.

I remembered Raven's comment from the prior night.

"Will you be teaching me more manners?" I said, half teasing, half not.

"Yeah, I'm a regular finishing school," Jackson chuckled, leading us around a corner and down a hall. Other tunnels branched off to either side, lit, but led to doors or sharp turns, so I couldn't see where they finished, although I got the idea that this place was enormous. "Today we'll just go clean the club, and then we'll see what Raven has in store for you later."

I wondered if our tour would conveniently include the prisoners' cages, so I could say hi to my dream-time friend. Then I realized that if we were up, probably everyone else was too.

"Will Lars be helping us?" I stroked one hand over the other—it was too easy to remember the feel of my knuckles hitting his ribs, the unreal strength I'd had, and the unfamiliar urge to use it on him.

"No. But he'll be there when Raven convenes us all tonight." We reached a set of stairs and Jackson headed up. I stood at the bottom, pondering.

"How did I know what to do? When he attacked me, that is."

Jackson stopped and turned. "The blood told you."

"What—how?"

"You're part of the system now. Blah blah death, blah blah life, black and white, yin and yang, epic struggle, entropy. You've heard it all before. What it means is that you're now on the dying side, and you'll naturally want to kill things."

"What?" I said, like I hadn't heard him.

"It's worse when the blood's fresh. Don't worry, it'll fade in time, unless you get a new transfusion."

"But I don't want to kill anything."

He snorted. "That's what everyone says in the beginning."

"No, really, I mean it—" I said, determined to convince him.

"Well, I've never met a vampire who could live without death before. But you're welcome to try to be the first." He turned around and kept walking up, and I trotted after him. I felt the need to prove myself.

"What would you have done, if you were me?"

He shrugged. "It's hard your first night. You seem to know the score, so you must have had some dealings with our system before now. And vampires don't give blood to complete idiots, so—well, I don't know. Before here I had what you would call a troubled past. Add to that the fact that I have a temper and I'm a man, and we're more prone to beating each other's heads in, and I'm older than I look—yeah. I probably would have killed him. And you should have no doubt in your mind that he was out to kill you."

The chip of rock Lars had taken off the floor with his first blow was a pretty big clue.

"I'm not telling you to sympathize with him, but the day you don't get enough blood to be able to fight back is usually the day you die." Jackson inhaled deeply. We'd reached the top of the stairs, and he pulled a large key ring off his belt. "If you and I had to share the same Master, I'm not sure what I would have done in his place. And if you'd been stupid, or complacent, or scared, or naive, well, his problem would have been solved, neatly. But he failed, and you didn't kill him, so we'll all have to keep on being one big happy vampire family."

I frowned. "The last time someone told me that, she died." And she'd been a daytimer too—Sike. I remembered her cruel smile and her red hair—and the lengths to which she'd gone to rescue Anna and her final sacrifice to save me. I had so much more sympathy for her now that I knew what it was like to be like this. And whatever being a daytimer was, it hadn't wrung all of the human out of her. I looked back up and found Jackson watching my face.

"Were you close to her?" he asked.

I shook my head. "Not as close as I am now." I didn't know what else to say—all the questions I wanted to ask him were too leading. I'd just said I didn't want to kill anyone, and yet killing Raven was my quickest ticket out of here. I could hardly ask Jackson for help with that, though.

"Stop worrying about hypotheticals," he said sagely. "The only thing you'll be killing today is germs in the bathroom with me."

CHAPTER SIX

He unlocked a closet, revealing a panoply of cleaning supplies, and then we carried the tools of our trade through two more locked doors. Locks were fine up here—because they were meant to keep prying people paying to dance out of the real catacombs below. The final door led into a basement, and I was hit by a wall of scent. Smoke, old and new, sweat, sex, fear—I stood in the doorway for a second, overwhelmed, but Jackson walked on in.

He gestured grandly. "May I present Hell. Like so many other things in life, it looks better in the dark."

The room was huge, with flames painted on the walls, in colors that were garish now but probably looked better when the club's light show was running. Mirrors curved up and down among the flames so that people could watch refracted images of themselves as they danced. A well-stocked bar stretched the entire length of one wall, two shelves of liquor illuminated by red lights from below.

"I thought it was called the Catacombs."

"The whole thing is. Hell's the first level." He reached

out and tapped the bucket I held with the end of a broom. "The sinks that fit these are only on the first floor. The club's three floors high, and there's a smoking patio out back."

"So it's Hell because we have to carry water upstairs?"

"No—because it gets nicer as you go up," he explained as a thick panel of something shiny set into the ceiling caught my eye. His gaze followed and he grunted. "One-way glass. The people upstairs can look down— and the people above them can, too. Stairs and bouncers limit access and—"

"Hell, Purgatory, and Heaven?" I guessed.

"Perg for short," Jackson said with a grin.

I walked underneath the glass and looked up; it was completely opaque from down here. But everyone who was dancing here would be wondering who was looking down at them from above, and the business model fell into place inside my mind. I assumed the vampire architect or whoever'd had the bright idea to install the glass had done it so that they could see attacks coming. But what it'd done to the club was something else. Access could be controlled via the stairs, and people on one floor knew there was another floor above them that for some reason they weren't quite good enough, attractive enough, or wealthy enough for. And those on higher floors could be as voyeuristic as they liked, looking down. I imagined them deciding to summon people dancing below—and those dancing below would have the thrill of knowing that they might be being watched and rescued.

I walked under the glass panel in a circle. "You have

parties you advertise heavily once or twice a year where you tell people they can go wherever they want, so people down here can see what they're missing—and you let people upstairs choose people below to call up. The people down here always feel like they're performing—and the people up there get to feel like kings."

Jackson nodded. "Just add in some extraordinarily attractive and attentive women, quality drugs, and truly frightening bouncers for safety and keeping cops out."

In a town as striving as I'd always heard LA was, it was genius—and to a degree foolproof. Dammit. "I bet there's a line out the door."

"Every night."

I looked at the broom I held. "This place must be a license to print money—so why the hell are we carrying buckets?"

"Paying employees comes with liabilities. We just cash the DJs and the bouncers out each night. The more people we have here during the day, the more we have to explain why our Masters only come out after sundown. Raven does have some dedicated bloodslaves, a few registered family donor lines, but, well"—his lips twisted to one side, as if he was weighing what to tell me—"it's been a lean year, let's just say." He reached into his bucket, pulled out a roll of trash bags, and handed me one. "Come on. I always start in the bathrooms. I like to get the worst parts done first."

Hell's bathrooms were stainless-steel affairs, all the easier to clean with harsh chemicals, but still gross.

Jackson claimed they had attendants in them, but I assumed those people were just there to make sure that people weren't doing drugs they hadn't purchased locally, and not keeping the place clean.

I tried to do a good job, within the limits of what could actually be done—I was a daytimer, not a magician. But keeping busy was good for me, it kept my mind off Lars's attack, and while I was scrubbing I could pretend that this was some sort of shitty summer camp where I could just bide my time until my parents returned to save me.

Only my mom probably thought I was dead, and if I was going to be kind to her I would have to keep it that way and not explain what had happened to me. She'd never even get to meet her own grandson.

Oh, baby—you'd love her. And she'd love you. She'd spoil you half to death, I know it. A wave of sadness hit me like a physical blow. What Lars had done wasn't half as bad as knowing I could never really go home.

"What's wrong?" Jackson asked from two stalls down. I inhaled, startled, and realized I'd been holding my breath.

Everything was wrong. Not that I could tell him that. I gathered myself up, using the wall of the stall I was in for strength. "I just feel like some sad vampire Cinderella in here."

"It's been a while since you cleaned a toilet, huh?"

"Yes. Not that I'm too good for this, but it has, as you say, been a while." I leaned back onto my heels. I couldn't imagine doing this while eight months' pregnant, either.

"What did you used to be?"

"I'm a nurse." I was unwilling to use the past tense just yet. Nursing wasn't something you ever gave up—either you were or you weren't one. It was a permanent state of being.

"So how did you find out about vampires?"

"I used to work on a secret hospital floor for sanctioned donors." I left out the occasional werecreatures and shapeshifters and daytimers and blood. No matter how safe I might feel around Jackson, the less anyone here knew about me the better.

I heard him stand and he appeared in the doorway of the stall—the brows on his forehead knit into almost one solid line. "You mean there's a place where they take care of donors? On purpose? Keep them in one piece?"

"Yeah." Which, I realized, implied that here was not like that.

His expression slowly relaxed as he considered things. "That sounds almost civilized. And it explains why Lars wasn't able to take you, plus or minus a pint. You knew about the system. Where was that?"

"Back east," I said, still being coy. He snorted and didn't press, but then he went quiet, clearly thinking hard. I felt compelled to say something. "It's not like it's equality central out there or anything."

He nodded, standing at attention with his mop. "Still. It's nice to know that there are different ways to be."

I nodded back at him. There was a chance that in the future he'd be a vampire too. Maybe if he was given a choice in the matter he'd run things differently. I hoped that I would, if it ever happened to me.

* * *

After we finished with Hell's bathroom, Jackson led the way to the stairs for the second floor. We passed a side hall with a door at the end of it and I stopped.

There was sunlight on the other side of that door. I knew it.

"Hey, no, don't even think it—" Jackson said, turning around.

"Why isn't it guarded?" I stared at it over his shoulder. It was locked, but it wasn't like the thick oak doors downstairs—it was just a normal-looking door. Wide, but mostly decorative. Impulsive muscles answered desires I hadn't voiced yet—I knew I had the strength to tear it in two. Jackson moved to stand in my way before I could do anything.

I was stronger than he was right now, I knew it. I could take this mop in my hands and snap it and stab it through his neck if I had to—what the hell part of me was thinking that?

The same part of me that hadn't been afraid of killing Lars.

I quieted in horror just as Jackson started speaking.

"Think things through, Edie. It's not locked from this side because it doesn't need to be. You could leave, but you wouldn't get far. And there's nowhere that you can hide; Raven would always be able to find you. You don't want to piss him off like that—you haven't seen him mad."

The human part of me was like a compass—I knew it was late afternoon in winter now, and the sun was beginning to dip. If I did leave I couldn't get far enough by nightfall, and after nightfall there'd be nowhere I was safe.

I didn't have any ID so I couldn't fly—and it's not like I had any money to buy tickets anyway. I could find a police station—and tell them what? That vampires were after me? Ask them to keep me safe inside a cell? I'd seen my share of crazy people working at the hospital, I knew exactly what the cops would think and say. Rightly so. And I'd seen before how vampires could command people to make them do what they wanted them to. If I gave any cops my real name they'd think I was insane—I was sure I was on the roster of those who'd gone down with the *Maraschino*. If I gave them a fake name, and seemed crazy enough, they might keep me in a holding cell overnight, which was when Raven would show up and convince everyone there that I didn't exist, after he told one of them to fetch me.

I could call Asher, but what then? Torture him and then put him in harm's way? Ask him to take on an entire vampire House on his own?

I stared at the door, a hundred different pathways spooling out inside my head, none of them ending well, like reading a choose-your-own-adventure book where every option made you die or, worse yet, killed someone you loved.

"I shouldn't have shown it to you this early. Please, trust me. If you left like that your lives would be in terrible danger." Jackson grabbed my wrist and gently pulled me toward the stairs. I stiffened and he quickly let go—but it wasn't because of his touch, it was the plural he'd used. "I'm sorry—I overheard Wolf and Raven talking before they left last night."

I swallowed. "Does everyone know?"

"Just them. And me."

I wondered what the outcome would have been if Lars had known—if his hammer would have been aimed at my belly instead of my head.

"They'll find out eventually, I mean, they can't help it—when it starts having its own heartbeat, they'll be able to hear it with fresh blood. We can hear babies here all the time, fetal alcohol syndrome ahoy. But I won't say anything to anyone before then, I swear."

Just how far could I trust him? I didn't know. I might not know until it was too late. It seemed like the only way to find out anything here was the hard way. He stepped back, giving me a little space. "Come on—we still have two more floors to go," he said, and I reluctantly followed.

Purgatory was nicer than Hell. While Hell had seemed a little on the garish carnival side, Perg had an Old World cathedral theme, mixed with a light S&M, stone walls with gargoyles grinning down from above, and wide black leather couches.

Heaven was the nicest by far, appropriately. It was white-on-white, and managed to feel both exotic and monied, with white leather chairs and white marble tables and white polar bear skins on the walls. It was more like an exclusive club than a dance hall, with the space devoted more to lounging than dancing—probably because most of the dancers on this floor were paid to do so—and it had the most extensive bar I'd ever seen. The bathrooms were far nicer here as well, with walls and floors of white marble, and they were less dirty—although they needed more meticulous work, as the white marble was unforgiving.

"How're you doing, Cinderelly?" Jackson asked when we were done.

"I think I've bleached my skirt. Does that mean I can throw it away and get a new one?"

His eyes glazed over for a second, as though he was listening to someone inside himself, and not to me. "We'll find out soon enough," he answered slowly.

I felt whatever it was, too. Like I'd just let the last bit of sand fall out of my hand, or let go of a bird I didn't know I'd been holding. Like a piece of me that had been mine was gone.

"It's always a little bit like dying when the sun goes down," Jackson said. "You'd think it'd be the reverse, but it's not, not for us."

"Are they up now?" I lowered my voice without thinking about it, and he nodded.

"Yeah. Raven will know you're alive and where you are, but he'll want to see you, to make sure you're still in one piece. We'd best go present ourselves," he said, and started leading us back down into the actual catacombs.

It was easier to pass by the door to the outside world at night. While I missed fresh air, it didn't tempt me like the thought of sunlight did. We put our supplies back into the closet and then started our trek below.

"Who built all these tunnels, anyhow?"

"Don't know. There's a huge network of them underneath LA, though. Most of them collapsed during assorted earthquakes, but apparently the ones we're in are stable. We'll know an earthquake's coming when all of our Masters run out the door."

"What if it happens during daylight?"

"Then we'll all die, and they'll slowly crawl their way out at night."

"Awesome."

"I try not to think about it too much."

He led us through to the chamber where I'd been introduced the morning before. Everyone else was already waiting. Celine was again impeccably dressed, this time in club wear, a tight-fitting red dress with holes cut out to show expanses of white skin that somehow managed to stay classy. She was behind her Mistress, whose name I hadn't learned yet, and who was dressed in a long skin-fitting white dress that flared at the neck and knees, intentionally modernizing a queen's silhouette, with high hair and an oversized beauty mark to match. The male vampire whose name I didn't know was dressed in leather pants with a fitted black shirt and a suggestively buckled collar. I assumed Celine would be in Hell, her Mistress in Heaven, and the unknown vampire in Perg, based on clothing alone.

Wolf was still Wolf, though, in a leather vest and T-shirt, more muscled than manly, and Raven was still Raven, lounging on his couch in head-to-toe purple-black—the shade certain bird feathers took on under the right light. He wore a coat that would have been a costume on anyone else, swirling down to his knees. Jackson nudged me forward to stand by Lars, who was dressed in a black business suit, hovering by Raven's side.

Lars didn't look any worse for our fight—and neither

did I. He was still angry at me, I could see it in his eyes, and almost feel the hate radiating off him. I wondered if he was worried that I would rat him out to our shared Master.

"Who put her in that?" Raven asked aloud as I took my place. I noticed he wasn't asking me.

Jackson stepped forward. "There wasn't any other clothing around, Master."

Raven's thin lips puckered in distaste. "She can't attend the bathrooms in that. Not even on the first floor."

The queenly female vampire looked to Celine, who bowed apologetically, while gesturing to her more petite form. "I don't have anything in her size." It was hard not to roll my eyes, but I managed.

Raven sighed as though my fashion troubles ought to be beneath him. "Jackson—"

Jackson stepped forward at the mention of his name. "If I may, Sire's Sire—"

Beside me, Lars tensed. Maybe he thought Jackson would be the weak link. Raven waved his hand in the air. "By all means," he said as ironically as possible.

Jackson went on, seeming used to being ironized. "I don't think she should be upstairs at all. She was a nurse before she came here." It was my turn to tense. I hadn't considered that Jackson might rat me out, instead. "It is possible that she may be of use to Natasha."

Raven made a thoughtful noise as I looked around the room for a person I hadn't met yet. And a cruel smile parted Raven's lips as he looked toward the door behind me, and I looked over my shoulder at the girl walking through. "Speak of the devil."

Her black hair was pulled into a high ponytail, which then spilled down her back in a thick wave. She had her father's ice-blue eyes and his widow's peak and his same aquiline nose, and was wearing an oddly modest black turtleneck—which I realized hid her neck—and jeans. A simple bracelet hung at her right wrist, charms dangling. Despite her youth and her casual-Friday outfit, I recognized her instantly—she looked exactly like her father, Nathaniel, the psychopath who'd infected and then sunk the *Maraschino*. He'd sacrificed four thousand innocent people in his attempt to raise a monster to obliterate the vampires that'd kidnapped her.

When she saw Raven she broke into the world's hugest smile. It was completely disconcerting.

"Hey baby," she said, and walked across the room to him as if the rest of us weren't there.

"Dear one," he replied, reaching out for her. She hopped onto the couch and folded under his arm and he held her the exact way Asher held me sometimes, closing his eyes and pulling her close.

I had no idea what to make of that. Her resemblance to her father was chilling—and he was why I was trapped here. But watching her snuggle with Raven—and him snuggle back—was like watching a nature program, viewing the intimate habits of an unknown beast, being both aghast and unable to look away. Beside me, Lars tensed. I wondered if Lars had known her father—or if he'd ever tried to kill her, too.

"How's work tonight?" Raven asked her solicitously, stroking a hand through her hair.

"It was good—I'm close, things are almost done,"

she told Raven, pulling back to smile up at him. "I just need two more test subjects. I want to be sure."

"Of course. I appreciate your thirst for perfection." And he smiled down at her, amused, showing teeth. It was as if the rest of us weren't even in the room anymore. While he couldn't give her warmth or real love, I realized he could give her his completely undivided attention, a particular talent of vampires—and she basked in it like a flower does the sun. I looked around quickly, and saw the male vampire I didn't know grimace.

Jackson did more than that. He groaned. She turned from Raven's shoulder to look at him with an irritated frown. "I wouldn't ask for them if I didn't need them."

"You said that last week," Jackson said. Wolf subtly moved his hand to stop him from speaking further, and I could almost see Jackson biting his tongue.

"Jackson's just upset that you're making so much extra work for him," Wolf apologized, as though Jackson were incapable of speaking for himself.

"Good. I would hate it if we no longer shared the same goals," Raven said, thin lips pulling into a dangerous smile above Natasha's head. He glanced at me again, then squeezed her, and pointed his chin at me. "Could you use the services of a nurse in your lab?"

She shrugged. "I could use-use her," she said, "and then lazy Jackson would only have to find me one more—"

"No, I need her alive, for now. I meant to help you. I worry that you're working too hard."

"Of course I am. I want to make things perfect for you," she said without the slightest hint of guile.

"I know. But maybe if she could help you some, you'd have more time to spend with me."

The look on her face was meltingly sweet. "I'd like that."

"It's done then." Raven looked over to me. "You will do whatever Natasha tells you to," he commanded. I could feel the order go through my body, as if he'd just chiseled it into my bones.

Natasha turned to regard me as my pulse began to race. I knew every vampire in the room could smell my fear—because I'd just been given over to a psychopath's daughter like some baby bunny to a toddler on Easter. Fuck you very much, Jackson.

She didn't catch my horror, though—or perhaps, she was so used to seeing people afraid of her that she was oblivious to it, even taking it as some sort of tribute.

Raven smiled indulgently at her, leaning forward, rubbing his cheek against her hair, before turning to regard the rest of us in the room. "We should be open already—unless there's anything else to deal with tonight?" No one moved or made a sound. "Let's get on with it then. And speaking of extra work, Jackson—I've left some trash at the crossroads for you to dispose of, although you should make sure to blame that on Lars."

Raven got up gracefully and offered his hand to Natasha, who took it to rise. He bowed deeply to her, kissing her hand in a formal fashion. "Soon," he told her, then released her hand and walked out.

The vampires left the room first, then Lars and Celine trailed after them toward the dance floors. Natasha watched Raven leave with a soft smile on her face. She looked young. Asher said she should have been my age—but if she'd been turned into a daytimer when Nathaniel's blood-testing scheme had been found out, that would have been seven years ago. She'd first gotten vampire blood when she was what, nineteen? Twenty? But she didn't look like she'd aged a day since sixteen.

When she turned to look at me, though, her eyes were ancient—and I realized Raven's command had given her utter power over me.

Jackson stepped up quickly as we became the last people in the room. "She'll help me tonight—she can be yours tomorrow," he warned.

"What, you don't trust me?" Natasha teased, giving him a lopsided grin. "Does Jackson have a crush?"

"What kind of lab is it?" I interrupted. Her father had been doing illegal research on humans for vampires when he'd gotten in trouble with the Consortium. If she'd continued it on her own and been successful where he'd failed—

"Stem cell. Have you ever done anything like that before?" She sounded genuinely hopeful. I shook my head. "But you're familiar with sterile procedures, yes?"

"Yeah."

"And you can draw blood?"

"Like a vampire," I said flippantly.

Natasha blinked, and then broke into a smile. "Good enough for me," she said. She looked to Jackson next, much more business-like. "I'll expect my subjects by dawn. I want a male and a female, and try to make sure they're not addicted to anything. The last set—"

"I'll get them to you after my disposal run," he said, cutting her off.

Natasha nodded curtly at him, then smiled again at me and walked out of the room. I turned to Jackson once she was gone. "You don't just clean the bathrooms, do you?"

CHAPTER SEVEN

Jackson raised a hand and pushed it through his hair while bowing his head a little. "Not really, no."

"Why did you sell me out to Raven?" Not that I should have expected any loyalty—I hardly knew him and he was a daytimer, come on. *Baby, your mother really ought to know better by now.*

"Everybody here has to pull their own weight—" he began, making excuses while I frowned, more at myself than him.

I'd never worked in a lab but I'd had to have been living under a rock not to have heard of stem cells—cells that were undifferentiated, that could grow into other cell types depending on where they were used and what factors they were exposed to. Scientists were busy trying to use them to cure all sorts of things, but the research, while promising, was complicated and slow.

What the hell was Natasha using stem cells for? Was she still trying create blood substitutes like her father had been? I realized that if she was—I needed to know. She couldn't be allowed to succeed. A world where vampires didn't need humans for blood would be a world overrun—*and no safe place for you, baby.*

At the thought of that dismal future, I frowned even harder. "And what's a disposal run?"

"It'd be easier to show you on the road. Assuming you want to come."

I hesitated. I should be volunteering to help Natasha immediately. The sooner I figured out what she was up to, the sooner I could report her to the Consortium. It was another possible way out of here: calling the group that seemed to loosely govern supernatural creatures down on her and Raven's heads. Unfortunately, the only time I'd met a representative from them they hadn't handed me a business card.

"She doesn't have any work for you yet—she's out of human-shaped lab mice," Jackson said. "And it does involve leaving here for about an hour in a car."

At the thought of getting outside and being able to ask Jackson questions in the car safely, like just what Natasha was testing, I was sold. "Let's roll."

Jackson led me through another warren of hallways until we reached a point where the walls widened and our tunnel was intersected by another one—and a prone person's leg was visible on the far side, as if whomever the leg had belonged to had fainted dead away. I looked at Jackson, whose demeanor said that this was normal for him, and then ran ahead.

"Are you okay?" The leg belonged to a man, a boy really, some pale club kid—made paler by blood loss. "Sir? Can you hear me?" I felt for a pulse, and it was there, but weak and slow. I shook him hard. "Hey!"

Jackson put restraining hands on the boy's chest. "Don't wake him up—it's not good for him, or us. He doesn't want to remember this, and it would only make our job harder." He easily picked the man up and hoisted him over his shoulder.

"What happened to him?"

"What do you think happened? Raven gave you a huge amount of blood the other night. He had to get it back from somewhere—or someone." Jackson shrugged and the man jiggled. "He's lucky to be alive—it's not as powerful for them when they don't kill the victim. Something about eating the spark of life fills them up faster."

"Psychophagy." Once upon a time, a vampire had wanted to eat me.

Jackson's eyebrows rose. "Is that what it's called?"

"Yeah." It was hard standing beside him when I ought to be calling 911 and starting warm IV fluids on the boy.

"Huh." Jackson turned to indicate where we were standing. "This is the crossroads." He pointed down two of the tunnels. "Those ones we don't go down. They belong to our Masters, and if you snoop you'll be killed on sight. And that one"—he pointed to a third—"is where Natasha's lab is."

I reached out for the dangling boy's hand, digging my fingers in for a pulse. "He needs medical attention—he's only barely alive—"

"I know. Let's get to the car," he said, and started going back the way we'd come.

Tunnels intersected, forming a map in my mind. I definitely knew how to get up to the club now—and how to get out to the garage. Jackson flipped open a metal box on one wall, revealing a wall of key hooks like what you'd find at a valet station. It was open—of course it was. The only person here who wanted to leave was me.

We walked down a row of cars until we reached a Honda Civic. "I don't get to drive the fancy ones. Wouldn't want to, either, with him on board." He clicked the doors open and settled the boy into the back. I crawled in through the opposite door to keep an eye on him. Jackson gave me a look, but closed the door and settled into the driver's seat.

"So it's like this all the time?" I asked, lips pursed into a frown.

"Yeah. Rex—the other male vampire—picks out a few candidates and dopes them up for himself and the others. GHB, MDMA, coke, whatever suits their moods. Do they want an easy meal? To fuck or to fight? Even without the drugs, they've got their own powers, the mind-control thing they can all do, and I don't have you tell you that they're strong."

I didn't respond. I didn't want to give him an out, for making something so awful sound so commonplace.

"Sorry if I sound clinical," Jackson said, after a long silence, looking back in the rearview mirror at both of us. "I realize this is your first time with it—but this sort of shit is my every night. Most times their victims are convinced, the way vampires are good at convincing people, that they were lucky to be chosen and that they had an amazing time. They got picked to go to Heaven and drank top-shelf drinks and danced with beautiful girls, and they got a little overdone. Sometimes there's sex, even willingly, and sometimes there's not. And sometimes I get to put on a plastic apron and cut corpses up with chain saws and put body parts into buckets of lye."

"So where are we going now?" If he said we were going to a chain-saw-and-lye-atorium, I would have to jump him.

But then what? Wreck the car and fight out by the roadside? If it were only me I could risk that—I wouldn't think twice. *But not with you here, baby.* I looked down at the slender cool wrist in my hand.

This boy beside me had been someone's baby once, too.

"Relax. We're getting him somewhere safe. And then we'll call him in. Between the drugs and the narcotics in vampire saliva, he won't remember what happened to him enough to explain it to the police." He took a right-hand turn. "You don't know how lonely this town is, Edie. And Rex has a way of picking out people who just got here—with no connections, no friends, no past."

"And sometimes no future," I said.

"I don't kill them, I just dispose of the bodies."

"And that makes it better somehow?"

He took his eyes off the road to look at the rearview mirror again. "What do you think you are now? What do you think you'll grow up to be?"

My lips thinned into a line. I hadn't gotten a choice. Natasha's dad had taken that away.

Jackson pulled over to a desolate side road in a bad neighborhood and put the car into PARK. I opened up the backseat door and got out, and he took the man out, laying him carefully on the side of the road. He flipped back a corner of the man's shirt. "See? One bite's self-sealing. There's no reason for anyone to find it. And they'll test what little blood he has left and find out that he went out and got drugged, only he won't remember where he was going." He reached into his pocket and pulled out a cell phone. I listened to him report hearing a gunshot and seeing someone fall by the side of the road, sounding like a gruffly concerned bystander too nervous to get out and check on his own, and I waited until he'd hung up to speak.

"You do this every night?"

"No—most of the people go home happy with strange hangovers they can't quite explain, and feel strangely exhausted the next day. They stumble out of the Catacombs on their own two feet—some of them even come back the next night. But our Masters live on blood, and it's either them, or donors—which we have precious few of right now, thanks to Natasha—or us."

He got back into the car, and I took the seat beside him this time. He kept speaking while he disassembled the cell phone. "I doubt they'll be here soon, but the system works. He's young, and if he's managed to hold on this long, he'll make it a few more hours." I was surprised when he turned the ignition key and slid the car into drive.

"Aren't we staying here? To make sure he's safe?"

"Can't be seen."

"But—"

"Edie, no matter your relationship with the Beast, you're a good person, I can tell." He pulled out and hit the gas. "I really like you. But in the Catacombs, having a heart is an expense you can't afford." When we hit the highway, he rolled down the window and flicked out the phone's sim card onto the asphalt like so much cigarette ash.

CHAPTER EIGHT

Looking out the window, I realized I'd been so involved in being worried about the boy that I'd missed my chance to run.

I already knew all the reasons why running would be a bad idea, and none of them had changed since I'd thought about them last. I reached for the door, for the window switch—and found it locked. Go figure. Jackson snorted and released it with a button on his door, and I set the window down a few inches so I could feel the night breeze. Los Angeles's air was much drier than Port Cavell's. We were cruising past what I assumed was downtown, where old roads that hadn't been built for such a big city were looped over one another like concrete shoelaces.

"I'm sorry. I know your last twenty-four hours have been rough." He sounded sincere.

"You could say that." I brushed my hands through my hair. If this was my safe chance to ask him questions I needed to hurry up. "So why did Anna save you?" he asked—and I realized I wasn't the only one in a querulous mood.

"We're friends."

"Friends," he repeated, like he didn't believe me. I shrugged.

"She moved heaven and earth to get blood for you. She warned it might take a lot. Many of the Houses were unwilling to risk it. If you give blood to someone, and you can't cure them or bring them over, then you have to take that blood back . . . and Anna said if anyone killed you, they'd die." He looked at me out of the corner of his eye. "You're sure you're not related somehow? Distantly?"

"No." I plucked at the elastic edge of my skirt. I'd saved Anna's life twice. The first time was after I'd accidentally killed her sickly guardian at work. With his dying breath, he'd asked me to find her—and I'd found her chained up and being abused, and saved her when he couldn't.

The second time wasn't so much a saving as just being willing to go back. I didn't run away from her when I could have—when I probably should have, since it might have saved me from getting stabbed. But I tried to save her and proved that someone cared, and that had been enough. She'd saved herself in the end, breaking free from the other vampires who'd chained her, but she might not have done it without me being willing to risk my own life for her first. There was no good way to put all that into words, and I didn't think it was a good idea to share it with Jackson besides.

"Do you know what she's been up to while you've been apart?"

I frowned. "I heard you all call her the Beast last night."

"Yeah. Other names for her haven't been quite so kind. She's consolidating her power. Either Houses and Thrones pledge to her and take her blood—so she knows where they are at all wakeful times—or they die. In less than a year the Rose Throne, under her leadership, has come to completely dominate the East Coast." He swung us into a wide turn. "You do know what she is, right?"

This time I nodded. "She's alive."

"Like the rest of them aren't. She can make an infinite amount of blood. Which gives her the ability to create an infinite number of vampires," he said.

I nodded again.

"And that doesn't worry you?"

"Should it?" I said. As much as I trusted Anna, an infinite number of vampires did sound bad.

Jackson wheeled over to the side of the road and parked, putting hazard lights on, then turned so he could look at me. "I'm going to take a big risk here, Edie, because this might be the only time we can get away from them to talk. You were horrified by what you did to Lars, and you didn't kick Celine out afterward. Hell, you didn't even make her sleep on the floor. And you tried to save that kid just now—you're not like one of us and you don't want to be. So I think that even if you disagree with what I tell you next, you can manage to keep it a secret."

I wondered what confession my agreement would bring. "I can't promise but I can try."

"I get the feeling you take your tries more seriously than most." He gave me a halfhearted smile, and then his expression became worried. "I'm not just with

Raven—I'm not just black and white. I'm Grey. With House Grey."

"No. No no no—" I backed up physically in the car seat, pressing against the door. Members of House Grey had tried to ruin Anna's ascension to the Rose Throne's ruling body. They were some secret organization inside the vampire Houses and Thrones that had their own obscure agenda—one that had it out for Anna and hadn't minded trying to kill me along the way.

"If I was going to hurt you, I wouldn't be telling you about it now, would I?"

I got my legs up on the seat so that if I had to I could kick him back. "Why are you telling me at all?"

"I know you've had some run-ins with us in the past, and I'm sorry for that. But we had reasons for doing what we did. Anna's messing up the game—the field, the ecosystem, whatever you want to call it. It's not supposed to be like this for us. There's only supposed to be scattered pockets of vampires, groups in urban areas, loners out in the rural ones. We're conniving and we're jealous as hell, and that keeps us self-policing. And when that doesn't work, House Grey steps in and starts killing to keep the numbers down." The sound of cars driving by at speed five feet away from us punctuated every other word of his.

"Why are you telling me this?"

"Because I want you to understand. House Grey isn't your enemy, Edie. We're here to maintain balance. Anna's not the first living vampire, you know. One comes along every few hundred years, blood runs in the streets, and we're almost discovered—or we are discovered, and hunted down. Back in the day our wars could be written off as plagues or genocides—but the world has changed now, there's too much technology. We won't get a second chance to hide this time around when things explode—and if we fight, we'll take a fair chunk of humanity out with us."

"But she's not like that—she's my friend—" I protested, shaking my head.

"You're right, she seems to be. But there might come a time when you're the only thing standing between her and her vampire army. I just want you to think about that."

I hugged my folded-up knees, trying not to think at all. "How can you claim that House Grey is on the side of humanity?"

"I know it's hard to believe, but we are. Or at least on the side where vampires stay the same. Vampires kill a few thousand people a year, or a few tens of thousands. It's less than heart disease or cancer. But an army of vampires, led by a dictator, no matter how benevolent, has to feed. And God forbid something does happen to her, and all of them are set free from their bonds—what then?"

"I'm not hurting her."

"I'm not putting a stake in your hand. I just want you to start to think. Please don't make me regret talking to you like this." He looked so earnest—I knew he believed what he was telling me.

I just hoped I wouldn't start believing it too. Anna was my friend. She'd saved me. She had to have her reasons for grabbing power back home—and hopefully she'd thought out all the repercussions of her actions. "I won't."

"Good."

I bit my lip. "Is Wolf Grey too?"

"Not in the least. He's Raven's lapdog, hook, line, and sinker."

"Then why are you?"

"I got into one hell of a bar fight back in the day. Wolf saw me brawl and decided to 'save' me." Jackson said the word as sarcastically as possible. "Never mind the fact that I had a wife and kid. Ever since then, I've wanted to get out." He saw the look of horror on my face and shook his head. "What, you think you're the first day-timer who wasn't happy about all this?"

"No," I lied. I'd actually never, ever considered that before. "When was that?"

"'Seventy-three." My guess about his age was right. Was I going to be trapped now, too, like he was, always thinking that the best of my life was behind me?

Maybe it was. I pushed that thought away. "What happened then?"

"House Grey said they could free me. Although it turns out their timetable's a lot longer than mine." His hands tightened around the steering wheel, and he turned the car back on.

We drove for five more minutes before I broke our silence. "You know you talk as if you're already one of them, even though you haven't changed."

"I'm close enough," he said, pulling us onto an expressway. "We have to get back. If I take any longer they'll notice, and I still have work to do tonight."

"Getting test subjects," I said with a frown.

"Right."

"What happens to them?" As much as I hoped Natasha's research was fruitless, I didn't want her to kill anyone to prove it.

"I don't rightly know. So far they've all died—but I'm not sure what goes on before that. It's why none of our Masters is allowed to kill anyone without permission—and why we don't have many donors anymore. Raven went through them first. Easier to keep things quiet."

"But you don't know what she does with them?"

"I'm not allowed to help in the lab. I don't know how." He shrugged. "I could learn, but she's not willing to teach me—and I was turned into a daytimer before science got so hard. I go in there to empty her trash cans, and deliver boxes of glassware, but that's it."

"So why did you rat me out to Raven?" I asked, but as I said it I realized I already knew. "Because you also want me to spy on her for you and House Grey. Great."

A sly smile lifted his lips, and he glanced at me out of the corner of his eye. "Anna's not the only one who worries them—and up close you'll have opportunities I won't."

"Even if I do, it won't mean I'm on your side."

"Fair enough." There was another long stretch of silence. "Besides, wouldn't you prefer working in the lab to being a janitor?"

Yes, if I didn't have a sinking feeling that she was carrying on her demented father's research. Nathaniel had been trying to create a synthetic blood replacement so that vampires would no longer need humans to survive. "Maybe," I admitted. I did need to know what she was up to.

"And she probably won't kill you if Raven tells her not to. Which is more than I can say for Lars."

The more I thought about Natasha and Raven, the more wrong it became. Her father'd been willing to kill thousands of people to save her—and she'd been playing house. "She's in love with him, isn't she?" I didn't know why it was so hard to believe it, even though I'd seen it with my own eyes. It just seemed so . . . unsafe. "Does he control her? Did he do that to her?"

"Nope. She came in that way. I was here the night she arrived."

"And he didn't command her to love him?"

"Not that I can tell. You can't really command emotions, besides. Behaviors, yes. He can tell you to act like you love him, but in your heart you'd know."

"Does he love her back?"

Jackson made a thoughtful noise. "Do vampires love? Does anyone? Who can say. He doesn't sleep around on the side, though—it's why Lars only gives him men, so as not to offend her. I've been watching them kiss for seven years now. Maybe it's close enough."

Asher's math was right—we were the same age, only she'd been frozen in time by being stolen away and given enough blood to stay looking perpetually young. And I bet seven years of captivity could earn you an epic case of Stockholm syndrome, regardless of your original feelings.

Jackson took the next few turns in silence as we

drove down surface streets, pausing to press a button for the garage door. When he drove us underground I watched the sky disappear and wondered when I would get to see it next.

CHAPTER NINE

We walked to the doors together, and Jackson hung the key back in the valet box on its hook. I followed along meekly, my mind a storm.

Baby, what have we gotten ourselves into?

Raven was waiting for us on the other side of the first set of doors. This startled me—and Jackson, who gave me a worried look, as if I'd somehow summoned Raven to betray his confidence. I didn't realize until that moment just how much he'd pinned on my secrecy.

"Master, I apologize for taking—" Jackson began.

Raven cut him off. "You may go."

Jackson bowed. "I'm sorry—"

"You may go," Raven said, sparing him a dark look.

Without raising his head, Jackson looked from Raven to me and pleaded at me with his eyes before leaving the room. When we were alone, Raven gave all of his attention to me.

"I'm afraid we haven't had a chance to be properly introduced yet. In private."

"I was led to believe that nowhere in the Catacombs was private," I said with a tight smile. I didn't want to follow him anywhere—at least in the hallway there was a chance someone might hear me scream. Not that they'd necessarily be inclined to come help.

"Jackson taught you well. But come, you wouldn't want to disappoint me, and I didn't save you to kill you just yet." He turned and started walking, and it was clear I was supposed to follow. With no other options, I did.

He led us back to the crossroads and then took one of the hallways Jackson said I shouldn't go down, walking half a block before opening the door to a private chamber then holding it for me, waiting. Feeling like a fly being invited into a spider's web, I walked past him.

Raven moved around me to sit on a low bed that occupied one half of the room. Everything was decorated much like his war room—in purple and black satin—but there was only one door, and I had no doubt he would be faster to it than I was. He patted the bed beside himself. I continued to stand, and he lifted his lips to show pointed teeth in an ironic grin.

"It's going to be like this between us?" His disappointment sounded genuine—and worse yet, caused me pain. "You're not a prisoner of war, you know. You're one of us. You're family."

I knew Raven was lying—Lars trying to kill me proved it—but part of me desperately wanted to believe him. A thick chill was coming on again, settling like sticky tar over the rational part of my mind. It was hard to look at the bittersweet smile on his face and hold firm, knowing that my resolve was in any way causing him pain.

"I want you to feel safe here, Edie," he said, stroking the empty space beside him on the bed. I wanted to feel safe too, so badly, more than anything else in the world—and how much more safe would I feel if I just took a step?

"Stop that," I said, not moving.

"Stop what?" he asked, then closed his eyes and shook his head. "Oh, that," he said, and gestured between the two of us, as if we were connected by a rope. "I can't. It's how we are."

I kept frowning, concentrating on staying still. "Will it always be like this?"

"It fades as the blood does, but to some degree, yes. I'm a part of you now, no matter how much you wish I weren't."

No wonder there were so many vampires scared of Anna, if after sharing blood she had this power over them. "Is there an antidote?"

"My blood is a poison then?" he asked, eyebrows rising. I didn't respond. "Only the ones I'm sure you've already thought of. Your death. Mine. You would find it hard to kill me now, though. Like calls to like, and seeks to keep it safe."

"I'm nothing like you."

He tilted his head. "And yet part of you, your very essence now, is me."

It was as though his attention were a weight, and the longer it was on me, the heavier it became. "Is that what happened with Natasha?" I asked.

He smiled softly. "No. She is mine by her choice. It is different between us."

How far off the mark had Nathaniel been? My God.

"I don't think you've appreciated the predicament you're in yet, Edie, so I've brought a prop." He reached into a pocket hidden by his coat and brought out a knife. "Do you know what this is?"

I nodded as my mouth went dry.

"Come here. Hold your hand out. Don't speak."

My body did as he commanded without thinking: I crossed the room with my hand out as if I were asking for a train ticket. Raven held the knife like he was going to slice open my belly. Everything in me was divided in two—the wise part of me that wanted to scream and run, and the part of me that was stock-still, forced to obey. *Oh baby, oh baby, oh baby*—

He reached out and tapped the blade on my palm. It burned like it was on fire. I couldn't see any blood, but surely he was cutting me, there was no way it could hurt any worse—he lifted the blade just as I thought I couldn't take anymore, and there was a white stripe across my palm where the blade had been, where I'd already scarred.

"It's silver. Hold it—gently now."

My fingers wrapped around the blade, and he let go of the hilt, leaving the weight of the knife in my hand. It burned, it burned, it burned, like fire on top of fire. It was as if the blade were serrated, even though I knew it wasn't; as if it were covered in spines that were stabbing into each of my nerves individually.

He was watching my reaction, and at some signal placed his hand back on the hilt. The weight transfer dug it in for a second, and I realized my mouth was open because I was trying to scream, even though I couldn't. He pulled it out of my hands, making it slide against my skin—the blade wasn't even sharp. It didn't need to be, not when silver hurt like this.

"Have you learned a lesson, Edie?"

My mouth was still open as the fire left me. I closed it, glaring at him.

"Feel free to speak now," he added as an after-thought.

"Don't touch silver," I said, because I knew it wasn't what he wanted to hear.

"Edie," he said, drawing out my name, waggling the weapon between us. Smart-Edie was still trying to make me jump back, but the rest of my body still wasn't listening.

"You can make me hurt myself. And there's nothing I can do to stop you."

"Good. Smart. Know, too, that I am imminently capable of violence," he said, seeming amused with his own honesty. "I am a vampire, after all."

"Did you rescue me just to brag?"

"No. I saved you to lure her here. She'll try to come and save you. I know it—I knew it the second she put out the call for your life. And you know it too, otherwise you'd have been groveling already." He finally put the knife away. "Do you have any powers or abilities you can use against me?" His voice was casual, but there was still the undertone that I had to answer.

I shook my head. "No. I'm normal."

"Then why does she want to save you?"

"She and I are friends."

"Why?"

There was no point in lying to him. "I saved her life."

There was a pause, and then the sound of Raven's laughter, cruel and long and harsh from disuse. "You? Saved her life? Please, tell me how."

I realized then that he didn't know everything—if he did, he wouldn't be asking me. And if he didn't tell me directly to tell him, with his awful-voice, the one I couldn't disobey, then I could say what I wanted to.

I'd been told once a long time ago that vampires love a loophole—well, so did this daytimer, now.

"There was a big fight. I was there, and I took her side," I said, as generically as possible.

"You expect me to believe that you were instrumental during the Dark Night? When she lured all of her Throne to one place to slaughter?" That wasn't quite how it'd gone down, but she hadn't exactly left any survivors to set the record straight. She'd been the prisoner of her countrymen for a century, tortured at their hands, and in that time anyone would develop a thirst for revenge. Anyone who'd made it out had probably wanted to believe they'd been the victims of a well-executed attack rather than a spectacular case of wrong-time-wrong-place-ness.

"I was there. I helped," I repeated. "What'll you do when she gets here?"

"What vampires always do. We'll have tea, play chess, trade the fascinating stories of our kind." His grin spread and became positively vulgar. "Or I'll slaughter her and make her watch while I eat her beating heart."

I still couldn't take a step back, but my face gave away my horror.

"What? Would you rather that I lie to you?"

"But you can't—" I began to protest.

"Who are you to tell me what I can and cannot do?" he said, in that horrible tone that I could not disobey. My mouth slammed shut and the thought of speaking vanished from my mind. "No one has commanded me for three hundred years. You would do well to remember just how much I could command you to do." He stood without saying another word and walked for the door.

I sagged in his wake. I had been dismissed.

Someone's throat cleared behind me, while I was still trying to reassemble the pieces of my mind into a cohesive whole. I whirled and saw Jackson there, looking apologetic.

"I just wanted to make sure you were intact."

"So far." He couldn't ask me out loud what he really wanted to know—if I'd told his secret. All I could do was shake my head when he had a questioning look in his eyes. "But it was awful. Is it always like that?"

"After they've freshly fed, yes. Plus it's worse when you're alone with them, and all their attention is focused on you."

Damn. How much night was left tonight? *Too much, baby.*

"I still have to go get test subjects—I don't think you want to come with me for that."

"No."

"I left a bag of food in Celine's room for you. You may not feel like you have to eat, but it's a good idea if you do. Makes the blood last longer in you when you're not running off it."

"Thanks." I'd rather run through the stuff if I could, so that Raven would have less power over me—but then I'd be all the weaker against future attacks. I exhaled roughly.

"You can find your way back?" Jackson asked, giving me a worried look.

"Yeah. Thanks," I said, nodding. A moment passed between us. Nothing sexual or even friendly, just a tacit acknowledgment that we were both fighters in the same war. In different trenches, but a trench was still a trench.

"See you tomorrow then." He nodded and left the room.

CHAPTER TEN

I waited for another thirty seconds. I could easily find my way back—but I still needed some time for myself, and it seemed unlikely Raven would immediately return to taunt me.

Without him in it, this room felt hollow. There wasn't anything here to let on much about him—no posters or furniture, other than the bed. I supposed the people he brought here were already so intoxicated with him that they didn't find the place a bit on the serial-killer side.

Which was what he was, no doubt. He could've killed me. Or, made me kill me. *And you, baby.*

Shit. Jackson was up there culling people like they were antelopes. I wanted to do something about it—Race upstairs? Pull a fire alarm?—but looking at the scar on my palm, I was too scared.

I was used to being nervous, and worried, and anxious—but what racked me now was a full-body fear. I might not have always had much concern for my own life, and I might have been too willing to trust in whatever luck had gotten me this far, but I couldn't bet my baby's life on it.

If it was always going to be like that with Raven, I didn't know how I could stop him. I had to figure out some way to warn Anna.

She had to know she was coming into a trap. She was too smart not to. But—even though I was frightened, I didn't want to believe I was impotent. Not doing anything would scar me worse than the silver had.

Yet how could I help her while I protected my baby?

I needed to learn as much as I could about this place, immediately. If there were safe places to hide, or alternative ways out, or ways I could somehow help Anna to get in. It didn't matter what he told me to do, or what my blood wanted, or that I was afraid—I knew who I was. *I want to be a mom you can be proud of, baby. Not enslaved to a horrible vampire for the rest of my too-long life.* I steeled myself and stepped outside.

On my right, the lights were stretched farther apart, like pinpricks into the darkness. The prisoner I'd met in my dream—was he down here too? Could he really free me? I had a good excuse to be here now, since Raven had brought me himself, but I might not get another. One hand protectively over my belly, I silently padded down the hall, glad I was in tennis shoes.

There were doors on either side—I listened at the first one I passed, holding my own breath, listening.

Storage? Or bodies? Or storage for bodies? I leaned in and tried to smell at the edges for blood but the only thing I could scent was pervasive musty damp, my own smell, skin, and the residue of Jackson's soap from earlier on today.

I decided it would be more useful to figure out how far the tunnel went than to open doors—door opening would be vastly safer during the day—so I trotted down to the end of the hall.

It sank and turned again. The tunnels under the Catacombs were just as tangled as Los Angeles's highways. I raced to the end of this one, bolder now that it seemed like everyone was busy upstairs in the club. The lights were farther apart; I counted off three of them and raced up to the last one, expecting to find another turn, then drew up short.

I'd reached the final light.

I was pretty sure the hall continued—it'd stopped being painted a long time ago, and the floors and ceiling were now smooth stone like you saw inside caves with stalagmites. But the power cable that'd been following my path ended with this last lightbulb; it was capped at the end.

Were these tunnels abandoned? Was it even a tunnel in front of me anymore? For all I knew it could open up into some massive cavern, or into an awful pit. I snapped my fingers once and heard the echoes reverberate into the blackness.

Did the vampires come down here at all? Was this where they slept? How could they see? Or were they hearing instead? Sonar? Heat vision? Scent trails, like ants? So much I didn't know, and so much that could kill me. I frowned into the dark. I'd seen all I could tonight—literally. After I swiped a lighter or a flashlight, I could risk coming back.

I wound through the halls I'd just come down, the stone rising subtly beneath my feet, and counted doors. There was a difference between the old ones and the worn ones. I assumed the old ones were unimportant, but I marked the worn ones in my mind—anything that was of use to a vampire might be of use to me.

I'd reached the land of paint again—was that Jackson's job too, I wondered?—when I heard a commotion near the crossroads, off to one side. I trotted up to the area I was allowed to be in right before the female vampire arrived.

She would have beaten me there if she weren't carrying a man along.

He was almost twice her size, and she had her arm around his waist, pulling him up against her the way a toddler sometimes carries a large doll. Her hair was wild, freed from its updo, pins hanging down akimbo. He had one hand sloppily beneath her collar around her shoulders and neck; his free hand was grasping for her breast, and she was laughing at him—until she saw/smell/heard me.

She stood straighter, wheeling him behind herself like she was hiding him from me, despite the fact there was no way that I could fail to see him around her. "What are you doing here?" she asked. Her voice sounded like a whipcrack in the silent hall, and I realized she was trying to control me—but it didn't quite work. What a relief.

"I got lost," I said, awkwardly bowing. "Mistress," I tacked onto the end, voice authentically unsure, peeking up at her from between strands of hair, meekly.

She looked at me like a bird would, one side then the next, as though her eyes were far apart and she needed to bring both of them to bear. The man was wearing a dark shirt with black stripes and a pattern with points of shininess. Some of her white makeup had transferred onto him, and his lips were stained the color of hers. He pushed her collar out of the way to try to kiss her neck. I wondered how he'd feel shortly once the tables were turned.

Would he be another of the satisfied customers that Jackson had told me about? Would he remember anything about how he got that makeup on his shirt tomorrow? She kept eyeing me while the man pawed at her. The weight of her gaze was far heavier than the tone of her voice—just because she couldn't control me didn't mean she couldn't hurt me. I didn't want her to drop the man and take up with me. I knelt lower, reaching one hand down to the cold ground, desperately trying to think of excuses for me to be down here. "I was hoping that I could find some clothing that would fit me better."

Her kohl-rimmed eyes narrowed and she let go of the man. He slid down her and to the floor without support, and then she flowed over to me, her heels hardly making a sound on the stone floor. It was hard not to move away after what I'd already been through with Raven. I wanted to scuttle backward and protect myself, cross my arms over my baby and curl into a ball, but I knew moving would be bad—in the same way that deer did, right before they got hit by cars.

She leaned down, putting one of her pale hands underneath my chin, lifting my head up until I was on my knees and her face was beside mine, her eyelashes batting against my cheek. She inhaled deeply, then exhaled. "You smell like him."

I didn't know what to say to that. She released my chin and looked at me as though she'd just found out a secret. "I could make you irresistible," she crooned, her voice an instrument played for me alone. "I know his needs. His wants. His desires. I could show you how to please him."

I had a feeling she wasn't talking about the incapacitated man on the floor. "No, thank you," I said, as politely as I could.

"Pity," she said. Her tone was mocking, but that could have just been her accent. "I can help you with clothing tomorrow, but if I do you a favor, you'll have to do me one."

I nodded, because that was generally how favors with vampires worked, and I didn't want to anger a creature that could snap me in two.

"Good." She bent over and picked the man off the ground, heaving him up to her shoulder as if he were a sack of flour, he didn't outweigh her by 150 pounds, and she weren't in heels.

"You're a strong one!" he laughed as he was manhandled aloft.

"They think we women are weak, but we know otherwise," she said, grinning at me with fangs out before turning to finish carrying him down the hall.

I waited until she was gone and hurried back to Celine's room.

I prayed I wouldn't see anyone on the way there, and I didn't. Jackson, true to his word, had left a bag of fast food for me. I had no idea how long my detour had taken, but the burger grease was congealed and the fries were cold. I supposed I should be glad it wasn't pickles and ice cream. I ate all the burger and half the fries and hoped that there was some folic acid in it somewhere, since I didn't think I could get anyone to go out for prenatal vitamins on my behalf.

While I ate, I thought. About the last time I had fries with Asher, on the *Maraschino*. It really hadn't been all that long ago, but it seemed like my life kept picking up speed, actions and consequences blurring into a red shift that was becoming harder to make sense of.

An unknown vampire had contacted me in my dreams, I didn't know what Natasha was researching yet, Raven wanted me to lure Anna in, Jackson wanted me to betray Anna to House Grey—and Anna was my only hope of ever seeing Asher again.

I missed him. I'd been so busy or scared since I'd gotten here that I'd hardly had a chance to breathe, but oh, I missed him. What I wouldn't give to be able to curl up into his arms and be safe—or put my back against his and fight our way out of here together.

I put my hand against my stomach. "I don't know if you can hear me, baby—but I love your father very much."

"We're honestly touched," muttered something from the bottom of my bag of fries, followed by a rustling sound.

I jumped, startled, and heard the sound of the Shadows laughing at me.

"Too rich by half!" they chortled.

I reddened with shame. "Stop it. You're not supposed to scare me, we're supposed to be a team. Have you been in there this whole time?"

"Long enough that you ought to feel foolish."

I had the temptation to walk the bag over to the vanity

and open it up beneath the light—they might not all die, but they'd have to hide under the last half of my fries.

"Temper, temper," they chided.

"How'd you get in there?" I asked, as I saw. There was a shadow extending from one of the posters on Celine's bed out to where Jackson had set the bag. "What were you hoping to accomplish?" I squinted at the bag's outside. "Were you hoping to get thrown out?"

"And crawl back across two thousand miles on our own? Not hardly. We were merely bored."

"I'm so glad I've been risking my life and dealing with insane vampires all night while you've been coming up with ways to startle me."

"You can't blame us," they said, their voices shifting. "We thought you might have died. In fact, we're surprised you're still alive, given your propensity toward self-sacrifice, although it's probably hard to find something worth dying for in here." I could see their form in the shadows created on the inside of the bag. They pulsed when they spoke, like a miniature heart. "What did you learn? Don't make us sift around in your brain. We're afraid the vacuity there might kill what's left of us."

I didn't appreciate their tone, but realized they were merely blustering. The portion of Shadows I held here had originally come from a much larger mass, a frightening powerful darkness, capable of, it seemed, almost anything. But this little group here—easily killed by exposure to light and half a world away from Port Cavell—was as lost as a lamb.

"Don't you dare feel sorry for us," they warned me with a growl.

"I didn't find any useful way out yet. I'm working on it."

"You do realize that with every moment here you weaken?"

"Thanks for the reminder."

"We're saying you need to hurry, girl. Not just for yourself, but for us."

Like them being in danger would hasten me to action. I snorted. Then their shadow inside the bag suddenly flattened completely, like a gopher dropping into a hole.

I shook the bag. "Shadows?"

The bell rang as Celine pushed open the door behind me, and I understood why they were hiding. She was carrying a bag of food just like I was, and eyed me, my fingers still covered in grease. "Club's closed, and mostly cleaned. Thanks for being so much help."

"You're welcome," I said back with equal sarcasm. "Do we have to present ourselves again?" I figured Jackson would have come and found me if so.

"No. Usually everyone drifts off when they're done."

"And all your ladies, they're through?"

"It's a Tuesday," she said with a shrug. "The promise of sex can only do so much—and only men who have to work tomorrow can afford them." She carefully took her shoes off, lining them up beside her bed, and then sat down on it and pulled out her burger. Maybe being a daytimer meant getting to eat all the hamburgers you wanted, hooray. I folded the top of the bag the Shadows were in to keep them safe and set it down nonchalantly.

"Do you enjoy being a daytimer?" I asked, to keep our conversation going and so she wouldn't ask why I'd been talking to a bag.

Celine made a face at me while she chewed. "Yeah. It's fantastic. Rainbows and ponies, the whole time." She took another huge bite of burger.

It was hard for me to imagine her being any other way, but clearly she hadn't always been a daytimer. She must have had, once upon a time, other hopes and dreams. They were probably pinned like butterflies underneath her framed head shots. "What were you before this? An actress? Or a model?"

She swallowed, then took another bite, rather than answer me. I watched her eat, trying to wait her out, but it didn't work. When she was done she pulled her legs up onto the bed. "Can it be bedtime now?"

"Is anyone else going to try to kill me tonight?"

"Only in my dreams." She dusted her hands off and then reached up to draw the curtains of her bed.

I went to set the bell over the door. Then, lying down in my nest of pillows and sheets again, I turned the light off.

CHAPTER ELEVEN

I heard a rustling sound from the bag. The Shadows were probably setting themselves free, or they were faking it and would be trying to hitch a ride to the dump with the trash tomorrow, agreement with me forgotten. There'd be no way to talk to them with Celine in the room, but right now they weren't my first priority. I needed to sleep first, to keep up my strength, and to see if I could find that strange vampire in my dreams.

As an ex-night-shift nurse I was good at operating tired—which would probably be a good thing if I managed to live long enough to be a parent. But the punishment for that was sometimes my body held on far longer than it ought to, as if I were fighting sleep itself. Between worrying about the baby, Asher, and Anna, I could be up for the next forty days straight.

Somehow though, in the abyssal dark of the catacombs, I finally slept.

Instead of dreaming about my house this time, I was in a land of rolling hills, covered in desert scrub. I spun around making sure I didn't have any company and muttered, "The hills are alive." I took another look in all directions. "I guess that's okay, as long as they don't have eyes."

"Why would hills have eyes?"

I jumped, startled anew, and found a man standing behind me. I decided to not honor his question with a discussion of seminal horror films. "Is it you?"

He nodded. He looked like he'd just stepped off a statue, because he was wearing a toga. He was a little shorter than I was, though far more muscular, and his skin was dark tan where it showed.

"What's your name?"

"It's not safe to tell you that. Right now, I could merely be a bad dream."

I grunted. In case Raven interrogated me. Even if I thought my dreams were real, there was currently no proof, and I supposed it was safer for both of us. "Can you really kill him?"

"Do you really want me to?"

Now that I was out of Raven's presence I had my right mind. "The sooner the better." Before he could trick me again, or me myself.

"Then yes, I can."

"How?"

"Because I am his Sire. If I command, he must obey. I could even command him to kill himself, and he would."

"I take it that's why you're a prisoner here?"

"Indeed."

This was sounding too easy. "Are you're sure you're not a dream?"

He raised his hand, and our surroundings changed.

The desert scrub folded away, replaced by sharp mountain peaks and drifts of snow. Then we were near a river, bridged by stone, and on an ocean shore, standing on rough rocks—"Okay, okay." I held my hands up. "You can stop shaking the snow globe now."

The world around us resolved into a pavilion in front of a temple, lined with columns, a statue standing between each pair. Roman—original. The statues were painted, not worn white by time. Each had a face not unlike my mysterious friend's.

"I have lived for very long and traveled well. These are my dreams, not yours."

"Agreed." My dreams would have had a lot more traffic in them, or involved me being back at school and having forgotten my locker combination. "But why are all of them in daylight?"

He looked taken aback, but quickly recovered. "Because you wouldn't want to see me in the dark."

Probably true—or even vampires missed the sun. It wasn't worth calling him on, though. I walked down the steps of the temple to the road outside and started smoothing sand for him to draw on. "Make a map and show me where you are."

He followed me, more slowly. "I . . . cannot. I was incapacitated when I was brought here. I do not know where I am."

Here at last was the much more familiar difficult part. "You're kidding me, right?" I dusted my hands off on my legs and stood. "You're aware that there's an apparently endless system of tunnels where you could be? Do you know anything about where you are?"

"In a hole. In the dark. My walls are stone, and my cell is grated with silver."

I'd finally found someone who could help me, and I didn't even know where to begin. I started pacing in a circle.

"But if you find me and free me—" he began.

"You'll kill him. I get it." I looked back at the temple behind us. He was like it, in a way. Hugely powerful, currently completely useless. "Why me? Why haven't you asked someone else for help?"

The temple shimmered like a mirage and we were in the hilly desert again, forcing me to look back at him. His face was serious and drawn. "You've already been a servant long enough to know that admitting weakness among our kind is halfway to defeat." I nodded, and he went on. "When I woke you from your last dream to save your life—did you kill the one who tried to take it?"

I closed my eyes. "No. Which was probably a mistake."

"Probably," he agreed. "But it shows that you are ruthless enough to contemplate your Master's death for freedom, but not ruthless enough to kill without thought."

So he was willing to help me because I seemed unlikely to kill him. Damned with faint praise, once again. "There are others here who want out. Why not one of them?"

"Because they're not also with a child they want to keep."

My baby was just a little extra assurance that I

wouldn't kill him for his blood once I found him. I hugged myself. "Why're you so weak?"

"I've been starved for the better part of three centuries. A servant shoves in pieces of half-drained corpses that I wouldn't feed a dog, then leaves them here to decay and foul me."

"A servant? Which one?"

"Different ones over time. This most recent one, I could not say. The scent they leave behind is artificial—your world, not mine. And no one ever visits at night. But they've been absent for a month now."

Was there a way I could ask the others, safely? Jackson, maybe, but none of the rest of them. "How long does it take a vampire to starve to death?" I wouldn't only have to free an angry vampire—I'd have to figure out how to feed one too.

"Hopefully not as long as it takes for you to find me," he said, lips pulled thin. "If you value your own life, and that of your child, you must find me quickly."

There were other things I wanted to know—how his dream powers worked, how he'd originally been trapped, and just how old he was—but for now the final thing I needed be sure of was my safety. "You promise you won't hurt my child? Or me? Or my friends?"

"Do you have any friends here?" he asked, eyebrows rising.

"Who knows how long it'll take me to find you. I might by then." I already knew I didn't want to kill Jackson. I frowned at myself. Dammit, Edie, *dammit.*

"Then I promise to not kill you, your child, or anyone you mark as friend. Just find me as soon as possible."

Easier said than done. But if the Shadows had stuck around overnight, maybe they could be convinced, or threatened, into helping me. "I'll start looking in the haystacks for you tomorrow."

A questioning look clouded his face. "There is no hay down here."

"It's called an idiom. You've missed out on some things. Let me go back to sleep, okay? I might need the rest."

He looked for a moment like he might refuse me, long enough for me to wonder if even vampires could get lonely, and then acquiesced. I slept.

I woke up feeling unrested, but at least no one had tried to kill me during the night. Or morning. Whatever it was right now. I hadn't felt the moment when the night had changed to dawn, but I had a feeling that Raven was asleep—it was as if a subtle weight had been lifted off my shoulders. I found the remote and clicked on the light and heard Celine complain inside her bed-palace.

"I'm going to the restroom. If I'm not back in fifteen minutes, send reinforcements."

Celine snorted. Her foot had pushed a corner of her curtain out of the way, and I could see her face pressed into a pillow, hiding from the light.

I took the bag of fast food with me, to throw away, or so I could confer with the Shadows in private. The sooner I could set them loose to look for the prisoner, the better.

I moved the bell and stepped out into the hallway— and found a pile of shirt boxes, with a nice note on top. *Now you owe me,* it said, and beneath that *Estrella,* with a flourish, as if she were signing an autograph for a fan.

So that was the female vampire's name.

The door opened up behind me and I jumped, afraid Celine was coming after me. She held her ground. "What? You're not the only one with a bladder," she protested. Then her eyes flicked to the hip-high boxes of clothes, and she saw the note. Her lips, still the color of last night's lipstick, puckered as if she'd just licked a lime.

"I didn't mean to—"

Celine held her hand up for silence, and then walked around me, hand still outstretched. After that she sauntered on to the bathroom, and I was afraid to follow her.

It was probably impossible to piss Celine off more than her Mistress's actions already had. I opened up the top box. It had a kilted skirt, pleats ironed neatly, and a folded white top below that. The second box held shoes, for the skirt in the next box—a slinky floor-length skirt with a tight black tube top?

Each box was as improbable as the next, and many of them came with suggested shoes or items of jewelry. Was she honestly suggesting I should wear any of these? They did look like they were my size, but they were uniformly hideous—and none of them would look good on me a month from now, or a month after that.

Maybe Natasha would at least give me a lab coat. Hopefully not made out of test subjects' skin. At that dark thought, I felt queasy for the first time since I'd left the *Maraschino* and cursed my overactive imagination—then wondered if the safety of Raven's blood had been breached. It wasn't only me "wearing" his blood out—it was my wonderfully immune and tenacious half-shapeshifter child too. I paused, trying to find a tickle of morning sickness in myself, not sure if I was hoping it was gone, or back—it would be nice to feel pregnant again, even if it meant throwing up some. *Things are going okay in there, right, baby?* Nothing in response. But I was only five or six weeks along. I hadn't had any bleeding or cramps. I'd have to assume the best for now, because I couldn't afford emotionally to think about anything else.

I opened up the next box from Estrella, expecting another hideous outfit and finding it. A romper, the sort of thing that I wouldn't have even worn back when I was thirteen. I prepared to toss it aside, and then thought better and checked. It, unlike all the other options so far, had pockets.

Outfit acquired.

I was wearing it by the time Celine came back, but I didn't dare talk to the Shadows with the chance of her hearing. She took one look at me and snorted before remounting her bed. I was hoping she'd draw the curtains closed and I could turn the light off again, but there was a polite knock at the door and I answered it, knowing no one but Jackson would bother.

His eyebrows rose, taking in my sartorial choice. "You're wearing that?"

"Yep."

"Well," he said, surveying the other boxes in the hall, "all right then. I came to get you—Natasha's up, and she's already sciencing away."

"Thanks." I was torn. Now there was no way to get to the Shadows safely. Even if I took the fast-food bag to the bathroom, Jackson would be right outside, listening in. Despite the fact that he'd trusted me with his secret, I didn't want to share them—if they managed to find the man in my dreams, they were my ticket out of here, maybe even before Anna got involved. I looked back into the room behind me. "Hey, Celine, I want to save these fries for later."

"I'll get more—" Jackson said.

"I like cold ones, and salt." I gave him an I'm-not-quite-in-control-of-my-hormones smile. He shrugged, and Celine groaned.

"Fine. Leave me the remote."

I turned off the light and tossed it into her bed.

After we'd walked down half the hall he turned toward me. "You realize when you get back, those fries'll be laced with cyanide?"

"I'm okay with that." I wished I'd been able to set the Shadows loose. At least I'd left them in the dark—assuming they were still in the room.

"So what's with the boxes?" Jackson asked, leading me back toward the crossroads.

"Estrella wants to be on my good side."

"Like a lamprey eel," he said with a snort.

"This is better than spandex."

"Not by much."

There was an awkward silence between us when I knew what I wanted to ask, but not how to ask it. "How'd the rest of last night go?"

"Did I find two more test subjects? Yes."

I twisted my lips to one side without saying anything.

"After a while it gets easy. Until people start coming in here and looking at me like you are." He turned away from me, as if there were something interesting passing by on the gray stone wall. "You do what you have to do to get by. The ends justify the means, and all that."

I had a lot of questions for him about how House Grey was "protecting" humanity by having him get people for Natasha to kill, but I knew they'd have to wait. "So all the bodies get lye'd afterward?"

"Yeah. But there haven't been any new ones for about a month."

"Why not?"

"I'm not sure. The cages are empty, and Natasha keeps needing new people—maybe she's doing her own cleanup now. There's more than one key to the lye chamber." He shrugged.

"Were all the bodies that you disposed of . . . intact?"

He gave me a surprised look. "No. Why?"

I shrugged. "No reason." I had a feeling I knew who was now feeding the prisoner, intermittently. *The plot thickens, baby.* I wondered what had changed with her research during the past month, though.

We were almost at the crossroads. I knew we wouldn't be going down the darker path I'd taken last night, and since I still wasn't sure about the Shadows, my search might be on my own. I didn't think I could ask for a flashlight, but maybe I could get away with a little less. "Jackson, can I borrow a lighter?"

His attention was back on me in an instant, perhaps imagining Celine's bed going up in flames like a pyre. "Why?"

"I used to smoke," I lied. "Might as well start again while I'm invulnerable now."

"No, you didn't. Your teeth are too nice. And you don't need to be going down dark hallways, besides. You have an assignment," he said with a tone. To spy on Natasha on House Grey's behalf. Right.

We reached a metal door, and Jackson opened it with one hand.

CHAPTER TWELVE

The doorway led to a short hall, and I could hear the whirring of ventilation ducts. "Negative air pressure?" How'd they manage that down here?

"Only the best for Raven's princess," Jackson said with a nod. He opened up the next door, and the stone floor changed to tile.

Natasha's room was a lab. It was twice as big as Celine's room, and had partitions with shiny fume hoods and brown glass light-proof jars of chemicals. Several machines thrummed—I recognized some of them from biology lab, centrifuges and a spectrometer, but others I couldn't name. Levered refrigerator doors lined one wall.

I'd been imagining something medieval-torture-chamber-esque, not white floors and shining metal. Then again, some of the worst atrocities known to man had been done in the name of science—and revenge, if you counted the *Maraschino*.

"Natasha! Delivery!" Jackson shouted beside me, then, more quietly, "She doesn't like it when I wander around in here."

"Of what?" Natasha yelled back.

"A co-scientist!"

Not hardly. I stuck my hands in my new pockets and waited for her to appear.

When she rounded the corner she was wearing a lab coat. Her hair was in a high ponytail again, safety goggles perched on top, and her lipstick was a childish shade of fuchsia pink, the only pop of color against the rest of her black. When she saw my outfit, she broke into an amused grin. Rompers were pretty nonthreatening; I'd accidentally made a good choice. She waved her hand in dismissal at Jackson. "I'm done with you now, janitor."

"I'm supposed to take her back whole at nightfall," he said.

"Yeah, yeah," she agreed, and kept waving.

Jackson's face wasn't as positive, but he left the way we'd come without comment. One of the machines in the room picked up speed, like a washing machine finishing its cycle.

I hadn't realized until right then how alone we'd be. The last time I'd been alone with her father he'd brutally dislocated my shoulder. Fear surged inside me at the memory—Nathaniel'd hurt me, he'd hurt Asher, and he'd killed four thousand people, all to rescue her. A tar-black flower blossomed in my heart, a petal for each dark idea of how to make her pay me back for what he'd done—

She leaned in, startling me from my line of thought. "I said, at least you have closed-toe shoes!" she shouted as though I were deaf.

I blinked and looked down. I was still wearing my trusty tennis shoes. The ones I'd been through hell and back in. "Yeah." Reality was back and the darkness was gone. I wanted to keep it that way. I curled my hands into fists, biting my nails into my palms.

"I'll order you safety goggles and a lab coat. Try to find some pants, okay? Sometimes we use phenol, and I don't want you melting spots into your legs. You won't need them today, I've already done all the work with the last sample batch." She turned and walked away, still talking, assuming I was following after her. The light caught the charm bracelet I'd seen before on her wrist and made it sparkle.

Natasha paused and looked back at me. "Well? Come!" she said expectantly. I trotted up to her like an obedient dog without thinking. I'd forgotten Raven had told me to do whatever she'd said until that exact moment.

She watched the surprise on my face and frowned. "I forgot he tied you to me, sorry. I'll try not to use it, as long as you don't go crazy, okay? What I'm going to show you next might startle you."

It felt weird to have her sympathy after I'd been guilty of such dark thoughts. "Okay," I said with trepidation.

She nodded and pushed the door open, revealing what was inside. "Meet test subject sixty-four."

I walked into a room that had a prone woman shackled to an autopsy table near one wall. She was naked and covered in wires on a table that had a basin at one end and a drain at the other. She was bound wrist and foot, with lockable leather restraints, and I bet Natasha had the only key.

It was odd that she was strapped down and still connected by cables to an ECG. All the leads on her chest were hooked to one monitor, showing a series of completely flat lines. There was another monitor beside it, one that I was less familiar with, and leads from her shaved head were connected to it, and I realized it was an EEG machine, for electroencephalography—brain, instead of heart. Its monitor was white and had twenty or so lines, just as flat as the others. An arm from the EEG jutted out, holding a camera. I'd only seen one of these twice before, both times in a hospital setting, on patients who'd had profound brain damage due to hypoxia after heart attacks or strokes. When family members couldn't believe that their loved ones were blinking just to blink, and wanted to read patterns into the spastic movements of the brain dead, doctors set up EEGs to prove that there was no controlled brain function left.

I was so used to seeing people with wires on them and over them, it took me a moment to process how profoundly strange all this was: Natasha was monitoring someone who was completely, head and heart, dead.

I looked back to her, and found her watching me. "So you really are a nurse," she said. I gave her a questioning look. "You didn't freak out," she explained.

Only on the inside. "What's going on here?"

"I'm running some delicate tests," she said coyly. "On people."

"I'm not asking for your approval." She sounded bemused.

"Good, because you wouldn't get it."

She actually laughed at this. "You're sassy. It's refreshing. The others are mostly scared of me."

Just like I probably should be. *I need to stop thinking with my mouth, baby.* I looked at her. She was young, yes, a little too pretty for her own good, yes, but she didn't look like a serial killer—which was probably test subjects one through sixty-three's last thought. "What's the EEG for?"

"So I know the exact moment when things work. Raven's right—I haven't gotten more than four hours of sleep in a row in months. I do need a helper, and I don't trust the rest of them. I don't trust you either," she said with a snort, "but you might actually be competent. Jackson's just a butcher, you know? And Celine's too obsessed with being pretty to be smart, and Lars—" She rolled her eyes. "He thinks he's too good for this because he's been Raven's servant longer than I have."

I looked to the monitors. There was a blood pressure cuff set up, reading question marks, and a blue oxygenation monitor cable stuck to the woman's right big toe, reading zero. At least all the alarms were off; otherwise everything that could be beeping a warning, would be. "But she's dead," I said.

"Yeah, she is. That's the whole point." Natasha gave me a smug smile. "Ever drawn blood from a dead person?" I shook my head, and she went on. "Of course not. Whatever, I can teach you. It's not that hard—and it's not like they're a moving target." She handed me gloves and a face shield. I'd learned in the past that if someone ever offered you a face shield, you put it on *immediately*. But I didn't think Miss No-Pulse here was going to start spitting. Natasha read the confusion on my face. "It won't spurt out at you—no heartbeat means no blood pressure. I just don't want you shedding skin cells and germs into my sample. Lean in and see."

I watched her work with the efficiency of someone who had done this sixty-three times before, possibly multiple times per patient. She swiped a cleaning agent over the woman's chest, and I saw several other tiny holes there in among the leads and cords.

"I try to go into the same hole, but the heart only has so much blood in it—it doesn't matter which ventricle you use. You don't just randomly jab in the torso—even if you do get blood, you'll get too many other tissues and by-products of decay. If you run out—sometimes Jackson gets lazy and the test subjects are small and their hearts don't hold that much—you can milk it from a subclavian or the fem, but then you have to squeeze their leg or arm while you're pulling the syringe plunger out—that'll be easier with extra hands, for sure. I tell him not to get women with fake breasts too, but this *is* LA."

By the time she was done talking, she'd pulled out ten ccs of blood. The charms on her bracelet dangled as she held up the syringe. There were only two of them, a heart with a *C* engraved on it, and ballet shoes. It didn't match the rest of her hand, holding up a syringe of a dead person's blood.

The question I wanted to shout to the heavens was,

Why? I assumed we were continuing her father's illegal research into creating blood substitutes. If so, there might be some value in blood samples, yes, but not in leaving all these leads hooked up—or shackles on. People who'd been poisoned by off-brand fake blood didn't wake up.

"I think from here on out, you'll be doing all the body work. I'll show you how to prep the subjects, shave the heads, affix the leads—both machines have diagrams on them to show you where the stickers go—"

"I know where to put ECG leads." There was probably value in letting her think I was dumb, but I still had some nursing pride. "What I don't get is why you're killing people."

She looked at the blood in the syringe she held and then at me. "Would you believe me if I told you it was for a greater good?"

Not in the least. But if I told her that, our conversation would shut down and I wouldn't discover anything. "I'm listening." It wasn't hard to sound realistically reluctant.

Natasha gestured at the body with the syringe. "You already know what vampire cells do for us. What if we could use them for other things? Like, say, to cure cancer?"

That struck remarkably close to home, and my mom. To think that once upon a time I'd tried to sign her up for this. With Dren, of all vampires. "But you're killing people."

"Be honest, Edie. If she was here, she probably wasn't going to amount to anything. I know everyone wants to think their kid's going to do something remarkable, but how often is that really the case? Your kid excluded, of course. I'm sure yours will be quite the special snowflake."

I tried not to react, but it was too late. She shook her head. "Raven doesn't hide anything from me—and I don't hide anything from him."

"So you're saying he wants you to cure cancer?" I found that hard to believe, and I wanted to get the topic off me and my baby.

"Among other things. But first I have to know fully how vampirism works. How the cells transfer and take hold, how they propagate—why they kill first, how they revive later, and what happens in between." Intellectually, I could see how that would be fascinating, apart from the killing-people part. She waggled the syringe between us. "Honestly, she wasn't going to amount to anything in the scheme of things."

"But how do you know?"

Natasha snorted. "Statistically, I think I'm pretty safe."

I frowned. "So you think only big things count?"

"Yeah. That's why they're big. Besides, why should life be more fair to someone else than it was to me?" She tossed the syringe into the air and caught it with the preternatural agility of a daytimer. "I've got to go start the cycle. I'll be right back," she said, and left me alone with the corpse.

Natasha's "body work" didn't involve washing the woman off—she still had on the smoky makeup she'd arrived at the Catacombs with, plucked eyebrows, and tastefully nude lips. Her arms ended in delicate fingertips with clear nail polish on them, and her toenails were painted red. If she hadn't had the leads on, she would have made the perfect mannequin. I assumed Natasha had just cut her clothes off her instead of wrestling her out of them.

She looked young, not just because of her makeup, but because she was. At the hospital, when people look a certain way—homeless, drugged out, worn out by alcohol or life—you shrug and say "Okay." A girl like this, though—she might have been running away, but someone knew she was gone. She wasn't old enough and didn't look lost enough to have fallen off the map yet. She looked like a sleeping beauty, waiting for a rescuing prince.

I stepped away from her, emotions welling up. I had a hard time being mad for things that happened to me, but I was good at standing up for other people, and I felt like this woman needed protecting.

What promises could I make to her, though, when she was already dead? I'd missed my chance when I hadn't tackled Jackson before he'd chosen her last night, and God or fate or karma had let her fall through the cracks. I stepped away from the table suddenly feeling exhausted and looked for a place to sit.

There was only one chair in this room—in front of a sleek computer. I heard a machine winding up from the other room, so I quickly sat down and touched the keyboard. The monitor woke, and a pad by the keyboard lit.

A biometric lock. Medication machines at the hospital used them so that visitors couldn't get bad ideas and sticky fingers. I pressed my forefinger to the pad; it glowed but didn't unlock. Of course not.

I sighed and played through my next three fingers, just to have something to do besides thinking about sharing a room with a cruelly used corpse. The computer glowed a warning about running out of attempts, but whatever, who were they sending it to? Raven wasn't up. And playing with it was a way to forget how I'd failed the woman the night before—a way to ignore her corpse.

The computer, assuming I was an idiot, gave up on me and went to a password prompt. I hadn't expected that—but maybe if Natasha was using solvents like phenol in her lab she wanted secondary access in case she ever burned the crucial fingerprint off.

Of course I didn't have a password for it either. I made sure to switch to caps before I typed RAVENISADICK in one and VAMPIRESSUCK in the next one and hit RETURN.

Not surprisingly, those didn't log me in. I went through a few more curse words, and then just bashed at the keys because it felt good. When I was done, I fumbled around the back of the screen to turn the monitor off.

"What are you doing?" Natasha asked, coming into the room.

"I just wanted to check my email," I said, deadpan.

"Yeah, no." Natasha rolled her eyes. "Two hours from now you're going to need to draw blood again. I'll be back by to supervise. You're welcome to wait here—if you leave, Jackson'll make you scrub more toilets." She glanced back at the prone woman. "And if anything happens with her—make sure you get on this side of the door and lock it."

My eyebrows rose. "You're kidding, right?"

She shook her head. "Nope!" she said and waved as she shut the door behind her.

CHAPTER THIRTEEN

A human body had ten pints of blood, roughly four liters. If we were taking ten ccs out at a time, and there were thirty ccs in an ounce, and sixteen ounces in a pint, and a northbound train was coming at sixty miles an hour while Jimmy was biking south on the tracks . . . I looked around the sterile room again, and then at the body. This was sort of how I imagined a waiting room in hell would be. Natasha did have a point. It wasn't like I had anywhere else, or better, to go. I didn't want to hang out with Celine after Estrella's earlier display, or try Jackson's patience—or have him try to pump me for information that I didn't have.

At least here I could snoop around.

I stood and walked over to the closed door, trying the handle. She hadn't locked it. I noticed the door itself was solid steel, and the frame had been reinforced, which seemed odd. I opened it, peeked out, and—finding myself alone—closed it and started opening drawers.

Most of the cabinets were empty, but there was a drawer full of neatly stacked medical supplies. Butterfly needles in all gauges for blood draws on normal people with blood pressure, boxes of alcohol wipes, rolls of tape, and individually wrapped packets of gauze. A drawer full of test tubes, another of sterile ten-cc syringes; one had a whole box of needles.

There were also more mysterious implements, loose, with flecks of blood. I made sure not to touch any of them. One of them was definitely a bone saw. I hadn't seen an autoclave on my way in, but maybe sterility didn't matter all that much since everyone Natasha experimented on died.

I was in the same position I'd been in since I'd gotten here—no power, no chance to fight back or even warn anyone. I could destroy her computer, but then what? There was a chance that I'd fatally piss off Raven, and Natasha would be shaving my head next. Maybe afterward she'd send my arm down to the prisoner.

Baby, usually the world is not this bleak, I swear.

I turned back to the woman on the table. If Natasha was waiting for someone to come back from the dead, I might be interested in getting a heads-up too. All her lines were still flat, and none of her had moved. It was easy to be freaked out because she was so lifelike.

Even though I didn't see dead bodies often, I knew they had signs. I leaned over to look at the backs of her legs, where her unused blood should have been pooling into vasodilated capillaries, making her look like she was half bruised, but it wasn't. And she wasn't bloated. There was a chance that she'd just finished being "subjected" before I got into the room. But still—I took her hand in mine. Her fingers slipped into my grasp and were as supple as they'd probably been in life.

She didn't feel dead. Or look dead. But—Natasha had

all as much admitted that she'd been dosed with vampire blood. The only question was how long ago—and from whom.

I set her hand back down where it had been—facing up, fingers slightly curved—carefully, as if I might wake her up. One of the services on floor Y4, where I'd been a nurse and gotten started on my supernatural path, was to stockpile blood for some of the local vampire Thrones. The Shadows had given the place enough security that they could feel comfortable banking blood there for later, should they need to change anyone fast. But it always-always-always took three days. I'd only seen one transfusion where a daytimer had gotten enough blood to change. At the time, it had seemed like that person had died. And once I'd kept a changed daytimer in my closet for three days to help out Anna. She'd seemed dead right up until she'd woken up hungry and gone berserk on an unlucky werewolf burglar.

I didn't know if this was the test subject Jackson had admitted to getting last night, but I had a feeling she was. If so, why did Natasha's warning to run for the door sound so sincere? She should be dead—or asleep, or whatever euphemism anyone used—for seventy-two hours straight. If that was the case, though, why was all the monitoring equipment running, as if it were waiting to chart the moment she woke? I stood up and paced, thinking, sure to keep a close eye on her.

Raven shouldn't have been able to make another daytimer so quickly after saving me—Lars's jealousy had made that clear. Ingesting mere human blood wasn't enough to even out the deficit of giving me so much of his. Just because you ate carrots didn't mean that you'd bleed carrots—there was a strange, possibly metaphysical, metabolic pathway for vampire blood that had to be followed in between.

But Natasha was unlikely to work for any of the other vampires, and Raven wasn't the type to allow any other of his flock to gain advantage on him. I faced the woman with crossed arms. Whose baby was she?

The only thing I knew for sure was that Natasha wasn't following in Nathaniel's footsteps anymore—human blood-substitute tests didn't involve turning people into vampires. Despite her altruistic claims, if she'd managed to turn someone from human to vampire in under one day's time, she was far worse for humanity than her dearly departed dad.

I circled to the computer again and sat down, elbows on the desk, holding my chin in my hands in thought while I stared at all her monitors' straight lines.

After three minutes of watching her not-breathe, I risked looking down at the keyboard.

HAVE I MENTIONED HOW MUCH THIS BLOWS? I typed out, hammering my frustration with each letter.

The monitor flickered to life, showing the login screen. It would have been awesome if that had somehow managed to be Natasha's username and password combination. My estimation of her would have shot way, way up.

A word-processing program opened and a cursor started blinking at the top of the screen.

The keyboard is monitored. Do not touch it again.

I put my hands by my sides like a child who'd just been caught. The window shrank in half and then another window opened, and an absolutely frightening face took its place.

I'd never been so happy to see an eyeless, lipless man in my life—his exposed gums and teeth made it look like a jack-o'-lantern was grinning at me.

"Gideon?" I whispered. Gideon was one of Anna's daytimers; he'd been working for her and been caught and tortured. They'd cut off portions of his fingers, and all of his ears and lips, then gouged out his eyes. He was helpless, and since everyone else Anna knew was nocturnal, he'd been dumped on me to babysit. At the same time Gideon was there, I'd been harboring a ghost in an old CD player. This ghost—who kind-of-sort-of claimed to be Wayland Smith, the legendary blacksmith from Nordic lore, but I called him Grandfather because he seemed old and generally disapproved of everything, up to and including the dragon he'd helped me kill—had talked Gideon into taking apart everything electronic I owned, down to my toaster oven, and inserting it into himself. So now he had a webcam on his shoulder, a CD player with the light still on in his chest, and some metal fingers. Grandfather and Gideon were one and the same.

Basically he was a cyborg who was really good with electronics. He still disapproved of a lot of things, though.

Hello again, Edie. There is no microphone on your side, or camera, so this is solely one-way. Hit the space bar now if now is unsafe to talk. The words blinked on the screen all at once.

I wished there were a camera, so he could see me

smiling back at him. I took the monitor between my hands as if I was going to kiss it.

Good. Hit the space bar if it becomes unsafe, and this transmission will instantly end. Until then, read. I leaned into the screen.

We are coming for you, but we must choose our moment. We are deciding on the safest course. It was hard not to take to the keyboard and type in HURRY! *Anna requests that you continue to play nice until we arrive, knowing how hard that is for you. Your man requested instead that you should play nice-enough.*

I grinned even more helplessly at the monitor, thinking of Asher.

Curse again on the keyboard the next time we can safely talk. I hope to have more information for you soon, but know that we have not abandoned you. We are glad that you are currently safe. From your keystrokes, I can tell you still have all your fingers. Good-bye.

Keystroke metrics. I had no idea how many computers in Los Angeles Gideon was monitoring right now to find me on this one, or how long he'd been looking, but I was so glad he was. Maybe House Grey and Jackson were right to be paranoid about Anna, if she was monitoring all the communications by other Thrones that she could.

Too damn bad.

I had the better part of another hour alone in the room. While I thought, I was mesmerized by the woman's monitors, with their continual proud declaration of her un-life.

Natasha came back in two hours to supervise my

blood draw. I think she was scared there wouldn't be any blood left in the heart, and I'd botch getting it out from the femoral artery—nurses never went there for IV starts or blood draws.

"Okay, yes. Just about that deep. Then withdraw it slowly, there's a chance you'll run dry, but you don't want to chase it down with your needle and hit muscle wall—" she said, watching me perform.

I levered up the syringe's plunger slowly, and the barrel filled as I watched. It looked just like any other ten ccs of dark red human blood I'd seen.

"Okay—she's clearly not dead all the way. Since I don't think you're Jesus, I'm pretty sure she's a vampire," I said as I handed it over. "Where's the other test subject? What's happening to him?" There was a chance that Natasha was splitting her time between here and another similar lab, machines hovering over another corpse.

"I'm holding him in reserve."

"What happens to her if she wakes up?"

"It's not if, it's when."

I frowned at her. "Three days, right?"

Her lips pursed in smugness. "I've figured out a way to speed the process up." Her voice was full of pride.

"How? And when?" How long did Anna have before Raven had another fighting member of his house?

"I'm still making my projections," she said, suddenly coy.

"The others stood for this?" If Lars was pissed at me for sharing Raven's blood and becoming a daytimer, how much worse would being skipped over to be changed anger him?

"The others don't get a vote." Natasha shrugged casually. "Only Raven's opinion matters."

Without the context of this room, she'd seem so . . . normal. More normal than someone related to Nathaniel, or held hostage, or even in love with a vampire had any right to be. "What's a nice girl like you doing with him?" I asked before I could help myself.

She blinked in surprise, and then laughed. "I'm not so nice. But he saved my life."

"From what?" I tried to imagine him swooping in and lifting buses, and I couldn't.

"From leukemia."

It was my turn to be surprised. "I got it when I was young. My dad tried everything to save me, but—" She shrugged, indicating how hopeless modern medicine sometimes was. "When science couldn't help, he tried other things, and that's when he found Raven." Her lips parted slightly at the mention of his name. "He saved me, just like he saved you. Only I was fourteen."

"Whoa."

She nodded. "My father worked for Raven after that. I hadn't gone to school in a while because I was always sick, so he had me help him in his lab, and taught me everything I needed to know. And I used to stay up every night, making western blots, hoping Raven would return."

I couldn't imagine what it would be like to be turned into a daytimer as a teen. If she'd been forced to feel the same strange connection to Raven that I'd felt—it seemed like the sort of thing that ought to be prohibited, but by whom?

"Eventually he came back. He visited the lab, and

my dad didn't shoo me away in time. After that, I caught him watching me sleep. He knew that I knew he was there—and I knew that I mattered to him. I just knew." Her face lit up at the memory. It was taking all my strength not to cringe.

"Around that time, my dad started moving us around. But Raven always found me. And then my mom died in a car accident, and my dad decided it was Raven's fault." She shook her head to indicate how wrong he was, according to her. "Things got worse, until Raven took me away."

I bit my lip and nodded sympathetically, while being fearful that her mother's death was somehow the Consortium's fault, a punishment doled out for consorting too much with vampires.

She shrugged again, a slightly girlish gesture, designed to deflect attention, as if to say, *Nothing bothers me, not the past, or the present, or you.* "I don't get to talk about it much. The others aren't very good listeners."

"And your dad? What does he think?"

"He's mad at me. I write him letters, but he doesn't ever write me back." That shrug again. "He loves me, but Raven and I are in love. It's a totally different thing."

I strongly doubted any of her letters made it into the mail. And I could hardly encourage her to write him again now, when I knew he was in the Leviathan's belly at the bottom of the sea. She hadn't gotten to have a normal life, between her illness and her dad—and I realized that I didn't need my freakish daytimer strength to hurt her. All I had to do was tell her what had happened to her father, and why, and I would break her heart.

Despite the fact that we were still in the room with a corpse she'd created, I found myself strangely unable to do so, so I looked away. "Being in love is nice."

"Yeah. It is," she agreed.

CHAPTER FOURTEEN

"Anyhow," Natasha said, leading me back into the lab with her syringe of blood, "ask Jackson for a watch and then come back after Raven receives us tonight. It should be near the right time."

"Awesome. Thanks." I gave her a kindly smile and walked unmolested toward the door.

I was so confused. Nothing about my time here was as I'd expected, and I found myself actually feeling *sorry* for Natasha. I couldn't believe I'd just been nice to someone who was a serial killer. Again.

I walked down the tunnel until I reached the first turn and then sat down on the stone. *Concentrate on the good things, Edie.* First off, I was away from the potentially hungry pre-vampire, yay. Asher. Anna. My engagement necklace. There was a prisoner hidden away somewhere who was willing to help me. I had all my fingers, as Gideon had so aptly pointed out. *And you're still stuck with me, baby.* Things were bad, but they could definitely be worse.

I wished I could feel happier about that, though.

Every time I closed my eyes I saw an image of that woman's wired corpse.

I knew how economies of blood worked—that was why House Grey was scared of Anna. She was a living vampire, born one as the child of two daytimer servants, and she could produce infinite amounts of blood, due to some combination of genetics, magic, and, for all I fucking knew, alchemy. But I'd been led to believe that the metabolism of all the other vampires on the planet worked much more slowly, providing a natural cap on the population, because vampires could only share their blood irregularly with servants, and changing a human into a vampire required a lot of it.

So why was Raven letting this random woman—someone who'd just been cornered and caught last night at the bar—cut ahead of Lars? And how'd he managed to do it after giving so much of his blood to me?

No answer to those questions could possibly be good. Anna might be on her way here . . . but it might not be fast enough. I might still have to find the prisoner. I wondered if the fries I'd left in my bag with the Shadows would taste like sorrow, or cyanide, or if the Shadows might have taken the taken the fries with them, fashioning them into a crude raft to hold above their heads as they crawled back to hide underneath Celine's bed.

Your mom is not crazy, baby. Just a little stressed out right now is all.

I heard footsteps and stood immediately—I didn't want anyone else to see me and think I was weak. I was surprised when Jackson rounded the bend, as was he. "Is Natasha still alive, too?"

"Yep."

"Things go okay?" Which was as close as he could come to asking what he really wanted to know.

"Hunky-fucking-dory." I was really going to have to work on not cussing in the next eight months. "Natasha said you should get me a cell phone, flashlight, and watch."

"No, no, and maybe. Why?"

"So I can be on time for science."

"Where science is . . . ," he prompted.

A creepy speed-vampire-creation program? I inhaled to tell him, and then we felt it together, the release of nightfall. I had to remind myself that it was winter outside; night was still the majority of each day.

Jackson broadly shook his head, and I nodded understanding. We'd talk later—and by then, I might know more.

We walked to Raven's war room together, and were the first ones there.

Lars was next, in a crisp business suit again. He had to be the most fashionable bookkeeper/drug dealer in Los Angeles. Wolf rolled in, and Jackson moved to his side.

When Estrella entered, she was as glamorous as when she'd begun her shift last night. I had no idea how she managed to do her hair so fast after getting up—maybe she set it on rollers before she died in the morning? Her orange hair was pressed down in sleek waves, covering half her face, swooping down so that the lowest curl of it hung underneath her left breast, and the cream-colored satin beaded dress she wore draped down to the ground.

She looked like an otherworldly Jessica Rabbit, until her eyes focused, hawk-like, on something behind me.

I turned to see Celine trotting in on impossible heels. She'd outdone herself. Her hair was down around her shoulders in chunky waves, her makeup was perfect, and her eyes were sparkling with life as her hips rolled when she walked by. She looked like she was out to have casual fun tonight, like someone on the far side of a welcome divorce. I knew everything about her appearance was preplanned and intentional, but so far she was the most lively-looking person here, and Estrella *noticed*.

The vampire I hadn't run into yet stalked in. I remembered Jackson said his name was Rex. He wore a tight black shirt and tight black jeans, and there was something about him that looked hot and flush, as if he'd just contracted a tropical disease.

Raven walked into the room electrically, hair slicked back into a braid, with a white tank top that made him look paler. I wondered what percentage of vampire whiteness was caused by lack of sun versus lack of circulating blood. He had low-slung black canvas pants on, with metal loops for buckles tabbed to the sides. It was quite a change from his normal look.

"How is everyone tonight?" he asked, looking around with a cunning smile. "Are there any concerns from last night I should know about?"

Wolf grunted. "Three cops tried to come in. I was able to send them away, but we need to keep an eye out for them tonight."

"Were they after the drugs or the women?" Raven asked, then smirked. "Or just off duty?"

"Pretty sure it's the drugs. I'll let one in tonight so

we can find out—Jackson can tail him. Everyone should keep it clean tonight just in case, though."

"What?" Rex protested.

"Just say our suppliers fell through," Wolf said. "We can't have a perfect record when it comes to keeping the cops out—that'll only make them more suspicious. Or maybe we can find someone low-level in your ranks that we can set up to take a fall—"

The male vampire started shaking his head. Lars raised his hand, and Raven nodded permission for him to speak.

"Master, no drugs tonight will cause a drop in alcohol sales—"

Raven looked to Celine. "Balanced out by cheaper women?"

She swept a long bang back from her face. "More women, perhaps, Master? I hate to devalue my product, but I can call all my off sites in—"

Estrella held up one delicate hand. "I do believe it's my birthday tonight—or, no—Celine. It's yours." She grinned, looking at her daytimer protégée. "You already look the part."

"Excellent idea!" Raven exclaimed. "Lars—two for one drink specials, and Celine, bring all the ladies in but tell them to just party, no sales—hell, let them drink for free. We'll take a cash-flow hit but keep our customers happy and our noses clean. Wolf—if cops do come, please make sure they wind their way up to Heaven—and point them out to Celine, so that she can make sure they have a good time with her there."

"I get to work in Heaven?" Celine said, then hurried to add, "Master?"

"Celine, my dearest, I'm in Heaven with you all the time," Raven said with a grin and a low bow, one arm flourished out.

Someone was in a good mood. Why?

Rex cleared his throat, and Raven's attention lit on him. "Yes?"

"I request permission to feed."

Raven shook his head, almost imperceptibly. "Denied."

"But, Master—" Rex pressed.

"Denied."

I knew they needed to drink blood each night—although they wouldn't die without it, not right away, the starving prisoner a case in point. I'd seen Estrella with her chosen donor the night before—and none of them, Raven, Wolf, Estrella, or Rex, looked starved. *Feed* must mean something more in this context.

"It's unfair that all our kills go to her. She's not even a vampire," he said, and I knew he meant Natasha.

"Since when has a House been based on fairness?" Raven asked, taking a step forward. "Do you think I don't know my business? Do you think I should open things up for a vote?"

Rex stood his ground. "I want to feed. It's been three months. The last one went to Estrella."

"You don't think I know how long it's been since any of you has taken fresh life?"

The mood in the chamber was darkening, just like our Master's. Even though I wasn't involved in their argument, listening to them was like standing on a hill in a thunderstorm while lightning charged. The part of me that was attuned to Raven felt his anger and desperately wanted to hide. I put my hands into my pockets and covered my belly with my fingers for whatever protection it would give my baby.

Rex held his ground. "I need life."

"The human drugs you deal shouldn't work on you—so there's no excuse for your insolence." Raven snorted and turned his back on Rex.

Rex jumped—and landed right where Raven would have been, if he hadn't lunged out of the way at the last moment. Rex snarled and Raven laughed.

"I invoke the right to fight you!" Rex exclaimed, hands empty.

"Done," Raven said.

What did any of that mean? Everyone else in the room backed up to the wall, and I followed them. I looked to Jackson to explain, but his eyes were on the fight. And beside him, Wolf was tensed, ready, I felt, to run in and take Raven's side.

Raven and Rex circled each other in the center of the room, keeping Raven's rounded couch between them. It made things awkward for both of them, and I wondered if that's why Raven had it there—whoever attacked first would have to leap over it or race around it and show his hand.

Rex was betting a lot on the fact that he ought to be stronger than Raven right now, so soon after rescuing me.

Raven didn't look weak, though. It was hard to tell with him how much of his strength was an act, but he wasn't afraid. He leaned forward and snatched the sheet off the couch, sending pillows rolling to the ground, and he held it to one side as if he were a bullfighter, taunting Rex with a laugh.

Then he backed up several steps. Rex took the initiative and stepped up onto the couch, prepared to throw himself at Raven again. Raven whirled the sheet around, making it snap in the air like a whip, then seemed to fall—and Rex leapt in.

Raven rushed forward to meet him and I realized his momentary weakness had been a ruse. Rex had to hope that it was real—but that gave Raven his chance. He slid to the side like a dancer, letting Rex rush forward, landing and completing his jump, and then pounced on him from behind, winding the sheet around him like a shroud. With a fluid movement he pulled Rex's hooded neck to one side and bit down through the fabric into his follower's neck.

Rex spasmed with surprise and tried to buck Raven off, but Raven had him trussed like a spider. His arms bound Rex down, and the fabric had a growing red stain from the free-flowing blood at his bite site. Every time Rex tried to move he'd growl and bite harder, making the stain spread.

Lars fell to his knees and crawled around and over to where Raven could see him, prostrating himself. "Please. Please." Why would Lars be begging on Rex's behalf?

Raven saw him, and squeezed Rex so hard we could hear the sounds of his bones breaking, but then he let him go, sliding him down to the ground, still wound in the purple sheet. "Our fight is over. You have lost. You are forbidden to speak, and you will lie still."

Then he turned his attention to Lars, lying completely on the ground, and kicked Rex's ruined body over to him, satin sliding over stone.

"You are mine now, and mine you will always be."

"Yes!" Lars shouted, his voice fading into an orgasmic hiss.

"Drink up, and I will greet you in three days."

Lars raised his head, hardly daring to believe, and then he scampered over to Rex's body, pushing back the sheet. I couldn't see Rex's face from here, or hear what if anything was said, but Lars pushed his face into the place where Raven's had just been tearing, licking blood away. Color came to him as he did so, and the sounds of him sucking and slurping grew louder as his hunger rose. I was repulsed by the sight of it, and by all the sounds, but also so jealous.

Was that . . . how the change was? I swallowed. My mouth was full of saliva, as if it were me drinking in Rex, not Lars.

Was that how it would be for me? When Anna changed me to take me away from here?

Only if I couldn't figure my own way out first.

Raven watched Lars feed with apparent satisfaction, breathing heavily, and I could see an erection pressing through his pants. His white tank top was covered in blood. He took it off, and underneath smears of red streaked across his skin like war paint. He threw it down to Lars. "Wring this out. Drink every last drop."

Lars paused and looked up, face gory with red, and started pushing drops that had gone down his chin into his mouth with such ferocity that I was worried he'd bite his own fingers off. He clutched at Raven's discarded shirt and set to almost eating it too, before he fell over. I started forward—To help him? To take my turn at Rex's bloody neck?—and Jackson's arm flung out, catching me like a seat belt.

Rex began to dust away. His fingertips disappeared just as his shoes tilted and fell to the side. Wolf came up to Raven and looked down at the mess of the dusting vampire and the newly dead Lars.

"That's one way to stop selling drugs for a while," Wolf said, and Raven laughed.

The door behind the show opened up and Natasha gasped and ran for Raven's side. "Are you hurt? Has someone hurt you?" She reached for Rex's blood on Raven's chest.

"No, dear one—" He took her hand up to his still red lips and kissed it. "This is what happens when someone challenges me. He insulted you. I could not bear it."

Natasha looked around, fearful, as though her beloved might still be under assault. But Raven's presence calmed her, as did his hand around her waist.

When she was sure that none of us was attacking, Natasha leaned up to whisper something in Raven's ear, and he made a growling sound of satisfaction, releasing her to gesture to our entire group. "I think it's time for everyone to know my Natasha's true worth. Follow," he commanded, and we all obeyed.

CHAPTER FIFTEEN

Raven led the way down to Natasha's lab, vampires first, eager to see, and all of us daytimers trailing behind.

Jackson's eyes asked me what we were walking toward, and all I could do was frown and shrug. While Raven believed in her science, Natasha was smart enough to know that the other vampires wouldn't understand without a visual component. None of them would be interested in seeing western blots or centrifuged tubes of blood.

I didn't want to think that the naked woman was already a vampire—she'd only been here for a day—but the second Raven opened the door we could hear her starved howling, as if she were a rabid dog. Jackson's eyes widened, and we all hurried in.

Natasha stopped everyone but Raven from coming near. The shackles were in full use—the woman was thrashing against them, and leads from her chest and head had been knocked free. Her voice was terrible, lost, and angry—if she got loose she'd try to kill everyone here without a second thought.

"But I just caught her a night ago—" Jackson said, following it up with a hurried, "Master," even though who knew whom he was speaking to.

"I know," Natasha said, beaming from ear to ear.

Jackson and I weren't the only ones who were concerned. Estrella and Wolf looked to each other. Their Master had changed someone they didn't know, essentially gone behind their backs and cheated on them. How did he have so much blood to go around—and if he had, why hadn't he shared?

And how had he, with Natasha's aid, managed to turn this woman overnight?

Raven reached out to touch the center of the woman's chest. She calmed, sensing him, blood-to-blood. "It would be unfair of me to eat without sharing a meal with you. Drink and through her drink of me."

Estrella and Wolf again looked at each other. Was this a trap? Poison? Wolf took the risk first, rounding the table to pull out the meat of the woman's left thigh and bite into her femoral artery, and the woman howled in pain. Estrella watched him carefully and then, worried about missing out, pushed the woman's head to one side while holding her down to drink from her right carotid.

I pressed my hands to my stomach again. It made sense that vampires could drink from other vampires—after all, blood was blood—but watching it caused a special kind of revulsion. Maybe it was the realization that they could have just as easily been feeding on me.

They were both neater eaters than Raven had been with Rex. The woman kicked and thrashed and it was horrible to watch but there was nothing I could do, even as bile rose in my throat. Her fate had been sealed when Jackson had picked her from the crowd the night before. Her struggles lessened, her eyes went glassy, and she started to pant.

Raven's arm found Natasha's waist again and pulled her close. "Would you like to go on a midnight drive?"

Her lips parted and she smiled up at him with complete adoration. "I'll go get my things."

He lowered his head to her ear and rumbled, "Meet you in the garage."

She skipped away. "Jackson, make sure you clean up!" she called before the lab door swung shut.

Jackson stiffened beside me but didn't say anything.

The blood pressure cuff around the woman's arm cycled, but didn't stop inflating, searching for numbers that her body could no longer give. Raven nodded at Wolf, whose eyes were on his Master, even as his face was buried in the strange woman's thigh. "I'll be out tonight. You're in charge. The plan's still the same. Open as soon as you can." Wolf nodded, raising his head, drops of blood trapped in his beard. Raven looked to Celine and gave her a chilling smile. "Have a wonderful birthday."

"Thank you, Master," Celine stuttered as Raven left the room.

This was exactly what I'd been afraid of happening this afternoon. How had Natasha done it? How had she managed to shorten the death-to-vampire change by three whole days? Anna could make an infinite number of vampires—but she couldn't make them change that fast.

At least I wasn't the only one in the dark—it'd surprised Wolf and Estrella too, and it would have surprised the fuck out of Rex if he'd been alive to see it. He'd bet on Raven not having enough fresh blood to be powerful, when what'd probably happened was that Raven had drunk all the lovely pre-vampired blood out of successful test subject sixty-three.

But how? I wasn't the only person wondering—all of us daytimers were looking at one another now, waiting patiently for the vampire buffet to end.

Wolf rose up first, but Estrella waited until the woman began to dust. Without clothing, the remaining leads stuck to her skin fell as the flesh that'd been beneath each of them crumbled away.

If I'd had a lighter now I could have blown them both up. Vampire dust was flammable—I'd found that out a very, very long time ago.

Wolf looked to Jackson with clots of blood in his beard. "I'll go open the front door and let the bouncers, bartenders, and DJs in. We'll tell them what they need to know and open thirty minutes after that. Estrella, you'll be a fallen angel tonight and monitor Hell, which'll mean you'll have to be on your toes alone in Heaven, Celine. Jackson, you'll run Purgatory, and Edie, you'll be cleanup on all floors, after you change for it. Jackson will show you what to do. Go."

Everyone else exited the room on their assignments, leaving Jackson and me behind with the woman's remains.

*　*　*

"So what the fuck just happened?" Jackson asked the second we were sure we were alone. "I brought this woman in less than twenty-four hours ago. There is no possible way this should have worked."

"But it did," I said, staring at the table, running through possibilities in my mind. Jackson started pacing in a tight circle. I opened my mouth to tell him not to do that—if he built up a static charge, there was a small chance he could light the very flammable dust. Then I realized I should keep the fact that I knew that to myself.

"It's not right. It's just not right," he went on without noticing me.

"You got her two test subjects last night, didn't you?" I asked, and Jackson nodded. "Where's the other one?"

"In the holding chamber. Locked up."

"And when's the last time you disposed of a corpse again?"

"A month ago. I figured Natasha was doing it on her own."

"Or this—whatever this precisely is—started working." If all the victims turned to dust, that also explained why the prisoner hadn't been recently fed. "Which was also how Raven was able to heal me and still be strong enough to fight Rex and win—and why he could afford to give the rest of Rex's blood to Lars. He's been doing this for a month."

Without a mask to protect myself, I cupped my hand over my face and went over to the body, looking for answers.

"But vampires frown on eating their own kind," Jackson said, despite what we'd just seen. "It's usually a losing proposition. You never get out as much blood as you put in to make them."

"Maybe he's not using his own blood." If Natasha's father had been searching for human blood substitutes—maybe Natasha had actually found one. Only for vampires.

"But what about entropy? That's how the world works. You don't get to make vampires easy-peasy for free. It costs blood to make blood. That's why we're us, and they're them."

He didn't know what I knew about Natasha's lineage, and I didn't want to share that with House Grey just yet. "Let's skip the how and get to the why. What's the point of being able to speed the process up?" I thought I knew the answer, but I wanted to hear someone else say it.

Jackson's face went dark. "You'd be able to make full vampires who're beholden to you immediately."

I reached in and grabbed a pinch of dust. The test subject had looked like a vampire, felt like a vampire, and died like a vampire. "I don't think Anna has the vampire army market cornered anymore."

"Fuck me," Jackson said. He exhaled raggedly and hit the counter nearest him with his fist. "We'll clean this up later. We need to open the club now."

It felt absurd shifting gears to go to work upstairs after Natasha's spectacle. I wanted time to think and time to plan. Anna needed to know what had happened here—I was afraid that Natasha's research had changed the game in ways I couldn't comprehend.

But I couldn't ditch my "job"—Wolf would know, and I didn't want to make him angry. I hoped watching over the club would keep him busy and that our paths wouldn't cross.

Jackson waited outside Celine's room for me to change. The light was on and my fry bag was where I'd left it, and there wasn't an ant trail of fries to underneath the bed—I'd figure out what was up with the Shadows later on tonight. I pulled on an all-black outfit: leggings and a dress. The top was low-cut, but I hoped if people were looking at my breasts they wouldn't be looking at my stomach. I pulled my hair into two quick low pony-tails on either side, and pushed my feet into heels. Asher's necklace at my throat made it look like I'd actually tried.

"Not bad," Jackson said when I emerged. "You'll pass for hired help."

My job was going to be to circulate and pick up glasses and bring them back to the bars on all three floors. Each floor had its own style of glasses so that people on higher floors could come down and mingle while still having something on them that showed that they were special—and Jackson warned me that sometimes people snagged empty glasses and tried to go up. He introduced me to the bouncers, so they'd know me, and so I'd know them if I needed to call for help. They were all big guys, and several of them carried barely concealed knives. "Remember how strong you are. If people get fresh, don't hurt them, just let the bouncers know."

I didn't feel strong in this outfit, but that wasn't the point—I just needed to not stick out for a few hours. DJs set up their booths, bartenders wiped down their bars, and voilà, the Catacombs were open.

CHAPTER SIXTEEN

I hung out in the back of Hell feeling like a mime. There was no work for me to do until people started to drink—but the announcement of two-for-one specials on all levels of the club was getting out; I could see people sending texts to tell friends. And music started to pound at the level you could feel in your chest when you walked by the speakers. *Hope this isn't giving you hearing damage, baby. Although it's never too early to learn to appreciate a good beat.*

I used to frequent clubs, back in the day. I'd met Asher at one, in fact, although I hadn't known it at the time. It was hard not to think of him when I saw people dancing, remembering how once upon a time he'd watched me.

Soon the crowds meant I was too busy to reminisce. Girls swirled out first, braver boys followed, and then I was having to press through them to get back and forth with payloads of glassware for the bar. I swept through one level at a time, and then started over again. It wasn't so bad and people were more interested in themselves—my clothes marked me clearly as unimportant, so I was completely ignored.

Celine and Estrella kept their eyes on me in their respective habitats, and I made sure to wave to Jackson each time I passed through Purgatory. By my twentieth pass even he began to look slightly more relaxed.

And I didn't have time not to work—people were drinking with abandon. On a round through Hell, someone pushed a door open, and a wave of smoky air flew in. I'd found the smokers' deck. Made sense that it was down in the inferno.

I glanced over at Estrella—she was dressed far more elegantly than anyone else in Hell, with her otherworldly beauty. Men and women were attracted to her, and she circled the bar like a shark, gracing groups of people with her presence, even dancing hypnotically at the edge of the floor to pull more people in. For someone who wasn't technically alive, moving among humans made her seem full of life, as if she were a mirror, reflecting their life back at them.

I waited three more passes as the crowds grew, until I was sure she couldn't see me, and then I bolted outside.

The smoking deck was protected from wind by buildings with brick walls on either side—it had a Garden of Eden theme, metal trellises supporting winter-dry vines, giving me a chance to see the bronze snakes that'd been welded on. Bushes circled the edges of the patio, and in the back were two large topiaries trimmed to look like genitalia, one carefully shaped penis with testicles on each side, the other a vulva with a spotlight pointed at its most sensitive part.

There were heat lamps at regular intervals, which girls in sleeveless club gear congregated around like moths. Ashtrays overflowed and small tables held an assortment of glasses from each of the floors, giving me a good excuse to be there. I picked up glasses slowly while scanning desperately for forgotten lighters.

If I did my job right, I'd be out here several times tonight—but Estrella or Jackson could come out at any moment and forbid me from leaving the Catacombs again, assigning a bouncer to the chore. I got an idea, and chose my mark.

"Trade you a pass up to Heaven for your lighter." I shook one of the Heaven-themed glasses in front of him. Hell had normal barware, sturdy and strong. Heaven's was more delicate, appropriately.

"I already get up there, thanks," he said, brushing me off. Entirely possible—since this was the only smoking deck, people from all levels were forced to mingle.

"I don't suppose I could just have your lighter?" I pressed. I needed it, to see in dark hallways to look for prisoners to help free me, and maybe also to light dusted vampire remains on fire.

"Nope."

My shoulders sagged, and I picked up the glasses I'd collected, looking for another mark, when someone tapped me on the shoulder.

I jumped, almost dropping the glasses I held as I whirled. I'd been caught, this was it—but no, it was a strange conventionally handsome man standing behind me, not Jackson or, worse yet, Estrella or Wolf.

"I heard you needed a light," he said, his voice kind, offering a lit lighter out with an expectant look on his face. I didn't recognize him, but something about him seemed familiar—oh, God, I wanted so badly to hope.

"I actually needed a lighter," I clarified. "For someone else," I went on to lie badly.

His face broke into an easy grin. "That's good, because smoking would be really bad for our baby."

My eyes went wide. It was him—Asher—wearing someone else's form. I didn't dare say his name, because if I did I would tackle him and cry. He stepped closer to me. "Did you honestly think I got back on some plane?"

I shook my head. "I hoped you had, though. You don't know how dangerous it is here—"

"All the more reason I should stay."

"If something happened to you, though—" I cast another nervous look around before turning back to him. "I couldn't do this without you." Where *this* was the next thirty minutes, or thirty years.

"I'm going to be fine. It's you that I'm worried about."

Says the shapeshifter who came into a vampire enclave, unarmed. After watching Raven dispatch Rex—I shook my head to dispel the thought.

"What do you need this for?" he asked, handing the lighter over. I took it from him, fingers thrilling at the slight touch.

"To go places I shouldn't. And also maybe set things on fire."

His lips pursed. "And you're worried about me?"

"Asher." I lowered my voice so that only he could hear. "It's bad. They've come up with some way to speed up the changing process, to turn someone overnight." I saw the look on his face and went on. "Don't tell me it's impossible—I saw it happen with my own two eyes."

His face turned grim. "That changes things."

"I know." As desperately as I wanted to be saved by

him right now, this very instant, Natasha's experiment trumped everything else. "I have to get back and figure out how so we can stop it."

"Don't do anything foolish," he warned, his voice low.

"I'll be as careful as I can," I said, taking a step back, even though I wanted to throw my arms around him and never let him go.

"You'd better be. We're coming for you."

"I know." I bit my lips together so I wouldn't say anything more, and then turned around quickly and counted to ten. When I looked back after that, he was gone. The only thing I had to prove he'd ever been there was the lighter in my hand. I pushed it into the cleavage Estrella's bra gave me, and scooped the bar glasses back up.

CHAPTER SEVENTEEN

A girl was puking into a bush outside the entrance to Hell and I stopped to help her to the bathroom—it gave me the perfect excuse for why glass retrieval was taking so long.

By the time I did make it back to Hell's bar to drop off its corresponding glasses, Estrella had noticed my absence. "Where've you been?" she asked, sniffing the air before stepping away.

"Someone puked. I had to clean it up." It was hard not to grin at her displeasure. *Your dad's coming for us, baby.*

She was still frowning, but I knew there was no way for her to monitor all three floors, much less their bathrooms. And smelling of puke was better than smelling of lighter fluid.

The rest of the night it was easy to stay busy. I worked without complaint through closing, and helped check the bathrooms for drunks and herd the last few of them out the door.

"Good job tonight," Jackson said after paying the last of the DJs out.

"Thanks, boss," I said with more than a little sarcasm.

He snorted. "Go change, and we'll get to vacuuming."

Nice to see that the industry standard for cleaning up vampire dust hadn't changed while I'd been trying to have a normal life.

I'd hardly seen Celine all night, she'd been so busy celebrating her "birthday" upstairs. She'd beaten me back to the room, though, since as soon as the bar closed all of her chores were done.

She'd showered and changed into something frilly, and was blow-drying her hair in front of her mirror. She hardly noticed me when I came in, and I changed quickly, middle-school-locker-room-style, not showing any skin. I managed to shift the lighter from my cleavage to the pocket of the rompers without her seeing it in her vanity.

Celine finished with the blow dryer, set it down, and opened up a makeup bag. She touched a roller ball of perfume to the inside of her wrists. It was such a subtle scent that I could hardly smell it.

"Why're you doing that?" The club was closed. Who cared anymore?

Celine looked back in the mirror at me. "So I don't smell like you."

"Sorry. I got puked on. And now I have to go clean up dust." I could see myself in her mirror now—after a night of hustling in the club I looked bedraggled.

She set the perfume down and pulled out lipstick instead. "He's never going to want you, looking like that." She dabbed a fingertip against the red, and then patted it against her own lips, giving them a calculated natural flush.

"What do you mean?"

"They're not just interested in blood. They're interested in life—what goes with the blood when they drink it, the life, the soul, the fragile part of you that wants to stay alive. That's what they like—and it's something only humans can give them." She smeared the same color from her fingers on her cheeks, livening herself up. "It's easy for us to forget that sometimes. We try to be too much like them, when that's not really what they want."

I bit my lips in thought. "Thanks." *Baby, I'd say we should always try to be uninteresting to vampires, but I'm afraid that it's too late.* "I'll try to be quiet when I get back."

She waved me off, and I headed for the door.

Jackson was waiting for me in Natasha's lab, where everything was just as we'd left it. They'd always wanted us to wear masks on Y4 when we were dealing with ash, but I hadn't seen any when I'd scouted the drawers earlier, which pissed me off. I was a daytimer now, true, but I didn't want particulate vampire crap in my lungs. I'd be really sad if I came down with mesothelioma later, and I didn't want to think about what it could do to my child.

Jackson had brought a vacuum cleaner with a long attachment, and I used paper towels and cleaning solution to start cleaning off the loose wire leads for the EEG and the ECG. Because each of the pad's sticky surfaces were completely bonded to vampire dust, there was none of that tape-sticking-to-fingertips-or-gloves action you got at the hospital. I put as many as I thought I could get away with in my pocket. Between them and the lighter, I could make a rudimentary bomb. If the Shadows could find the prisoner and his silver grate, I might actually be able to set him free.

"Jackson," I began when he'd turned the vacuum cleaner off, hoping talking would distract him from my last palmed handful of stickers. "Celine told me something just now."

"I'm sure it was profound." He was scrubbing at the tabletop angrily.

It sort of had been. "About vampires being more interested in life than blood."

He paused, mid-arc. "I suppose that's true."

"Is life blood? Is blood life? Where's the line?" Dren had once wanted to murder me for my soul. Was that the same sort of thing?

"I couldn't say."

"Do vampires have souls? Or lives, really? As daytimers, do we?" I didn't ask what I really wanted to know—if I was losing my soul because of vampire blood, what did it mean for my baby? I wouldn't have ever believed in a soul if vampires hadn't once threatened to take it from me.

"I don't know, Edie." Jackson sounded exasperated, and started scrubbing again. "I feel alive. Do you?"

"So far." Alive, but not the same as I had been before I'd gotten Raven's blood. I'd never been violent before—or been in helpless thrall.

"Then I think there's more important topics to discuss. Did you figure anything out while you were shuffling glasses around?"

"No. I'm hoping Natasha will want to brag tomorrow, though, now that the cat's out of the bag."

"I wish the cat had swallowed the bag and then choked on it." He finished the table with one last swipe and leaned over to look at his own reflection, just like Celine had—maybe wondering the same as her about his future—then hoisted the vacuum cleaner again. "One down, one more to go."

I waited until we'd reached the war room to keep bugging him. "Who does Wolf feed on?"

"Usually the drunks at the end of the night. A little here, a little there, then he shoos them out the door. He's not like the others, he doesn't put on airs. He learned not to be picky in his past life." Jackson sounded like he agreed with the philosophy. "And speaking of past lives—" Jackson looked at Lars, sprawled out in the middle of Rex's dust, snorted in disgust, then started unspooling a really long extension cord.

Lars had been left where he'd landed, facedown. Now that he was helpless, I almost felt bad for him. I lifted his head and saw ash on his forehead, nose, and tongue from his last bite of Rex. Mouthwash wouldn't even begin to cover it once he woke up. "Can I put him on the couch?"

"Sure," Jackson said, from his expedition to find an electrical socket at the edge of the room.

I picked Lars up and settled him the way I would a sedated patient at the hospital, heels up, arms up, pillow behind his head. Except for the smears of dust across his face and staining his clothing, he looked like a king in repose.

By then Jackson had returned with the vacuum cleaner. He knotted up the corners of the sheet that Rex had died on and set it aside so he could run the vacuum cleaner over the dust that remained.

"Do they kill each other often?" I asked when he was done, pointing at the sack.

"I've seen it happen a few times. Raven doesn't tolerate dissent." Jackson shook his head at the whole situation. "I'm ready to call it a night, even if it's not dawn yet. We can regroup and compare notes again tomorrow."

"Sure." I still had things to do, and I needed to be alone to do them.

Jackson picked up the sack and carried Rex out like a mockery of Santa Claus, trailed by a small dusty cloud, leaving me alone with Lars.

I looked down at the dead daytimer. Had the most defining moment of his life actually been his death? What was happening to him now, inside him—would he be the same person when he came out on the other side?

Would I, if it ever happened to me?

I hope I never have to find out, baby.

CHAPTER EIGHTEEN

Celine was still in our room when I returned, sitting on her bed-throne, and back to being disappointed to see me. She looked like someone had stood her up, and I felt bad for her until I realized who that was.

I wanted to change and put the lighter somewhere safe and fold the rompers back up and keep them separate from my other stuff, but I was uncomfortable with her still being in the room.

"I think I'll go take a shower now," I said. I'd picked up my towel and started to slink back out the door when there came a loud knock from outside. Celine hopped off the bed instantly.

"Yes?" She trotted to the door, pushing me out of the way.

The door opened, and Estrella stood outside. When she saw Celine's face, with her no-makeup makeup on, hair tousled gently to her waist, she smiled. "My lovely, come attend."

And just like that, I had the room to myself.

* * *

I didn't have that much time before dawn—if I was going to set the Shadows out to look for the prisoner, I needed to hurry while everyone else was occupied.

Did I really need his help if Anna was on her way? I might have hesitated before Natasha's demonstration tonight. But now that I didn't know how many test subjects Raven would turn into vampires before Anna got here—what was that saying, that the enemy of my enemy was my friend? In that context, the prisoner and I should be besties.

I flicked off the lights, bent down, and set my hand down onto the ground.

"Shadows? Are you still here?"

For a time, silence. And then a sarcastic voice. "What, you want us to shake your hand?"

"Remember how we're on the same team? It's time for you to help out."

"With what?" Their voices were closer.

"There's a prisoner here who's trapped down in the tunnels in the dark. I need you go to looking for him for me."

"Do you know where he is?"

"No clue. His cell is covered with a silver grate—that's how you'll know you've found it."

"How many tunnels are there?" They sounded unsure.

"I don't know. But at least they're in utter dark, and they're under here, so you can still feed."

"Why should we help him?"

"Because he's Raven's Sire. He's promised to kill him, and once he does, we can go." I didn't want to tell them about Anna or Gideon just yet; there was always the chance they might try to sell me out.

A chill viscous fluid rolled into my hand. Was it just me, or did the Shadows have a little more substance to them? I knew they were still feeding on all the turbulent emotions happening above in the club.

"Why does your hand taste like vampire dust and shapeshifter?"

"It's been a very long night."

I grit my teeth and poured them into my tennis shoe again, so I'd know where they were and they could stay in the dark. "One second. I need to change—hide, okay?" I warned, and flipped on the light.

I took the fistful of vampire-dusted leads I'd plucked from cleaning the autopsy table and looked for a place to hide them. I settled on sticking them underneath the zebra rug's neck, under the ridge of its mane. Then I took off my rompers, put them back into a box, and safely set the lighter back into my bra.

Then I pulled on the spandex outfit I'd been given earlier and put my tennis shoes back on. Inside the Shadows were cold on my foot and sloshed up between each of my toes.

"Could you make this experience any more disgusting?"

"Do you really want to know?"

I didn't answer them, I just started walking.

I ran when I felt safe running, and I walked when I thought I should walk. Asher had told me not to do anything foolish—but Natasha's experiments called for desperate actions. Even if Anna bled herself silly, she couldn't do what Natasha'd just done.

Strangely, for once luck was with me. I reached the end of the tunnel—where it opened into unknown darkness—without incident and took three steps inside. Even that was far enough to give me a claustrophobic feeling, as if the tunnel were closing off behind me.

I knelt, pulled off my shoe, and let the Shadows spill on the ground.

"Can you keep track of time?" I asked them.

"Yes. It's an hour until dawn."

"How fast can you search?" The quicker Raven was dead, the safer the world would be.

"Depends on where he is. We can return here once we've found him, we'll remember the way." The utter darkness that made *here* creepy for me served them well. They could probably keep dividing an infinite number of times, sending smaller pieces of themselves down every possible passageway.

"I'll come back here then—but I might have to wait until it's safe."

"When will you learn there's no safe place for you here?" they chided.

"I know that. I do." Now more than ever. "Hurry."

They slunk away, and it felt like the darkness around me pressed in. I leapt back into the lit portion of the hall and raced the whole way back to Celine's.

After that I decided to risk taking a shower. A lot had happened since my last one—I felt like I was covered in a thin coat of dust and darkness. I emerged afterward and made my way back to Celine's room, only to find Jackson leaving it with a bag.

"I grabbed some of your clothes for the laundry

service—smelled like someone puked on you last night, sorry." He looked apologetic. Maybe because I smelled like his soap again. No—he was too sincere for that.

"That's fine, thanks," I said, even as my heartbeat rose in worry.

"You did good tonight. See you tomorrow." He moved around me and headed down the hall. It was hard not to fling the door open after he'd left.

Celine was still with Estrella, so he'd had his run of the place. My rompers were gone—and the hammerhead I'd put into Celine's bed—and the vampire-dust-impregnated stickers I'd hidden under the zebra's mane.

The only thing I had anymore was the lighter that'd come to the shower with me. Fuck.

Jackson knew vampire dust was flammable—and he knew that I knew, so he'd searched the room and taken anything I could use as a weapon away from me. He wanted me to play both sides, to betray the friend who was trying to rescue me, to stay here and play our Master's monster games—how dare he disarm me. I could chase after him in the hall but I could hardly cop to wanting to blow things up.

Or I *could* chase after him in the hall, tackle him, and break both of his legs just like I'd broken Lars's. Cold darkness began unfurling inside me—

"No!" I whirled and hit Celine's mattress without thinking first. It gave, rebounding violently back up, and I caught myself, startled.

That wasn't me. That was just Raven's stupid blood talking again. I wanted to be rid of it—I only wanted to be me. Plain mistake-making but well-intentioned human me. I just didn't know how to get back to that yet—and hell, I couldn't afford to be just human right now, not when I was swimming with so many sharks.

I flipped the zebra skin back and sat down among the pillows, hugging my knees to my chest, feeling helpless and angry. *I'm usually not like this, baby. I promise I'll make a good mom. You'll see.*

I curled up into a ball on the floor and waited for sleep to come, and hoped that I wouldn't have any dreams.

CHAPTER NINETEEN

Nothing was ever that easy.

The second my eyes were shut, the prisoner appeared. "Are you on your way?"

We were in the desert again, and I lay down in my dream as I was lying down in real life. I just wanted to be quiet and calm. "Can I get ten seconds to myself?"

He was quiet, but I could almost hear him counting down. I waited for twenty-five seconds, then rolled up to sitting and sighed. "Yes. The Shadows are on their way."

"Who are they?"

"Friends of mine. They're hard to explain." And they weren't exactly friends. "They can only live in the dark. They're searching the tunnels for you now, and when they find you they'll let me know."

He nodded his head. "That's good."

"You're sure you can kill him?" I studied his face, watching for any deception as he answered me.

"Yes." His brow furrowed. "What's changed?"

I didn't know if it was wise to tell him. Whatever Raven was doing, if another vampire figured it out—then I realized he might be able to read my mind.

"It's working, isn't it? That's why they no longer need me." His face darkened before I could voice my fears.

"You tell me," I said, trying to sound cagey.

"Your friends are really on their way?" His voice went low, and he looked at me just as intently as I'd been looking at him.

"I swear they are. Are you able to read my mind?"

He paused long enough that I became scared of his answer. "Not entirely. Only your surface thoughts. That's how I was able to re-create your living space, and your man. And that's how I know you won't be scared by this." He stepped away from me and concentrated, and the picture of him inside my mind shimmered just like my fireplace had. "The image I present to you now is how I used to be. It is not how I look now."

Here was where I'd find out he had no legs and I'd have to carry him—I shushed my grim imagination as the new image of him resolved.

Clothed, he looked the same. But he tilted his head and moved his hair back so that I could see a band of white around his neck, and then the top half of his toga disappeared to show me the skin of his chest. Like a chameleon changing colors, his dark skin became marred with white stripes, some thick, some thin.

"Do you know how long it takes a vampire to scar?"

I shook my head. "What are those from? Silver chains?"

"Yes. And weapons to hollow me out with." He pulled the cotton covering his hip away to show me scars spiraling out on him like blurry galaxies.

"With me too weak to fight back, chained down by enough silver to kill anyone else."

"Then why didn't you die?"

"Because of Raven." A dark smile spread across his lips, and I backed away, suddenly fearful of being too close. "Without his interference, I would have joined the rest of them. Osiris the Unrepentant, Constantine the Immortal, countless others with names just as fanciful. One by one, they all disappeared. What do you think keeps a vampire going as the eons pass us by? As we become more separate from the world, and the world itself more complex?"

"I have no idea," I confessed.

"Only the will to survive. Having to drink your blood keeps us among you, makes us change, keeps us fighting. We may kill humans, but without being dragged into your lives, we would die.

"The others of my kind, dark siblings from my past, became tired of you. Of trying to walk among your kind, learning new ways to be. And their histories became so heavy—imagine living centuries and being able to remember every victory and every loss with perfect clarity. Even we lose sometimes, and the perfect knowledge of each failure sits and burns in the belly like coal. Eventually even we, who ought to live forever, for as long as there are human footsteps on the ground, realize what we've lost—or we go insane."

"All your friends are dead?" I asked, and he subtly nodded. "But if they'd lived so long—what killed them?"

"At the end, if it is of our choosing, we drift off into the dark places and let the waters swallow us whole."

I wondered if they felt how I had after the *Maraschino* sank, when I'd jumped off the life raft and been ready for the Leviathan to swallow me—maybe they too had been filled with a profound longing to finally be somewhere quiet and rest.

"Without Raven's interference, that might have also happened to me. Perhaps I should be pleased he's trapped me here, and given me this opportunity to be fueled by anger far past my normal time."

"How old are you?" I could guess from his clothing, but I wanted to hear him say it.

"I was created during what you all call the Roman Empire."

If he and all those like him had managed to keep wringing enough life out of humanity for themselves to live, over thousands of years—how many people had they killed? If I thought about it like that, he deserved whatever Raven had done to him—it was a small measure of payback for thousands of years of him killing us.

He looked at me like he knew what I was thinking. "If you hate me, then you will soon hate yourself."

"I'm a girl. I have so much practice at hating myself, you wouldn't believe." It was safe to pace in the prisoner's dreamland, no vampire dust to set on fire. I wanted to ask him a hundred questions—why did holy water work on vampires if they predated Christ? What was it like to live that long? I couldn't even imagine what the world would look like in the next twenty years, with so much new technology—the thought of being changed and then clinging on for another few hundred years exhausted me, especially if I took the thought to its logical conclusion: once changed, I would outlive Asher, my child, and anyone else I'd ever known.

But I didn't have time to fall into that rabbit hole just

yet. The prisoner stood still, watching me think, scars like tiger stripes across his skin.

"Show me where they hurt you."

He pointed to his iliac crest, the high point on his pelvis, his voice taut with emotion. "I watched them shove in tools and pull out pieces of meat, the marrow of my bone."

My brain caught the tail of an idea. "No." I could only think of one reason why you'd dig around inside someone's iliac crest. Marrow transplants. Which someone who'd been treated for leukemia would know all about. "No way."

His eyebrows rose, and the image of his clothing resolved in a heartbeat.

Oh, God. Of course the prisoner wouldn't know what they were doing—he'd been trapped in here for most of the advent of Western science. But Raven was younger and had younger blood and knew he'd have to change to stay alive. He'd been willing to take big risks—especially when he had a donor who would heal up between tests.

"What?"

"Hang on." What had changed? Why weren't they using the prisoner anymore?

Because Natasha had finally figured out how to make things work. They hadn't needed the prisoner's bone marrow because they'd switched over to Raven's.

Vampires couldn't make an infinite amount of blood, but they were fast healing. So instead of giving test subjects vampire blood infusions, weakening the vampire that donated each time, Natasha had skipped back a step. Why transfuse blood when you could transplant bone marrow itself, the tissue that generated blood cells?

If the transplant worked, test subjects would immediately start making their own vampire blood.

It was as ingenious as it was awful.

All they needed was a donor, willing or un, as the prisoner proved. And who knew how many bone grafts they could take? I'd seen vampires knit bones together quickly before—Dren had done it; even daytimer Lars had done it when I'd broken his ribs and leg.

"What?" the prisoner asked again, hovering near in concern.

"I don't even know how to explain it to you." There must be more to the process—it'd taken Natasha years to perfect it, even with all her opportunities and a world-class lab. But with her help Raven had found a way to be almost as prolific as Anna.

And if any other vampires figured it out—then they could be too. A world full of vampires would be no place to raise a child. *Oh, baby.*

I looked over at the prisoner. "We don't just need to kill Raven—we need to burn this place to the ground."

At this, the prisoner finally smiled. "That is fine with me."

CHAPTER TWENTY

A sound interrupted us, a distant jingling bell. I sat up with a gasp, dream forgotten, and found Celine coming in.

She was disheveled but looked pleased, and there was a hint of color to her lips that hadn't been there before she'd put on lipstick. Celine had gotten blood.

She strode over to me, standing tall. "I want my pillows back."

I didn't know how much blood she'd gotten. I assumed that I still had more on board than her, but I didn't want to be wrong. I think the only way we'd really know who'd win would be to fight, and that might be dangerous for my baby. I shrugged as if it didn't matter to me, and threw all her pillows back onto her bed except one.

Her eyes narrowed at me in superiority. I could see her considering demanding the final pillow; then she thought better of it just in case. I realized she'd bluffed, I'd folded, and neither one of us was really sure who would have come out on top.

I put the remote on the ground and skidded it over to her feet, then lay back down as if I weren't afraid. "I'm going back to sleep now. Turn the lights off when you're done." When I heard her crawl into her own bed, I finally relaxed. By the time I fell asleep, though, the prisoner was gone. I had neither dreams nor nightmares for the rest of the night.

I got up to the sound of a knock at the door. The room was pitch black, but I had a feeling it was now day.

"Hey sleepyhead," Jackson said. I was still mad at him for disarming me.

"Yo." Celine was snoring behind me, secure in her pillow fort. I stepped outside and closed the door behind me.

"Want breakfast?" he asked, holding out a bag. "It's more of a late lunch—"

Just because I was mad didn't mean I wasn't hungry. "Yeah." Hunger was a new thing. I hadn't been legitimately hungry before. A sign of pregnancy? Or Raven's blood wearing off?

I took the bag, and then he held out a watch. "For when you help Natasha." I set the bag down and latched the watch around my wrist. I'd almost forgotten that I'd have to do that today—and what I'd found out from the prisoner last night.

"You okay? You look green."

"I'm fine." I needed to focus. If any information got out of here, if a hundred different Thrones started doing marrow transplants to create twenty new vampires each—the math was bad. And no vampire group would stand idly by while others gained in numbers.

"I'm sorry. About yesterday," Jackson said, taking my thoughtful silence for reprobation.

You should be, was what I wanted to say. Instead I shrugged. "How many test subjects are left?"

"Just one. Why?"

"Where are they?"

Jackson's left eyebrow rose. "Why?"

I knew Anna was coming, but not when. I needed to disrupt the cycle somehow to buy her some time.

"I need you to trust me."

"You know something more, don't you?" His eyes narrowed.

"Anna's not the big threat anymore. She's a genetic freak, a one-in-a-million mutation." I couldn't explain the specifics; the fewer people who knew, the better. But Jackson was smart enough to catch on. "However—if what Raven had Natasha do is repeatable, then anyone can, and will, do it. I don't know how often you get new orders, but your priorities need to change."

I saw his jaw clench and set. He knew I was right, even if he didn't want to go off script. "All right. But it's an electronic lock."

"Just show me where it is."

"We're not even supposed to go," he began, then paused. "Wait—I have an idea."

We went back to Raven's war room where Lars was still passed out, sprawled exactly as I'd left him. "We'll take him to Rex's old feeding room. It's nearby." And despite the fact that either of us could have picked up Lars alone, we shared the burden so that we would both have an excuse.

Swinging Lars between us, we went through the crossroads and down one of the forbidden halls. "Two doors down from here." When we got inside the room,

I let Lars's feet fall to the ground and trotted back outside. The doors were metal with no windows; another biometric keypad was set in the door. I darkly considered snapping Natasha's hand off and going through fingers until I found the right one.

"See? Impossible. She meets me when I bring them down," Jackson said, meeting me outside.

Just like the prisoner, he was a product of his times. They didn't have biometric keypads in the 1970s.

"Every lock has a key," I said. And I had a Gideon.

Jackson left me outside Natasha's lab, and I went inside alone. The door was unlocked, just as we'd left it last night when we were done cleaning the woman's dust. I went back to see if we'd missed anything, but we hadn't: The table was still gleaming, and there was polish on the tile.

I could destroy things in here—make the computers and electronics short out, open all the refrigerator doors, throw their contents on the floor, or wash them down the sink—but that wouldn't get at the heart of it all. For that, I'd have to kill Natasha. The sooner the better, too, before word of this got out.

But I wasn't a killer type, despite the thoughts I'd been having recently. I looked down at my hands. When I was myself I didn't want to hurt anyone. I only wanted to do what I had to to protect my baby and escape. Now, though, I had to add firebombing here to my ever-growing list of mayhem.

First things first; I needed to tell the few people I did trust what was going on. I was about to sit at the computer and type out a curse word when the door opened and Natasha walked in. She looked glamorous, but tired.

"Long night?" I asked, embarrassed.

"Yeah," she said with a shy grin. "In a good way."

"Glad to hear it. Or rather, glad to not actually hear it because that would have been weird."

Natasha's eyes went wide, and then she laughed. "Thanks, yeah, moving on, okay?"

"Please," I encouraged her.

"So what'd I miss last night? Before I got there?" she asked.

It took a second for me to process what she wanted to know. But she hadn't gotten to see Raven and Rex fight over her, and what was more intoxicating for a high school girl than that? I gave her the blow-by-blow and she listened, rapt.

"He never liked me. It serves him right."

"Well, no one's going to make that mistake again."

"Estrella and Wolf wouldn't anyhow. They trust Raven. That's why they've lasted so long."

"How long is long?"

"A century or two, respectively."

"So . . . when will he change you? I mean, aren't you more important to him than Lars?"

She snorted. "Definitely. But it's going to be a while. There's rules to follow. You can't be turned when you still have relatives left. They don't want you getting ideas about re-creating your own vampire family. I can't be turned until my dad dies."

I nodded as if I hadn't seen her father die myself. Did Raven know, and was he keeping that information from her? It wouldn't be that long until the manifest from the *Maraschino* was searchable online, if she bothered to look. Maybe that was why Nathaniel hadn't changed his name, so that there would always be a way for her to find him.

But why should Raven ever change her? If he did, she could possibly become a free agent. Easier to have her trapped in puppy love as if it were amber.

"Who did you leave behind?" she turned and asked me.

"My fiancé, my brother, and my mom."

"It'll be a long time for you then. Who knows, though, after you have your baby you might not want to be turned."

"Probably not." Ever. I was still having a hard time figuring Natasha out. She was still double-checking the job Jackson and I had done, making sure everything was cleaned to her specifications. "What's going to happen to the next subject?"

"I'll run them through tonight. I want to make sure I've got it dialed in now."

"How on earth did you manage to speed things up?"

"Trade secrets." She gave me a prideful smile.

"So you're going to turn them into a vampire? For nothing?"

"No, I'm going to make sure my numbers are good. I know they are, but it never hurts to repeat an experiment."

I decided to walk as far out on my branch as I could, and hoped I wouldn't fall off. "I believed you when you said you wanted to cure cancer—but I don't see how changing people into vampires helps that."

"Easy. Vampire blood cures everything. If we could get an infinite supply of it—we could wipe all sorts of suffering off the face of the earth."

"But doesn't an infinite supply of vampire blood come with an infinite supply of vampires? Who then eat all of the lovely people you're saving?"

"Not when they're all controlled by my Raven. And we wouldn't turn everyone into vampires, we'd just make a lot of daytimers. Imagine if people just got vampire blood instead of going into hospitals—think of all the people with incurable diseases that we'd be able to save."

It was impossible for my jaw not to drop. "You're talking about changing the very fabric of society, Natasha. You realize that, right?"

She smiled at me and nodded and did that shrug, as if it were my fault that my mind was too small to understand her vision.

This was what happened when you froze fourteen-year-olds in time. They were ignorant of history and too stupid to know any better.

"Raven's got everything worked out perfectly. And my research is winding down—or up, really," she said with a cheerful grin. "Soon we'll be ready to start."

I couldn't turn off whatever horrified face I was currently making, and she laughed at me. "Edie—Raven's blood saved me. The more people I can give that gift to, the better."

It was hard to throw stones. I'd been in her position less than a year ago with my mom. Only I'd been old enough and smart enough to realize it was a bad idea. I also hadn't been in love with a vampire at the time.

"Indebting people to vampires isn't like handing out organ donor cards."

"But it could be. Wouldn't people rather be daytimers than dead?"

"Have you thought past that? To the part where Raven has a jillion followers?"

"So? Better him than some big pharma corporation, doing endless drug trials, then using their research to wring cash out of the ill," she said, her voice tinged with spite. I had a feeling her words came from personal experience.

I bit my lips rather than speak again. I knew there'd be no changing her—but she still wanted to change me.

"Heart disease, HIV, cancer, all of it. And people would start to age more slowly, like us. Who wouldn't want to sign on for that?"

I didn't have a good answer for her. She waited for me to speak, and then sighed.

"Look, I know you're upset about the test subjects, I get that. But people die all the time, usually for much less noble reasons. I kill a few people but could possibly save a few million, in the first year alone. It's going to be worth it."

Test subjects one through sixty-four, were they present, might disagree.

"Besides, you're friends with some of them. You don't believe they're all evil, do you?"

"Most of them are." I'd met my fair share of vampires out in the world. I knew Dren had been an indiscriminate killer, probably still was. Even though I cared about Anna, I'd seen her do awful, violent things. She'd had her reasons at the time, but—no one person, or vampire, should rule the world. Absolute power corrupts absolutely—and the thought of Raven with a million daytimers was too much to bear.

"No. They're misunderstood. But not evil. Not Raven."

Her voice dropped so we could talk woman-to-woman. "Someone hurt him a lot, a very long time ago. He doesn't like to talk about it, but he's not as black-and-white as he seems. I can help him get over it. I know how he truly is. I know what's deep down in his heart. I love him and he loves me, and together we can change the world for the better. You'll see."

Every girl had to have that one stupid relationship. The one where she thought she could change the guy, if not in high school then in college. I knew I'd had two or three bred from all the insecurities that came with growing up and a fear of going into adulthood alone.

I had a sinking feeling this was Natasha's, but she'd never get a chance to outgrow it. Thanks to the vampire blood surging around inside her, she'd never get the chance to grow again.

"Anyhow," she went on, giving me a peaceful smile, "I'm going to go out and go shopping to celebrate. You're not allowed to leave the Catacombs yet, though, sorry." Her snub was matter-of-fact. "Go tell Jackson to keep you busy today."

I was both jealous of and mystified by her naïveté, and I left the lab with a millstone of too much knowledge hanging from my neck.

I went down to the crossroads and waited until Natasha was probably gone—and then I went back and tried the lab door. She'd locked it behind her, dammit. But it wasn't fancy, it was just a plain lock. I went up into the Catacombs and found Jackson looking out of place scrubbing the floor on his knees in Heaven. "You're supposed to keep me busy today," I said, because Natasha had told me to. She hadn't told me what to say after that, though, so I was on my own. "Do you have duplicates for all the keys?"

"Some of them." He put down the sponge he was using. "Why?"

"I need the key to the lab. Natasha's off on a shopping trip, and she kicked me out. I'll get it back to you right away—she doesn't have to know."

He put his hand to the key ring on his belt. "What are you hoping to find?"

If I tell you I might have to kill you. I put my hands impotently at my sides. "I'd tell you if I could, Jackson, but it's better you don't know."

He measured me with his gaze. "Is this because you're mad that I won't let you blow things up?"

"I am mad. Going through my things was a dick move. But this is bigger than that. Give me the keys. Please," I added, belatedly.

His hand sank to his waist as if he were a gunslinger, and he unclipped the set of keys. "Bring these right back. Don't get caught," he said, chucking them at me.

I caught them easily. "I'll meet you in Hell in a little bit."

I raced back down with the keys tight in my hand so they wouldn't jingle, and heard Celine taking a shower.

I unlocked the lab door and slipped inside, let it close softly, and then ran back into the autopsy-table computer room.

There was no way I was supposed to be here now—Natasha would know who it'd been if she looked at the keystroke log, and I'd get Jackson and myself busted. But how often would she need to look at it if she was the only person who had access? She was going to turn someone else into a vampire tonight. I couldn't stand idly by.

Then again, I was pregnant. Maybe now was a great time to be a bystander for fucking once. My hands paused over the keyboard.

The thing about saving the world is that it's hardly ever the last-minute choice that does it—it's the infinite number of choices you make on the way there that wind up making you who you want to be.

Did I want to be a person who just let another person die?

The part of me that was infected with Raven's blood could, easily. But the rest of me, the mom in me, and the fiancée in me, and most especially the nurse in me could not.

If I didn't disrupt their testing somehow, and buy Anna some time—what kind of world would be left for my baby? If the daytimer and vampire population exploded rapidly—

Before I could change my mind, I typed out four letters.

F-U-C-K.

The screen flickered to life, and a cursor appeared in the corner.

"Still have all your fingers?" Gideon asked. "If so, turn around and hold them up."

I blinked, but followed instructions—and the motion-sensitive camera for the EEG that'd been focused on the female vampire earlier turned toward me. I held my fingers out and waved.

"Good," said the screen. "We need fifty-six more hours for our assault. Can you manage to live that long?"

I nodded strongly, but held a finger up for attention.

"Yes?" And I realized we still didn't have a microphone set up. Gideon and I were going to have to play charades.

I pinched my thumb and fingers together as if I were turning a key in a lock where the camera could see and then looked over my shoulder.

Gideon, being Gideon, instantly listed off fifty things I might mean. They flooded the screen faster than I could read. I waved him down so that they didn't start to scroll off and pointed at the one I wanted when I saw it. *Lock.*

"There are five electronically locked doors in this facility, counting the garage. Do you need me to open one of these?"

I nodded emphatically. If I had pen and paper I could draw and hold up a map—and then tear it up into pieces and eat it to hide it afterward.

"Garage?"

I shook my head.

"The next nearest door is approximately four hundred feet from here." That sounded about right. I nodded emphatically.

There was a pause longer than I knew he needed on the other side while he considered options.

"Do not go in there. It is not safe for you, or your child."

I spread my arms wide, and then slowly brought my two palms together, shortening things up. Could Anna get here any faster?

"No." The camera's head shook as though it were him while he typed. "It will take the full fifty-six hours to mobilize and travel. You do not need to save that person's life."

But it wasn't just about saving his life—it was everything. What I'd seen Natasha do last night. Freeing that test subject was the only way I could think of to trip her up.

I gave the camera a jovial thumbs-up and mouthed the words *Yes I do*. I couldn't do it without his help, though. As much as I wanted to see my Asher or Anna, I was really glad neither of them was with Gideon right now to give him second opinions on my sanity.

There was a long pause while I thought Gideon might have run off to consult someone, or just started ignoring me for my own good. Then the typing began again.

"Mag locks default to open when there's no electricity. There's a utility truck doing scheduled maintenance nearby at six thirty tonight. They will have an accident during their repairs and take the transformer down. You will have a window of approximately five minutes when the power is off before the generators kick in. You will need a light, as with the power out everything will go dark." The cursor paused in place, blinking.

"The time is now five forty-five plus thirteen seconds," he said, and I looked down at my cheesy electronic watch. It was fifteen seconds slow; I'd have to account for that in my mind. When I glanced back up at the screen, Gideon had skipped a line.

"Sundown is at six forty-five."

CHAPTER TWENTY-ONE

Which meant that I'd only have a fifteen-minute head start before Raven woke up.

That was long enough. I could get into the room and out again in five minutes, haul the victim to the garage, give him some keys, and set him free. I might not even be seen, and his escape could be passed over as ingenuity and luck. If Raven hadn't had any of his blood, or given any of his own, he wouldn't be able to follow him as he could me. If he broke out of here, drove fast, ditched the car, called 911, and went to a hospital—chances were no one would believe his story but he'd be safe, and the whole testing process would be delayed a day, hopefully buying Anna some extra time.

It wasn't a great plan, but it was a plan, and I felt better for having one. I turned around to draw the outline of a heart in the air with my forefingers at the camera.

"I will let the others know of your affection."

I pointed at the camera emphatically, including it.

"Thank you," Gideon typed on the screen, and then it turned off, and the camera went dark.

*   *   *

I stood up, set the chair exactly back the way it was before I'd first sat down, slunk out of the lab's annex, and made my way to the hall, relocking the door quietly behind me. I trotted back to meet Jackson with the keys. I turned the corner—into a surprised-looking, fresh-from-the-shower Celine.

My instinct was to freeze, but the keys were too big to hide in my hand, and if I tucked anything behind my back, she'd know.

I couldn't get Jackson busted—or interrupt my plan. I had half a second to do what I needed to do, so without thinking I grit my teeth, raced up to her like a crazy person, and punched her in the face. The dark part of me that I'd been denying exalted at the sudden violence.

"Don't think that you're better than me just because you got blood!" I shouted to cover for myself.

She sagged into the wall, stunned, maybe more by my actions than by my blow. I'd broken her nose and blood poured down her face, spilling onto her clean towel. She was healing slowly. Estrella may have finally been kind to her, but she'd been stingy. The look of hatred on Celine's face as she held her bleeding nose was so hot it could have burned me. I was still stronger than she was, and now we both knew it. I strode down the hall, keeping my hand with the keys hidden by my stomach.

As soon as I turned the corner I started jogging. Not that Celine wasn't already an enemy, but there'd be no redeeming myself now. Good thing Anna was on her way. The second I opened the door to Hell, Jackson was appeared, and I handed his keys back.

"Were you seen?"

"Seen, but not caught." I looked down and there were flecks of Celine's blood across the back of my hand. *You're gonna have to do what I say, not what I do, okay, baby?*

"Is it still 'better that I don't know?'" he said in imitation of me.

I nodded and wiped my hand off on my skirt.

"You realize that only makes me want to know what's going on more?"

"I know. I'd feel the same if our positions were reversed." I still wanted to trust Jackson but I didn't know how much he'd tell House Grey—or what his true loyalties were to Wolf and, through him, to Raven. We could sort everything out fifty-five and a half hours from now.

He frowned deeply, latching his keys onto his belt one-handed. "I'm not an idiot, you know. I'd understand if you'd just tell me. I may be from the past, but I'm not stuck there."

I was tempted to say, *Your mustache disagrees with you,* but I kept it to myself. "I'd honestly tell you if I could, but if I'm going to do something stupid, it's better for you that you don't know."

"That, I can believe." He shook his head, and then himself, as if he were shaking off a dream. Then he nudged the bucket beside his foot with a toe. "Come on. While you're still alive, you should earn your keep."

It was hard not to keep checking the time on my watch or being paranoid about getting it wet. But doing something was better than avoiding Celine in the halls, even if Jackson kept giving me pointed looks.

At six twenty-four P.M. I stood, and so did he. "Please. Stay here. It's not safe to follow me."

"What am I supposed to tell Wolf if he asks me?"

"That I went down to the bathroom. The less you know, the less you can be forced to confess."

"I'm taking a big chance believing in you."

"I know." I leaned in and pecked him on the cheek, right where his wide mustache ended, before running back to the bottom of Hell.

With all the vampires asleep, including Lars, Natasha gone, and Celine cowed—unless she had a gun—I was feeling pretty good. I reached the crossroads, went down the forbidden hall, and stationed myself outside the test subject holding room door. I pulled the lighter out of my bra and flicked it on.

At six thirty Gideon, true to his word, turned all the power off.

I heard the door lock disengage and pushed into the room, lighter first. "Hello? Hello?" I didn't know how big the room would be, or where the test subject was.

The first thing I saw were huge machines with stickers. I recognized the symbols on them with growing horror.

Radiation. Hot pink atom-like shapes on yellow backgrounds. Of course—being a leukemia survivor meant that Natasha knew all about full-body radiation treatments too.

How many test subjects had she irradiated to make the vampire marrow cells take in early testing days?

I drew back, ready to run away. The machines weren't on now, but in minutes they could be. *Oh, baby. We are not going to be here then.*

I turned slowly with the lighter, unwilling to walk in. Luckily I saw the man with my daytimer eyes, hiding at the back of his cage.

Hiding, I realized, from me.

"Hey. Are you all right?" I skirted the machines and focused on my goal. The room smelled like puke and excrement, and I had to get him out of here.

"Who are you? Where are we?"

"I'm Edie. I've come to save you." I tested the cage with one hand. Strong, but I was stronger.

His eyes were wild. "Are you one of them?"

"No. I'm like you—I'm going to turn this light off now, but I'm going to get you free." I took in the lock mechanism of the cage at a glance and set the lighter down. Then I muscled the cage apart, hinges breaking—vampire blood was good for something. I picked the lighter back up with one hand and reached in as I turned it on.

He shrank back. "You are one of them—"

Ripping a metal door off its hinges had probably not been the most trust-inspiring move. "I'm still getting you out of here. Come on—" I reached in for him, and he shrank back even farther.

Then he lunged for me—I couldn't blame him, I was standing between him and the open door. He ran for me, arms out, to tackle me and escape.

Without thinking twice I swatted him back like I was a cat and he was a toy.

He bounced backward into the cage, his head hitting one of the metal bars, and he went down like a rock.

"Shit," I hissed. I reached for his ankles, pulled him toward me, and then turned on the lighter again. "Guy—wake up. Wake up!"

He had a pulse, he wasn't dead, but in my panic—in the moment when I hadn't controlled my dark side—I'd knocked him out cold. "Fuck fuck fuck," I whispered.

What was next? If I was going to get him out I had to do it now. I turned the lighter off, ignoring its heat when I shoved it back into my bra, picked up his floppy body, and ran for the door.

I remembered the hallways well enough even in the dark, and my footsteps acted as a kind of sonar for me—I was up to the garage just as the lights started to flicker back on. Carrying him along had probably been faster than trying to coax him down strange hallways would have been.

But I'd assumed I'd just be setting him up with car keys and letting him go—not that he'd need me to drive him off. It was go with him—or give up.

Fuck that.

The valet box of car keys was still unlocked. I pulled out a set with a symbol I recognized—the Honda Civic from the other night. I knew where it was parked, too. I unlocked it and hurled him into the passenger side, and then slid across the front of the car cop-movie-style to get to the driver's seat.

The engine came to life, I found a garage opener clipped to the visor, and we were out on the streets of LA.

"Wake up and tell me where to go." I careened down a side street as other drivers honked at me, distracted by shaking his limp form. "Where do you live? Where's a hospital? Where the fuck should we go?"

He made a groaning noise.

"Come on. You're alive, you're free, bounce back." I followed signs for the nearest highway—the larger the road, the faster I could drive. The sun was dipping down at the horizon, flickering in between larger buildings. Getting him free had taken too long—soon the sun wouldn't be up at all. "Come on, come on." I shook him one-handedly carefully so that I wouldn't hurt him again.

His head swung up and he blinked to life, looking at his surroundings, and then at me. "I'm free—fuck." His hand lunged for the door handle, and I was already going sixty. I hit the all-door-lock to my left with lightning speed.

"I'm not one of them—but I can't just let you fling yourself out the door and die. What's near here? Where can I drop you off?"

His eyes were wild and he started patting the door and the dashboard in front of him, covering the car with fingerprints on purpose.

"Stop that—help me help you!" I pleaded with him. The only thing I could think of to do right now was get as far away as fast as I could. My reflexes were off the charts; it was easy to gas and brake the car as I wove through traffic like I was in a car commercial on TV.

I glanced over again after a particularly sweet turn, and found his seat belt off as he wedged himself against the door, preparing to kick out at me.

"Calm down!" I shouted at him, realizing that that was the opposite of calming. He kicked his legs at me, and caught me in my shoulder. The car swerved to one side as I dodged his blow, and the person I cut off honked.

I gasped—not in pain, but because the sun went down.

The feeling that I'd been holding on to a taut cord some-one else had just cut began. "Shit shit shit—" I swung my arm out and lassoed his legs down.

"Stop it—please, stop."

I started changing lanes back to the left-hand side. I'd slow down and he'd get out and run away. This would have to be far enough, wherever this was. I didn't even know how to get back to the Catacombs from here—but I had a feeling someone would come and find me. I signaled—like a fool—and swung over one more time.

I'd been so busy trying to figure out how to drop him off without hurting him that I'd stopped looking at my surroundings. A black car split away from the pack be-hind us and zoomed up. I knew without looking who was behind the wheel, and when its sloped hood went under the Civic's tail, as we were propelled up and forward, I couldn't say I was surprised.

CHAPTER TWENTY-TWO

The car spun. I hadn't put my seat belt on so I was loose inside it like a doll in a dryer. I tried to brace off the wheel to protect my stomach, but when the car landed the wheel wasn't on top anymore. I heard one of my legs crunch, and felt the pain of it breaking, along with the strange sensation of it knitting again. The driver's-side door was crumpled, and the man I'd been trying to save had been flung out through the now shattered passenger window.

"Fuck." I checked the rest of myself quickly. All of me was sore for a second, but that was healing too. There were no bruises or scratches anywhere on me. I was intact—and my abdomen was okay. I lay my hands briefly on it. *I'm so so so sorry, baby.* I reached up for the passenger window to get myself out.

I couldn't see anyone else—we'd landed on one of the grassy islands between roads. Other cars had slowed down, but once the ones that'd seen our original descent moved on, it was hard to see us in the dark, since the Civic's one functioning headlight was pointing into the ground.

Not a single Good Samaritan in this town—although I thought I knew why.

"Guy?" I asked quietly. I hadn't had a chance to even find out his name. I scanned around, hoping he wasn't impaled on any of the brush or fenders forgotten here. I heard an answering groan, and spotted him, crawling away.

"Hey, guy—" I walked over to him. It was entirely unfair that I was whole and he was not.

There was a hissing noise coming out from him, as if he'd sprung a leak. Since there was no way I was going to convince him I wasn't evil tonight, I reached down and flipped him over like a bug. He'd landed on a stick, and it'd pierced the space between two of his ribs. With each inhalation air was hissing out around this imperfect seal. His lung was deflating like a pool toy.

"Shit." I applied pressure at the site. He had a pneumothorax. I needed to seal this wound up, and make another one to let out the air that'd gotten trapped on the wrong side of his pleural cavity.

Even though he was dying, he still swung at me. The magic of life. "Hang on—" I began. I heard the sound of boots on gravel and turned, just in time to see a kick coming. It landed in my jaw and sent me up in the air, reeling back, to land on the remnants of the car.

I bounced off the hood and landed on my stomach on the ground. My jaw had been loose, I'd almost bitten through my tongue, my mouth had had one hot second full of blood before Raven's blood inside me healed the tear. Same for when I hit the Civic, felt my spine stretch and bend wrong, and then recover the same way my leg had as I sprawled on the ground. I was whole, but poorly used, and no guarantees how long I could keep it up.

"Traitorous girl," Raven said, crouching down beside me, out of my striking range. I could feel the heat from the Civic's still-grinding engine and hear fluids leaking out, along with the omnipresent hiss of the man's fighting lung.

"People saw us. Someone called the police."

"So? I know this city like the back of my hand. You're ten minutes from anything here. A lot can happen in ten minutes—as you well seem to know."

"He's dying."

"He was going to die before. You haven't even accomplished anything." He lay down almost beside me, as a mockery of me. "Tell me what you know," he demanded, his voice a wave of power, hitting me harder than his kick had.

I clutched my hands into the dirt, trying to fight the overwhelming compulsion to tell him everything. I bit down hard and found part of my jaw still soft; I whimpered.

"Anna's coming for me," I whispered through gritted teeth.

"Oh, I already know that. Tell me something new. Something interesting." He flipped me over and grabbed my shoulders, pulling me up. He grabbed my chin and pulled it back, and I cried out as new bone ground. "Tell me everything."

"The computer in the lab isn't secure. Anna knows what you've done. She'll be here in fifty-three hours."

The bile of betrayal rose up inside me as vast and dark as a nighttime sea.

Raven laughed and let me drop back to the ground. Somewhere behind me, the man's injured lung was hissing more quietly as the wound worsened. I flung one arm out toward him, and the other toward Raven's foot.

I'd failed at everything. I sold out Anna, I'd exposed myself—and now I couldn't even save this one sad man.

"Please," I whispered. There was no way to abase myself further; I was already prostrate on the ground. All I could do was to seem as pathetic as possible and hope.

Raven stood and for a moment of horror I imagined him kicking me again, and hurting my baby. I'd been trying to play a bigger game, to help protect the world, when I should have just been trying to save myself. I fought curling up, knowing to do so would be to show more weakness, and then he would kick me just because he could. I held my breath and closed my eyes.

What happened instead was that he placed the flat of his boot on my cheek, grinding my opposite cheek into the gravel. I felt the stone of Asher's necklace press into my sternum, caught between me and the ground, as the stink of melting plastic rose nearby. Raven's phone rang, and he answered it. I couldn't hear what they told him, and he didn't verbally answer; he just put the phone back down and looked at me. The pressure on my face didn't change.

He knelt nearer my level. "I want you to admit that you're like us, Edie. You pretend to be innocent, but you plot and you scheme. My blood knows you, from the inside out. You and I—we are the same. Admit it."

Jagged shards of gravel pressed into my cheek, and his boot pressed down and he could finish his step and squash my head like a bug. "No," I spat out, tears welling in my eyes.

His lips lifted into a wicked grin. "Admit it—and I'll let you save him."

I swallowed dry. What was worth more, one life, or my pride? "We are the same," I whispered, from underneath his boot.

The pressure eased, and his eyes narrowed to slits like a cat's. He took a step back. "Good. You may save him now, if you can. But even if you can't, you and I still know the truth."

It took me a second to get to my hands and knees, and then I crawled over the gravel and road debris to get back to the man. He'd gotten cut on his way out of the car, but it wasn't the blood loss that was killing him; I knew on some primal level there wasn't enough blood in the air for that. It was the extra air in his chest, displacing his heart and squeezing his blood flow.

The median was full of random trash. I scrabbled until I found the two things that I needed, a plastic bag and a straw.

I tore the bag in two then pulled the stick out and shoved the plastic bag over the hole, creating a seal with the man's own blood. Then I felt down his ribs and lined up the straw with his nipple—if I hadn't had a daytimer's strength it wouldn't have worked, but I plunged it into him about three inches deep. I pulled out the straw, full of material from his chest wall, blew on the end of it to clear it, and then shoved it back in the hole that I'd made. The air that'd been trapped outside his lung started hissing out, along with serosanguineous fluid. I nestled the straw down, then made a dressing out of the other half of the bag, painting it onto the man with his own blood along three sides, leaving the fourth open intentionally. When he inhaled, the dressing would collapse against the straw, creating a seal for his lung. But when he exhaled, the fourth side of the dressing would lift enough to let any new trapped air out.

It was totally not sterile, but it would be better than dying.

Raven watched from the sidelines. I doubted he'd ever seen anyone try to save anyone else before. The Civic was burning now, upholstery caught on fire, giving him the aura of a demon newly risen from hell.

The man took a breath, and then another breath, and my seal system worked. His arm was bent wrong, but there were no bones sticking out. He'd been tough enough to live this long—he might make it a bit longer. I heard the sounds of sirens, and so did Raven. He stalked over to me and grabbed my arm. "Time to go," he said, lifting me up like a cat would a kitten. My pride in my work evaporated, replaced by utter fear.

"He'll live. We'll say he stole the car from us. By the time he gets out of the hospital, telling everyone his crazy story, everyone will think he's insane, and we won't even have to prosecute." He dragged me over to his car—there were scrapes all over the hood from where he'd shoved us off the road—and the door swung up like a wing. "Get inside."

I got in and sat down. The door swung down again, trapping me.

CHAPTER TWENTY-THREE

This time I put my seat belt on. I wondered bleakly if Natasha ever wore hers on their midnight drives.

Your mom's not a traitor, baby. She just got in over her head, is all. I hoped I could convince my unborn child. I hoped I could convince myself.

"Shall I read your mind for you?" Raven asked me.

I didn't respond. He swung his car around impossible corners, going up onto the shoulder, confident in his own ability to make sure he wasn't seen. I'd once watched Dren convince a train car full of people that we didn't exist—this was the same kind of thing, writ large, and on the go.

"I think that for the first time since you've gotten here, you're scared," Raven said.

I bit my lip and kept staring out the window, my expression dead.

"You've always known Anna would come for you, and you've always known that your man would stay true. You're not even scared of dying, although you should be." The car pulled into the Catacombs' garage again, and he let it idle for a moment.

"What you're really scared of, Edie, is that given enough time, and enough blood, you'd become like me. That eventually, you'd enjoy it."

I didn't speak, didn't move, didn't breathe. Raven laughed at me, and then got out of the car, leaving me behind.

It took me a shameful amount of time to figure out how to get out of the gull-winged car on my own. I wanted to take my frustrations out on something, and I thought about breaking out all the expensive car's windows, but I'd seen enough vehicular damage tonight. I slunk back into the Catacombs, exhausted by everything, not sure where to go or what to do. Suddenly the fifty or so hours left until Anna's arrival seemed impossibly long.

Wolf was waiting for me inside. "You thought you'd just waltz right back in?" He was pissed, and I didn't have a good answer for him—not that he would have listened to one. He lunged for me and caught me and took me under one arm down one of the forbidden hallways.

I fought with him because I thought I was supposed to, but I knew I couldn't win. It was night out, he was stronger than me, and I had no idea where the hell we were, especially once we reached the dark and he kept going, until the lights disappeared. Instead of fighting with him now I clung to him, hoping that he would take me back, afraid he'd just throw me somewhere and turn off the lights and leave me—which wound up being almost what he did. He pried me off his side and tossed me against stone. Rock hit my head and scraped my back and I landed on hands and knees in unseen sand. Before I could do anything, metal ground over metal and closed with a thunk, and I heard the jingling sound of keys being put away.

"You're in here until I hear otherwise. I hope you rot." Then the echoes of his voice ended just before his footsteps disappeared and I was alone in a stone cell.

I still had the lighter in my bra. It felt like the darkness itself was a beast and I was inside its mouth. I didn't want Wolf to see the light, hear the sound, or smell the butane and come back to take it from me. But I was afraid to move until I knew where I was and what was around me. I didn't want to put out a hand and feel someone else's bones.

I waited until I thought I couldn't stand it anymore, and then flicked the lighter on. The golden flame cast light in all directions. My cell was about eight by eight, and I was its only occupant, alive or dead. It was inside a tunnel, which looked like it got more cavernous at one end. Hard to say without reaching out farther, but I was scared I'd drop the lighter and lose it. The door was metal, wrought from heavy bars of iron. I put the lighter back into my bra, and then wrestled with the bars, hoping one of them would give, but none did. The lock was newer too, and solid. This wasn't connected to the electrical grid. Gideon wouldn't be able to open it. I'd just have to wait it out—and hope that someone on my side would still be alive at the end of things to find me.

CHAPTER TWENTY-FOUR

The stone was cold, and being alone in the dark was frightening. The thought of what Raven would do to me was worse.

There was no way to break his power over me. And some craven part of me wanted to please him. I hated that part of me—but it would take more than one lighter's worth of butane to burn it out. My hand found my necklace and I held on to it like a talisman. Anna knew I was here, and so did Asher. But a lot could happen in fifty hours. Too much.

I set my back against the wall and curled my legs up to my chin, trying to make myself small, staring into the dark.

Eventually, I must have slept, because I found myself back on the prisoner's plain.

"What has changed?" he asked me the instant I realized where I was.

I was sitting in his world the same way I'd been when I'd fallen asleep. He was kneeling beside me, frowning. "You're not the only person imprisoned now."

The line of his jaw tensed. "And your friends?"

"They're still looking for you. But I'm not sure how I can help them even if they do find you now. I'm sorry."

He nodded slowly and relaxed, rocking back. "You're not the first person to disappoint me."

"Great. Thanks." Sleep had been a brief window of respite. But now that I was "up" again, there was no place to hide from my fears. What if at the end of the night Raven came down here to get me? "I've got to get away from him."

He spread his hands. "Killing him is the only way."

"Surely someone has fought you off before, in all your centuries of being alive. Hasn't anyone ever managed to deny you?"

"No. That's the whole point. They can't deny you. When he calls, you'll go."

"How did you get trapped then?"

"Raven found out where I slept. His daytimers killed mine, and banded my coffin with silver. Then they transported me into a cave that was sealed off, and left me there until I nearly starved. Since then I've been moved from cell to cell. He makes sure to never visit me himself, only sending in daytimers he trusts."

"I saw another vampire invoke a right to fight him—"

"Vampires may invoke rights with one another; it's how leaders are deposed. As a vampire, you may request to fight as equals—and your request may be denied, so you must ask for it in a public space. But as a daytimer you have no natural rights, and vampires feel no need to prove themselves against you. No one requires honor to dispose of an insect."

"So why did he keep you alive all this time?"

"To torture me? To gloat? Habit? At first, I believed he was scared. Being without a Master is freeing, but freedom is fearful for some. Becoming a rogue means that you are alone in the world, that there is no one you can rely on—if only for the consistency of their hatred," the prisoner said, then snorted. "Some people are not meant to face eternity alone. Perhaps none of us is."

I didn't want to contemplate the thought, staying the same while everyone else around me grew old. "I have friends—other than the ones I sent to look for you. They're coming for me, but they won't be here for two days. How can I stay strong until then?"

"If you want to stay alive?"

"I do."

"Then you must think of that as your only job. Whatever that takes, whatever that means you must do. You gain nothing by struggling to the point that he crushes you, or by reaching for knives. Your children cannot eat pride, your man cannot make love to pride at night. You must be a thing without pride—like a beast. That is the only way."

Like Anna had been forced to become. I swallowed drily.

The prisoner stood. "I will leave you to rest now, before you think too hard and wake. When you are chained such as we are, dreams are the only freedom we have."

He faded, and the world changed around me, and I was back in Asher's living room. The fireplace was roaring and Minnie was stretched out on the couch. I joined her there, lying down, hauling her to rest beside me, stroking my hands against the soft fur on her stomach.

I knew it was a lie, but I was okay with that.

CHAPTER TWENTY-FIVE

The next thing I remembered feeling was a greasy coldness covering my lips and nose. I tried to breathe, couldn't get air—I was in the darkness of space and I didn't have a helmet on, all the air had left my body and I'd never draw another breath—I threw my head back in panic and hit my head on stone.

"Stop that," said a voice beside me in the dark. I found I could breathe again, and took in huge gulping lungsful.

I wasn't at home with my Minnie anymore. I was in a cell, in the dark—and I'd just heard a voice.

"What are you doing here?" the voice asked me. It was so quiet it was hard to hear.

"Shadows?"

"We waited at the entrance for you for a day—we thought you'd abandoned us."

I shook my head in the dark. It hurt where I'd walloped it on the ground. Raven's blood in me was slowing down.

"After a while we got tired of waiting and divided again to look for another way out."

I scooted myself to sit up. "Did you find the prisoner?"

"Of course. Stay still, so you may hold us."

I crouched, waiting, one hand stretched out. A small wet weight crawled to the center of my palm. "Why were you choking me?"

"We were spread out to search. Also, we were hungry."

"I'm so glad my terror at suffocating was good for something."

"As are we. Let us take you to your friend now, so that this can end. We want to go home."

"Join the club. But I'm locked in here."

The portion of the Shadows in my hand made a mocking noise. "Oh, really?"

It took a second, but with their instructions, and using the lighter once, I placed my hand up on the rusty lock that Wolf had used. They slid inside and shortly afterward the latch came undone. I unlooped it from the metal bars and set it down open.

"Hurry. The others wait."

"What time is it?" In the utter black, I couldn't see my watch.

"Night, a few hours until dawn."

Maybe enough. "How will I know where to go?"

"Don't worry—we'll hold your hand."

The Shadows oozed back and forth depending on the direction they wanted me to take, and I followed them. It was hard to trust them—my imagination had them walking me off endless cliffs and me falling onto stalagmites below—but the lighter didn't have endless fuel, and I needed to save what was left of it. Soon I didn't know how far we'd gone, and there was no way I'd be able to find my way back without their help.

"Stop," they said. "Let us down. Not on the silver!" they cried, rolling back and forth across my palm like mercury. I swung my arm farther out to one side and felt them sluice through my fingers.

"He's . . . here?"

"You told us to look for a silver grate, so we found one. If there's more than one person trapped under silver in this forsaken wasteland, we will have to start over." They sounded irritated. "We couldn't cross the barrier to go looking inside for ourselves."

I still couldn't see. "I'm going to turn on a light. Hide, okay?" I counted to ten before pulling the lighter out of my bra and flicking it on.

We were in a small room, carved out of more stone. I wondered at the people who'd taken so much time making these catacombs. The lighter's flame made the shadows jump off every imperfection in the rough-hewn wall. In front of me, just as the Shadows had promised, was an ornately carved grate, decorated with the image of a scorpion, looking archaeologically old.

I leaned over it to see inside, but the light from the flame didn't travel far, and the scorpion emblem scattered shadows. I had an impression of a person at the bottom of it—or a person-sized bundle of rags.

"Prisoner?" I whispered.

It was night out; he should be awake. But he said he'd been starved—maybe he wasn't strong enough? Or maybe he was fooling me? Or maybe it was a corpse at the bottom of the well, and my vampire was in another castle.

I reached forward for the grate itself. "Don't!" the Shadows warned, but too late.

I gasped in pain and almost dropped the lighter. "What the—"

"Just because it's tarnished doesn't mean it's not silver."

"Oh." I rubbed the fingertips of my left hand.

"Careful, you'll scar," said a parched voice that wasn't the Shadows'.

"Prisoner?" I crouched forward. "Is that you?"

There was a groan from below.

I held the lighter up again, and then bit the meat of my thumb, hard, and flicked the blood that welled up there down into the pit before I could heal.

The trapped creature at the bottom rushed up in a burst. It crawled up the sides of the well like someone was pushing FAST-FORWARD. It had a gaunt and drawn face, teeth straining out from a withered skull. It was the stuff of nightmares, the exact image of the last thing you see before you know you're going to die.

I yelped and jumped back into the dark. The sound of my shout echoed, echoed, and echoed behind me.

In the darkness, the first thing I was afraid of was that somehow he'd gotten out, that he was in the same room as I was. It took a moment for me to swallow my panic and start feeling around on the floor until I found the lighter. I flicked it on again, because I needed to look around and make sure I was still alone.

"Didn't mean—starved," hissed a voice, now much closer than it had been.

"Prisoner?" I asked, my voice rising.

"Yes. Don't look," he recommended, from inside his cell.

I nodded, eager to agree. Just a second of the silver had felt like fire—and it looked like it was three inches thick. I was strong, but was I that strong?

"We can't help you. It burns us," the Shadows said, as if reading my mind.

I leaned toward the pit. "Your promises are still good?"

"Always," whispered a too-close voice.

"Then get back." I wished there were a way I could keep the lighter on while holding it with my teeth. Then again, seeing him get nearer would only help me to imagine him breaking off my fingers and sucking on the stumps like bloody teats. My imagination didn't need any help. I set the lighter down again, and before I could think about it reached in, grabbed hold of the grate, and pulled.

It didn't budge. Not even a fraction of an inch.

I tried again, hands on fire, and it felt like the silver was cutting through my fingers as I pulled.

"Fuck." I reeled back, holding my fists up to my chest, teeth grinding together so I wouldn't scream.

There was a harsh laughing sound—it took a moment for me to realize it was the prisoner, not the Shadows, mocking me.

"If it were so easy, don't you think I would already be out?"

"I just need gloves," I spit out, when the pain let me breathe next. "And three other people to help me."

"If I could have one entire life—I might be able to get free," the prisoner said from inside his cell.

I clasped my hands together. They'd gone from burning to aching, as if they'd almost gotten frostbite.

"I'll work on it." I didn't even know where I was, or how I could get someone else back here—to kill them. Fuck fuck fuck. "I need some time, though."

"Will you be able to escape your own cell again?" the prisoner asked with a voice raspy from disuse.

I honestly didn't know. "Shadows?"

"For now, yes. But we expect you to come up with answers soon."

Of course they did. I stood, dusting my burning hands off on my short skirt. "I'll be back. Assuming I'm still alive." I put the lighter back inside my bra.

"Before you go—" I heard a shifting noise from inside the silver cell. "Another drop?"

I closed my eyes in the dark. He was starving, and we both knew there were no guarantees I'd be able to even come back here, much less free him.

"Please," he said.

"Of course." I pretended there'd never been any question. I squatted down beside his cell, savagely bit my thumb again, and milked it. I heard the first few drops spatter and hiss as they hit the silver. I swung to the right two inches and, hearing nothing, assumed they dripped down. When the blood stopped, I put my hand down, and the Shadows that were here with me rolled into my palm.

CHAPTER TWENTY-SIX

The Shadows took me back to the cell where Wolf had abandoned me. I got back inside and replaced the lock. Then I held it in place while the Shadows swam inside and acted like Wolf's key. Feeling it click shut felt like I was sentencing myself.

"Half of us are going to gather our brethren. The rest of us will stay here and await whatever genius next falls from your lips."

"I'll be sure to speak up then," I said, and curled up into a ball with my back against the wall and my knees beneath my chin.

It was hard not to flick on the lighter to check the time. Every passing minute got my hopes up that maybe Raven had forgotten about me, and that I'd sit out the final fight.

Baby—after all of this, the rest of our life is going to be really boring. I promise.

Just when I'd almost convinced myself that it had to be daytime, and began pulling the lighter out, I heard heavy steps approaching in the dark. The cell opened and I wasn't alone anymore. Rough hands grabbed for me with poor aim, proving that Wolf wasn't completely nocturnal. "Your Master awaits," he said, picking me up and hauling me out of the stone room. I held on to one of the bars as we passed, but he wrenched me loose.

We went back to the Catacombs, and Wolf deposited me in Raven's feeding chamber without saying another word. He didn't lock the door behind himself. I could have run, but what would be the point? I knew it was still night.

I looked down at myself in the dim room. My clothes were torn from the car accident, and I had splashes of that man's blood on me, and my hands—I gasped as I held them up to the lamp's weak glow. They were striped, like the prisoner's skin, worse than they had been from Raven's knife—burned from all the silver I'd touched.

"I'm surprised you didn't make another run for it," Raven said as he came in, firmly shutting the door behind himself. I put my arms to my sides, caught.

He stood, waiting, enjoying my discomfiture as I bit my lips not to speak.

"And so now you're the silent type. Of course." Raven leaned back against the door, one hand behind his back. He grinned malevolently. We both knew I was trapped.

"You don't look like someone who wants to cure cancer to me."

He paused, and then laughed. "That's Natasha's fight, not mine. I have enjoyed the fringe benefits of her research, though, I'll admit."

When he was this close it wasn't hard to imagine

why she was with him. I was still scared, but being in his presence was like being made of iron and fighting a magnet. "Why're you with her?"

"Would you believe that I want to protect her?"

My face must have said I didn't, because he laughed again. "I like seeing her hair lighten from the sun in the summer. I like seeing the light in her eyes. She still has hopes and dreams and the certainty of the very young. Instead of my blood, she wants my affection. She's the first in four hundred years, do you know what that's like?" It was not the answer I was expecting—nor was the expression on his face as he said it. He meant it. He honestly loved her.

"Then Anna's not your enemy—"

"You are the only person to tell me that she's not. Don't be offended if I consider you an unreliable witness."

"But I don't—"

"Sit. Kneel. Beg," he commanded in quick succession, and I found myself on the ground as if thrown there, forehead pressed against the dirt. "It's not much fun being controlled, is it?" he asked rhetorically. "No one will ever get to control me again."

"It doesn't have to be this way, though," I said, my lips brushing the ground. "What if you could come to an agreement? Make a treaty? If you gave me back to her—if Natasha stopped her research—"

"Ah, see? People in power are never inclined to share. That's the whole point of being powerful." I could see his boots approaching and feel the reverberation of his footsteps through the ground. He knelt down, caught my hair, and pulled me to my feet, his eyes cold and cruel.

"You would understand if I cared enough to break you properly. I learned from the best, and I know that to do it right you must do it slow. Give, and then take, give, and then take again." He licked his thumb and then wiped it across my forehead where I'd touched the ground, as a mother might clean the face of a child. I closed my eyes without thinking, and he chuckled. "It's been a long time since I've broken someone, though. It would take more time than we both have to do it right, and your Beast is on her way."

"What did your Master do to you make you like this?"

At the memory of the prisoner, a dark frown pulled his lips. "Nothing. He did nothing for me. Stay." He let go of me and I was forced to wait as he left the room, wondering what would happen next.

He returned with Lars—and two short lengths of chain. I tried to back up but couldn't, feet weighted to the spot by his command.

"Unfortunately, Edie, you're not as valuable to me as you once were, even mere hours ago. I could kill you now, and the outcome of events would be the same." He walked over to his couch and kicked it to the side, revealing a series of low metal rings bolted into the stone behind. "It's bad luck to wake up near a sleeping vampire—a newborn vampire, doubly so," he said, holding up a metal cuff.

"No—" I protested, getting some inkling of his idea as he bent the cuff around Lars's ankle, and then fastened him in turn to the wall. "No no no—" I tried to pull back, but my feet were fastened to the ground.

"Come here. Hand out," he demanded.

I couldn't refuse—and I watched in horror as he chained my wrist to Lars's.

"It's only temporary," Raven calmly explained. "Until he wakes up, that is. And I don't even know when he'll turn. It's an individual process—or was, until lovely Natasha figured out how to speed it up. But for you, it will be like playing Russian roulette. Will the Beast get here in time to save you, and fight through my sleeping army above? Or will you decide to rip his arm off to save yourself? The woman I saw groveling yesterday to save some human would never think of doing that. But already you're not that same woman anymore."

"Army?" I flailed against the chain in panic, the cuff cutting in.

"We've been busy upstairs while you've been locked up." He stood and surveyed his handiwork—me and Lars, Lars and the wall—and nodded. "This is the exact sort of thing my old Master would approve of. I command you to stay in the building, Edie. Learn how to become a vampire—or learn how to feed one," he said, and then left the room.

CHAPTER TWENTY-SEVEN

I moved as far away from Lars as I could get, his whole body splayed out, my arm outstretched. I tried to kick out to things—the bed, the lamp. I felt my arm loosen in its socket as I snowflaked, trying desperately to get ahold of anything I could use to sever us, or as a weapon.

How long did I have? I counted back. The traditional length of time it took to become a vampire was three nights—up until Natasha had perfected her bone marrow transplant technique. But Lars had been changed the original way, and this was nearing the end of his second night. I didn't know if vampire metabolic clocks were precise, but I figured that sometime in the next twenty-four hours Lars would wake up desperately hungry—and he wouldn't think twice about eating me alive.

I stretched even farther, finding new length, the rusty cuff slicing into my wrist, the wound healing—it seemed to me that it was healing more slowly. Was it, or was I imagining things? And would the scent of blood so nearby help wake him up?

Then I had that sensation again, as if I'd just read the last page of a book, and I looked at the watch on my free hand. It was daylight now. I was safe, until night. I gathered myself up, massaged blood into my cuffed hand, and considered my options.

The only way I could get the cuff off myself was to tear my own hand off. Raven'd made sure the cuff was too tight for anything less.

Or I could rip off Lars's arm. He was dead, or dying, or whatever the fuck it was now that was happening to him inside—it wasn't as if he'd feel it. It also wasn't as if I could kill him—he was technically already dead. But as I crept closer to him, contemplating somehow putting my feet against his ribs and neck and just pulling on his arm like a reluctant drumstick, my conscience got the better of me.

Baby, I don't know if I can do this. Even if it's for us.

"Just tear it off," said a voice. I almost jumped—I'd forgotten about the Shadows. Their voice was coming from inside my left shoe—they must have tagged along from inside my cell. "Yours, or his. Either way there has to be tearing. Or we can kill you, if you'd like to just give up now."

"No," I protested, sitting up. I saw them slide out into the shadow my leg had cast. "Shut up. Just let me think." I had all day to come up with something, he wouldn't wake up until it was nightfall—

"Technically, we've satisfied our promise to you, Edie. Even we can't get you free, and if you're no longer free, then you cannot help us."

I closed my eyes, blocking out the entire room, trying to ignore the rusty metal cuff cutting into my wrist. "That's fair."

"Not fair enough yet," said a female voice from behind me. I whirled to see Celine leaning against the door. Her face was perfectly healed now, and she was dressed in her club gear, with the addition of opera-length black gloves. "It's beginning to be fair, but—" She stepped into the room, her head shaking at my predicament. "—not yet." She was swinging a heavy cross on a chain, and I realized she must have liberated it from one of the people being changed into a vampire soldier upstairs.

I wasn't afraid of the cross, but I was afraid that it might be silver.

I carefully grabbed hold of the chain between Lars and me. If it came down to ripping his arm out to protect my baby from Celine, I'd do it, no question. "Anna's coming for me." No need to hide it now, since Raven knew.

"But she's not here right now, is she?" Celine made an arc around the room. I might have been stronger than her, but I was a sitting target.

She darted forward, and I jumped back, bumping into Lars, only able to use one arm to protect myself. My arms were bare and she had the gloves and her dress on. I felt the sting of silver as the chain wrapped itself around my forearm, before she yanked down and ripped it away to swing again, this time for my face. I yelped, bringing up my chained arm, but not fast enough: Silver slapped against the back of my hands, and I closed my eyes trying to protect them. She lunged for my throat and I felt a freeing snap from behind my neck at the same time as a line the length of my forearm burned, bone-deep. I swung for her blindly, but she was back at the door.

"That's what you get for hurting my face," she shouted. "See how long it takes you to heal that without blood." The cross dangled from one of her hands, spattering drops of my blood on the floor with each swing of its chain. Her other hand held my necklace, the gift Asher had given me after his proposal on the *Maraschino*.

"Have a fun time meeting Lars. I can't wait to hear you scream," she said, stalking out the door. She stepped in a shadow and I saw the Shadows surge to join her, as if they'd been sewn on. They were leaving with her, because she could leave. I couldn't blame them.

It's just me and you again, baby.

And Lars.

CHAPTER TWENTY-EIGHT

I could smell my own blood. I hoped that that wouldn't encourage Lars to wake up faster. My skin was trying to heal, some property of the silver wasn't allowing it to suture up—I could move my arm and wrist but it stung, and I was sure I'd scar.

I put my hand to the spot on my neck where my necklace had been. I'd taken it for granted this whole time. One more piece of my former life, gone.

Well, baby, there goes your inheritance.

I wanted to cry—out of exhaustion, frustration, and pain—but was too afraid to. And I needed to make a choice, sometime—I checked my watch—between now and about ten hours from now. About ripping a man's arm off or getting eaten alive.

It would be one thing if there was a way to get out after leaving here. Even if I could bludgeon my way out, pulling Lars's dead arm along behind me, I'd still be trapped by Raven's command to stay in the building. Until Anna killed him—and to do that she'd have to fight through who knew how many baby vampires upstairs first?

I sighed and put my head against my knees, my chained arm listless on the floor.

"There has to be a way," I whispered to myself, hoping that faking that there was one would give me greater strength.

"Glad to hear it," said a very small disembodied voice. I blinked and jerked upright. "Over here," said the voice. There was a tiny oilslick of blackness behind Lars's ear, a thumbnail's worth of Shadows.

"What are you still doing here?" I crouched down to their level. What remained of them would only barely fill a thimble.

"We have followed you this far from home. We are not giving up on you quite yet," they said, swirling as they spoke.

Their faith in me was as charming as it was misplaced. "Thanks."

"Protect us over here, will you?" they asked, and despite my desires to be anywhere else at that moment, I moved closer to Lars so that they could have the run of him and the wall.

"You're a lot more polite than the rest of them."

The tiny patch of darkness made an affronted snort. "We never liked them anyhow."

I couldn't see what they were doing as they dispersed, but they gave me occasional commands to move right or left, and I did so, within the confines of the chains.

"Your cuff and his are beyond our capacity, and yours. But the bolts that shackle him to the wall are short and old. It is possible you could pry him off it."

Thus giving me mobility, as long as I was willing to

drag a corpse around. I knelt down beside the chain around Lars's ankle, grabbed it, and pulled with all my might. Nothing gave. I tried again, setting both my feet on opposite sides of the bolt and hauling again. Chain ripped through my fingers, friction burning to no avail.

"Try harder," the Shadows encouraged. I dusted my hands off on myself, and on Lars's pant leg—and that's when I realized that his jeans were still covered in a fine layer of Rex's dust. And I still had a lighter in my bra.

"Hang on," I said, and started undoing Lars's belt. If I could knot his flammable pants around the bolt and light them as I pulled, I might be able to rattle the anchor bolts free.

I was concentrating so hard that I didn't hear Jackson sneaking up behind me. "What are you doing?" he asked, enunciating each word.

I looked down at Lars, whom I now had half naked. No wonder Jackson was surprised—it looked like I was about to have sex with a corpse. "Um. It's not what it looks like."

"I should hope not."

I stopped disrobing Lars and tried to act nonchalant about being chained to him. "What happened upstairs last night? And what's happening now?"

Jackson squatted down to talk to me at my level. His eyes were serious and dark. "They closed the doors before last call last night and trapped everyone inside. Then they held up each room, taking all their phones, and drugging them, a floor at a time, even the DJs and bouncers. We're the only people left awake—and Natasha's been making us bring everyone downstairs and divide groups of people by weight."

"How many of them are there?"

"Seventy or so. Lying down side by side, they're taking up all of Hell and most of Purgatory."

How many people was Anna bringing along? "You know what he's doing, right?"

Jackson nodded. "Turning them."

I yanked on the chain between Lars and me. "You've got to help me get free, Jackson—"

"And then what?" he asked, not moving an inch.

"Then we get out, we stop Natasha and warn Anna and—"

Jackson started shaking his head. "And what happens when night comes?"

"We can find where Wolf sleeps between now and then."

"Can we? Wolf, and Raven, and Estrella? And Anna won't get here until nightfall—you forget that she's one of them, too. Will she be able to protect you in time?"

"Jackson, he's making an army—" I protested. "If we work together—"

Jackson shook his head and gave me a serious look. "What happens to me if Anna wins?"

"Then Anna could take you in—"

"Really? Knowing who I am? You'd let her?" he asked, forcing the truth.

"I don't know. I could explain things—make her understand. And maybe you'd understand her then, too—"

"I'm afraid you've mistaken me for a hero, Edie. When Wolf changed me—I was losing that fight. Just like I'd lost all the other ones I'd ever started, stupid and drunk. He gave me blood because it amused him to have a loser like me for his daytimer. Someone he knew would be easy to control." Jackson rocked back onto his heels and stood. "I didn't go with House Grey to be noble for all the bullshit reasons I fed you—I went with them because for once I wanted to be on the winning side."

I rattled the chain in frustration. "So what's your plan then? Let Raven succeed? Let Anna be surprised by a seventy-person vampire army?"

Jackson's face was implacable—it was probably the same face he had when he was dipping corpses into lye. "Something like that. If I'm lucky they'll take each other out; it'll be like drowning two kittens in the same sack. Either way, I'll report back and House Grey will be pleased enough with me to finally change me over. And I'll be free."

"You're hedging your bets and you know it, Jackson." I strained at the chain, but it held me back like a dog leash.

"No one is coming to rescue me. My bets are all I have." He shrugged with a grunt. "Celine's wearing your necklace now. I assumed you were dead. I'm going to keep on assuming that. I don't know what you're doing down here and I don't care to. That's all the slack I can give you, Edie. I'm sorry. This is my one chance to get out and I'm taking it."

He wheeled and walked back into the hallway before I could think of anything else to say.

The second he was gone I started ripping off Rex's pants with a vengeance.

CHAPTER TWENTY-NINE

I threaded the pants around the chain between Lars and the wall. I couldn't get the fabric under the cuff to come free, but I was able to knot most of it around the anchor bolt that chained him. I tried to create a loose nest of the fabric there, so that the fire would have enough oxygen to breathe and be hot and fast.

Then I put my hand out in the shadow his form created. The Shadows pooled underneath, and I pulled them back toward myself as if I were scraping mercury across the floor, making a bridge of shadow so that they could hide in my shoe again. I'd seen vampire dust light before; I knew my clothing might get burned off me by the blast.

I was banking a lot on the hope that it would be enough to loosen the bolts so I could pry them free, but not enough to injure me beyond what my hyped-up blood could heal. I coiled into a ball to protect my stomach, then stretched out and lit the portion of the hem that I'd pulled out to use as a fuse.

Here go we go. Baby, hang on.

The fuse took and hissed like silver felt, racing up

the fabric to create a bright blue flame. The fire jumped from the fuse to the bulk of the fabric, and the particulate amounts of vampire dust still present caught hold. I saw a bright blue ball and then everything went very loud, and then very quiet.

I was in a place I recognized, unfortunately, curled up on the ground, with the prisoner looking down at me. "Am I dead?"

"I don't think so. Concussed, perhaps. What did you do?"

It took a moment for the precise chain of events to reassemble. There was Jackson, and Lars, and then fire— "Is my baby okay? Why am I here?"

The prisoner knelt, just as Jackson had. "I don't know the answer to either of those. You weren't dreaming, and then you were."

I could be bleeding out right now, lying beside Lars. "Send me back."

The prisoner nodded, and then closed his eyes, concentrating—but neither of us moved.

"Is it because you're weaker during the day?" I guessed with hope.

"No. Your mind—" He shook his head. "You still have his blood in you. You'll heal. Give it time."

"But I don't have any." I looked down at myself. I was still wearing what I'd had on above, minus the chain. My watch was still on my wrist, but the numbers on the screen were blurred. If I concentrated on what I wanted them to be they'd change, but that wasn't actually the time. Who knew how long I'd been out before I'd slipped into here? And how long it would be until I got back? "He's chained me to a sleeping vampire. If I don't wake up before he does—" The prisoner's lips parted into a cruel smile as I talked. "Why do you look pleased about that?"

"Because he remembers me. In all of this time I've been imprisoned, I thought maybe he'd forgotten I exist. But if he remembers the lessons I taught him, then he remembers me. Some."

I rose up. "What exactly did you teach him?"

"I culled him young, at an age when he had no choice but to look up to me. He was called Corvus then, and he haunted me like his namesake, trailing along behind me like a curious crow. I made him warm my bed, and help bury me each morning before daylight. I made him fight for every dram of affection I gave him, like he was a hyena fighting for scraps, and in return he worshipped me like a god. There was no Apollo or Mars for him, there was only me. I taught him to be cruel with my own cruelty, and capricious due to my whim. He shuddered when I walked by, never knowing whether to expect a blow or a kiss." The prisoner seemed to get lost in his tale, and he didn't sound contrite. Something like pride tinged his voice. "Maybe once upon a time I did feel something for the boy—I must have, to have bothered to change him—but three hundred years of imprisonment have dried that fountain up."

"I'm chained to a sleeping vampire because you taught him to assume the worst and fear being controlled? All of this is because of you?" My voice rose in anger, and the prisoner nodded, unashamed. "That's it. That. Is. It." I stood up and started pacing the plain of his imagination. "You remember your promise to me earlier? To not kill anyone unless I tell you to? I'm going to need a lot more promises from you."

His eyebrows rose on his forehead. "Which ones?"

"You can bleed people, but you can't take life without my permission. You can't create daytimers without my permission. You can't coerce me or anyone I love—or even anyone I don't—to try to get my permission. You will not plot against me or try to injure me or anyone I know." I inhaled deeply, hoping I'd covered all my bases. "I will be fair with you—but you will limit your interactions with human society to the bare minimum to survive."

The prisoner stood. He was beautiful—it was hard to superimpose the horrific thing I'd seen inside the well over him—and he was angry.

"A vampire has never been bent to a mortal's will thus. I would be trading his chains for yours."

"You're the one that created a monster, not me. I can't set you free in good conscience if you're going to be creating more vampires like him. You're bad company."

He stared hard, and I wondered for how many thousands of people his face had been the last thing they'd ever seen. "You are still in chains. You admitted it yourself."

"Take a chance that I can free you, or don't. I know where you are. There's going to be a war soon above, and it's possible that everyone who knows of you will be wiped out. What happens if the survivors move on and leave you behind? How much longer can you starve then?" I let the implications hang between us for a moment before continuing. "At least I'm going to try to free you. That's more than you'll get from anyone else."

"At the cost of my pride. Even if you do manage to free me, I will be fangless."

"Be glad I'm not asking you for those too."

"You're more like one of us than you know," he said, and the words stung. "All right. I will be bound by you, as no other vampire has been bound before. I don't know if I should hope for you to succeed, or be relieved when you fail."

"Doesn't matter to me—try to send me back. And keep trying until it works." I stretched out on the desert plain and willed my mind to go back to my body.

CHAPTER THIRTY

I didn't know how much time had passed when I woke. I looked at my watch first—it was four o'clock. Still daylight. I sat up, my brain rattling around inside my skull, and patted myself. Half of my skirt had been singed off—it would hang like a sari now—but my stomach and my skin were intact.

Had my skin been as burned as my skirt? I placed a worried hand on my belly. I wished I were far enough along to feel him moving inside me; I would feel better knowing that he was all right. But he wasn't just my child, he was half Asher's, and shapeshifters were tenacious and strong. I had to believe that everything was all right. I finished surveying myself while my headache made lights flash. The silver scar on my arm was still there from Celine's attack. While the time I'd spent passed out had healed the rest of me, the silver wound was still tender and oozing fluid. I blinked the spots out of my eyes and got to my knees to look at Lars.

The blast had broken his foot badly, and had burned his skin. Whatever superpowered healing vampires possessed didn't work until after you became one, apparently, because I could see bone. Luckily, being dead, he wasn't possessed of any blood pressure, so while there was a red stain on the ground, he hadn't exsanguinated.

"Are you finally back among the living?" the Shadows, now hiding inside my cleavage, asked.

"Yep."

"Good, because the bolts holding him to the wall are loose."

I nodded, grabbed hold of the chain, and pulled.

It was either hold Lars in a cradle carry or drag him along the hallway behind me. Carrying him like I would a child—my child—felt too intimate and overexposed, his head slumped forward against my breast where I knew he'd bite me without thinking when he woke. The Shadows had slid up my arm to settle behind my ear—hidden by my hair—to whisper to themselves and to me.

"Are you sure this will work?"

I shook my head.

"Then why are we doing it?"

"Because." I had no idea how many people Anna was bringing with her. If Jackson was right and there were going to be seventy ravenous baby vampires upstairs, loyal only to Raven, then we needed to even the odds. "What would happen if I put him out in the sun?" I asked, hefting Lars up.

"Nothing today. Not until tomorrow, after he's fully born." We reached the end of the tunnel, with only darkness stretching ahead of us. "We don't trust the monster here," the Shadows admitted.

"Neither do I. But he's our best bet. Help me find him again, please."

"Go left," the Shadows whispered, and I took the turn as I was told.

Each step was carrying me farther past the point of no return. Blood dribbled out of Lars's wounds, leaving a trail. There was no point in trying to clean it up—either freeing the prisoner would work, or it wouldn't. It did smell good, though, a little sweet, like the first blush of decomposition, or like overly sugared wine. I tried to ignore the part of me that thought like that as the Shadows led me into the dark.

"Here. He's below us. Watch yourself."

I nodded in the dark and set Lars down beside me. It was tempting to pull the lighter out of my bra to check my watch.

"Can you warn me before the sun goes down?" I asked the Shadows.

"Of course."

I nodded at their help, and then I swallowed. I was here too early—I had too much time left to think.

This was the only way to free the prisoner. To do what Anna needed me to do, what Asher needed me to do, what my baby needed me to do—to survive.

I'd assumed that'd meant doing what I was told to by Raven. Not doing something of my own accord . . . like this.

Lars and I hadn't gotten along. He'd tried to kill me,

and I'd blown him partially up, so I figured we were even. But what I was planning to do to him now was the kind of thing there was no going back from. It wasn't an impulse or an accident; it was the kind of decision I'd have to live with for the rest of my life.

I'd better make our lives worth it.

"Three minutes, girl," the Shadows whispered by my ear, like a lover. I felt over Lars in the dark for his arm that wasn't cuffed to me and reached out for the silver grate, finding it when my hands stung. Then I pushed his arm through and listened to the silver burn him as I wedged him in.

"Prisoner," I whispered, then I realized it was all or nothing. Three minutes until the prisoner woke up—three minutes until Raven woke up—three minutes until Lars woke up.

Three minutes until there were seventy hungry vampires upstairs.

"Prisoner—" I whispered louder. "Prisoner—wake up."

What if he'd decided dying was preferable to being enslaved to me? I'd never seen a vampire wake up before. Lars stirred beneath me.

I don't know what I would have done if he'd said something human first. If he'd said *Ow,* or *This hurts,* or *Get the fuck off of me.* But what he did was snarl like an animal, and that's the only thing that gave me strength to keep pressing him down. Even though he was stronger than I was, I was more desperate.

"Prisoner!" I shouted, and there was a scurrying sound from below, like dry leaves scraping over leather. Then I heard a horrible crunching noise and Lars began to howl.

I am the bad person here. There is no way to deny it—I have chosen to take Lars's life over mine. I may not be killing him personally, but I am the one who has made it possible for him to die.

Knowing that he wouldn't have thought twice about killing me feels like it should make it easier, but it doesn't. Because it's me who's sitting on top on him, listening to the sucking and gnawing below, trying to ignore the sound of Lars's pain. I curl myself down trying to protect my baby from the violence, the awful eating that won't end and Lars's whimpering, being born into the life as a vampire that he'd waited for so long to become only to then die, fed to another one.

I couldn't stand it anymore; I crawled away from Lars on all fours as the prisoner's hunger trapped him.

The taut chain between Lars and I dropped with sudden slack, and I heard metal hitting metal in the fresh silence.

Lars, who'd been dead for three days, was now dead anew, fallen into dust. I pulled the chain back toward me, and it rattled over the grate. There was nothing in Lars's cuff anymore, so I wound the loose chain around my silver-injured arm like a shield.

"That was good," the prisoner said from inside his cage.

It took all my strength not to cry. "Are you—" I began, not sure of what words I should use to finish.

"My name is Gemellus."

I nodded. He wouldn't be telling me that if this weren't all real. "Can you get out now?"

"I think so."

I reached my hand for my lighter, then realized this

entire room was impregnated with vampire dust, courtesy of Lars. If I lit him up, everything would blow.

It was my last chance to keep the prisoner trapped.

"And your promises to me?" I asked, because who knew if the dream promises counted as much as ones said aloud did.

"I will keep them. Back away."

I stepped backward wildly, hoping I wouldn't fall off a cliff in the dark. There was a sound of motion from inside the cell and then the noise of impact. Metal groaned but didn't give, and Gemellus cursed.

I took a step forward.

"I said stay away," he growled. "This is going to burn."

I crouched down, and he flung himself up at the silver. I heard the hissing of his flesh and closed my eyes, wincing, and the metal whined before giving up. The whole of the grate came free like the top of a beer bottle. I knew it because I heard it land and I coughed on the dust that it kicked up.

And now instead of being in the dark with a baby vampire, I was in the dark with Gemellus.

CHAPTER THIRTY-ONE

I stood slowly. My daytimer senses were aware of movement around me, but nothing I could pinpoint. The Shadows were a cold spot behind my jaw, like the pre-headache feeling of drinking something too cold too fast.

Hands grabbed hold of me, found my shoulders, and I screamed.

"Are you well?" the prisoner asked, releasing me.

"It's not that—I can't see."

"From the injury to your head?" Hands found me again, more carefully, fingers stroking into the tangle of my hair to feel my skull.

"No," I said, stepping away, hoping again I wasn't about to go off a cliff. "Because it's dark," I said, quietly.

There was a pause between us. And then he laughed for a long time, at me or at himself. It had that manic edge to it, loud because he could be, showing the world that he was finally free.

"The darkness does not bother me." One of his hands slid down my arm, rubbing over the chains I'd wound there, to find my hand. "Come. Let us leave this place and never return."

As scared as I was of him, and of what was waiting for us upstairs, I was more scared of being left here in the dark with what I'd done. "Let's go."

For all that Gemellus could see, he'd never been awake during his transport into the Catacombs. So the Shadows guided both of us out, whispering directions in my ear, Gemellus holding on to my hand. His fingers felt firm, different from the skeletal thing I'd seen in his cell before. I had no idea about the rest of him, although my imagination was having a marvelous time making hideous guesses.

"You smell like blood."

"One of their servants cut me with silver." The wound Celine had given me ached.

"You'll scar then."

We reached the light of the hallway. It made my eyes burn, and Gemellus had to let go of me to shield his eyes from it. I realized he hadn't seen any light in centuries—and it'd been over a thousand years since he'd seen the sun.

The light finally gave me a chance to look at him. Lars's blood had filled him out. He wasn't the resplendent man from my dreams, but he could be, if he were given more blood. He was a little shorter than I was, which made sense—back when he'd been born, he'd probably been considered tall. He was lean and covered in muscles and naked, which would have been awkward except that as a nurse I'd had occasion to see far too many naked men. I was more concerned with his limp. I hadn't felt it when we'd been walking—he'd hidden it from me—but now that we were going forward, I could see his left foot drag a little with each step.

"The injury is old," Gemellus said, brushing away my gaze.

"Do you know where Raven is?"

"Somewhere above us. The blood calling is not as precise as we led you to believe." He looked around the hallway, specifically at the light. I didn't know if electricity was common yet when he'd been trapped. "Where is Raven likely to hide? Assuming you'll grant me permission to kill him."

If the Catacombs were a castle, I'd guess on the battlements. He knew Anna was coming into town—I hoped I still had time to warn her. I needed to get to the computer in Natasha's lab, though; what was there was more important. "You can kill him on sight—but I need you to get me into somewhere else first."

He opened his mouth to complain, then remembered his promises. With Gemellus at my side, I raced up the hall.

The door to Natasha's lab was open. I'd assumed it'd be locked, but why should it be? Raven's army was rising above. I was sure if you asked Natasha there was no way he could lose. I walked in, listening, but all the machinery was silent.

"Who's here?" a female voice shouted from the back. "Jackson? Come back here!"

Gemellus started forward, but I put a hand out and called, "Natasha?"

"Edie! Come save me!"

Compelled, I ran into the next room.

Natasha was on the table, shackled as test subject sixty-four had been, with a swelling black eye. She looked hopeful when she saw me, less so when she saw Gemellus. "Set me free," she pleaded—and then remembered she could order me to do so. I saw it cross her face, but my hands were already reaching for the latches of my own accord. They were buckled, but not locked. Her charm bracelet had been bruised into her skin.

"What's happening upstairs?" she asked me, then looked at Gemellus. "Who's he?"

"You mean you don't know?" She shook her head, and I looked back at the naked Roman. "Have you seen her before?"

"I would remember if I had," he said lecherously.

"I thought you'd tested on him."

Natasha wiped tears off her face. "No. I didn't know where my samples came from. Raven told me not to ask, so I didn't. Jackson's the one who brought them to me—"

"It was never a woman," Gemellus said. "Always a man."

I whirled on him. "Why didn't you tell me that earlier?"

"Who would trust a woman more than a man?"

"I forgot you came from an incredibly misogynist time." I had to resist hitting myself. Or him. Jackson made the most sense. Of course Raven wouldn't risk Natasha, or make her burn herself picking up silver. I just hadn't wanted to ask him, because I'd wanted to have a friend—

"If your sleeping place is being threatened, you want men fighting on your side," Gemellus explained.

"Shut up." I stalked over to a drawer, pulled out a fistful of individually wrapped gauze, and handed them to him. "Open these," I demanded, and then refocused my attention on Natasha.

"What happened here?"

"Raven locked me in here for my own safety. And then Jackson came in with his keys and said he needed something, and stole my computer. I tried to stop him but—" She was trying to stop herself from crying at the memory. He'd hit her. And then shackled her to the table. Jackson had had blood more recently than she had—because Raven never needed to curry favor with her. "He didn't even lock the door when he left."

"How many are there upstairs?"

"I dosed seventy people. I didn't get to the last five. It should be enough, though. The Beast's only bringing five vampires, our spies said so—Raven's going to be fine, right? He's going to win?"

Natasha was looking to me to support her power-hungry boyfriend. I didn't know what to say.

"I honestly don't know."

"Because the stories are true, aren't they?" Natasha said, fear growing in her eyes. "If we were going to win, why would Jackson betray us? Maybe he knows something we don't. The Beast's a killer. We knew this was dangerous—" She touched her swollen eye, and then hopped off the autopsy table.

I looked over and found Gemellus watching her like a cat, gauze packets unopened in his hand. "Natasha— Raven's right. You should hide."

"She is one Raven cares for?" Gemellus said. I could almost read his mind.

"No." I couldn't let her get out of here with everything she knew. But I wasn't going to feed her to Gemellus either. "Just let me think, okay?" I announced to the world at large.

But the world wasn't into waiting for me. Natasha walked into the next room with purpose. "Wait!"

She had the refrigerator door open in a second, and a syringe in her hand a moment after that. There was no needle on it, but you don't need a needle if you're willing to hit yourself hard enough.

"Stop!" I shouted, and Gemellus lunged, but it was too late. She started sinking, three inches of syringe embedded in her thigh, plunger depressed. "Shit—" I ran to her side just as her head hit the ground. Her body went still, and there was no light in her eyes.

"Natasha?" I shook her, and pulled the syringe out. Blood, her own and whatever vampire concoction she'd been using on test subjects, welled sluggishly from of her wound. If I were willing to suck on it like a snakebite, could I get the venom out? She still had her charm bracelet on, and the heart with a C was twinkling under the fluorescent lights. I understood it now—it was a gift from Corvus.

"She's dead. How?" Gemellus stood over us both, then slowly turned around, placing a hand against the metal of the nearest refrigerator. "What is this place? What happened here? How were these made?"

"I cannot even begin to explain all this to you right now." I set Natasha down and stood. Looking up, I saw that the camera from the EEG machine had tracked us, and was watching us from inside the autopsy room. Gideon was still on.

Now that there was no computer I didn't have another way to communicate with him. All I could do was draw a big 7-0 in the air between us. The camera nodded, and then went limp.

Seventy against five. The odds were going to suck.

But if you counted Gemellus and me, that made it seventy against seven.

CHAPTER THIRTY-TWO

"Give me those," I said, and snatched the packets of gauze from him, to rip off all their tops at once. I shoved the gauze inside my silver wound with a hiss—it wouldn't heal it but it might stop me from smelling like blood—then I wound the rest of the chain around it.

"You should have let me kill her," he said.

From my position on the ground it was easy to see the injury that'd broken his leg and healed wrong. And then his leg lashed out to kick her, sending her body skidding across the room.

"Hey!"

"I made no promises about desecrating the dead," he reminded me. It occurred to me that there was probably a reason for the scorpion inlay on his silver grate. I hoped the promises I'd had him make were tight enough—no time to think about that now, though. "I need to feed, if I'm to fight him. How did she change herself?" He swept up the syringe she'd held. "What tool is this? Did it once hold blood?"

"Yes—I'll explain later." Maybe. The fewer people that knew, the better. We needed to find Jackson—

Gemellus crushed the syringe in his hand. "This is what I will do to him. Can we continue?"

"We can—but we need to destroy everything here first." This whole room was too dangerous to leave intact. I didn't know who Anna'd brought with her, or who would survive tonight. Everything in here had to go.

I had no idea if Natasha kept off-site backups. I hoped not, but I couldn't guarantee it. All I could do was destroy what was here. I started opening up the refrigerators and yanking out the contents, letting petri dishes and Erlenmeyer flasks fall to the floor, spilling sticky contents. I opened up a drawer full of blood draw supplies and stared into it. Test tubes, needles, tourniquets . . .

"If we may help," the Shadows at my ear asked.

"Yes?"

"We can destroy all that is in here, if you but turn off the light."

"Everything? Inside the machines too? I need you to ruin all of it, make it unworkable, unsalvageable." There wasn't much of them left; they'd be spread very thin.

As if sensing my worries, they clucked like a mother hen. "You would be surprised how quickly we can move in the dark. Swear to return for us, and we will start."

"Done." I stared into the drawer I had open. How many times had I been told that blood was power? I reached in and grabbed a full set of anything I might need to get some extra blood for myself. Then I stepped over Natasha's form and turned off the light. "Gemellus, get into the hall."

The chill of the Shadows rolled down my neck, down my back, buttock, and thigh, like a cold grape; then it fell away from me and I stepped into the dimly lit hallway. I closed the door behind myself so that they could work in complete darkness.

"So you trust them, but you don't trust me?" Gemellus asked.

"I've known them longer."

Gemellus snorted. Then his face became serious and his hands curled into fists at his side. "I need to feed so that I can fight Raven."

"I know." I didn't want to run upstairs into seventy hungry new vampires—but I didn't want to stay trapped in the catacombs like a rat, either.

Which way is safest, baby? I wished I knew.

"You will let me feed, won't you?" Gemellus pressed.

"Yes," I said, exasperated. Raven knew all the passageways down here. All these rooms could be barricaded or overwhelmed; there were no good defensible places, which was probably the point—and Jackson had already proved the uselessness of locks.

I was considering running to the garage when I heard the sound of footsteps running down the hallway at full speed. Gemellus grabbed me and wrenched me back, putting me against the wall behind him.

It was one of the bouncers Jackson had introduced me to—only it wasn't him anymore. I'd seen the bloodlust of the newly born before, and he was the textbook definition of it, twice as big as Gemellus and crazy-eyed. He hurled himself at Gemellus, trying to take the older vampire to the ground.

But Gemellus was faster, even with his limp. He feinted back, making the other man overstep himself, and Gemellus caught his hair with his hand and yanked his head down hard against his naked knee. For a second I was worried he was going to rip the man's scalp off—and then there came the sounds of more footsteps running down the hall.

"May I?" Gemellus asked while the new vampire was concussed. I nodded in wild fear. Gemellus grinned evilly. Fangs came out and he bit into the man's neck. He didn't even look for the carotid, he just bit through it, windpipe and all. He spit the cartilage on the ground as the man dusted. The only thing left of him was the dust powdering the bloodstain on Gemellus's chest. The bouncer had had cargo pants on—pockets galore. I shook them free of dust before pulling them on.

"May I?" Gemellus requested again. I glanced up—another newborn was on the way. Gemellus met this new one head-on, running into him at speed, bowling him down to pull both his arms off.

"Yes!" I jumped into the pants and pulled them up, buckling them around my waist. I shoved needles into one pocket, and the test tubes into the other.

Gemellus shouted, "May I?" from twenty feet farther up the hall.

"Yes!" I called back, and then heard him laugh again, like he'd laughed when he was first freed. I heard the wrenching sound of breaking bone; by the time I looked up again, Gemellus was covered in another vampire's particulate mist.

A third one ran in, then a fourth—Gemellus had the advantage because the hall was narrow, and their hunger made them too stupid not to get in one another's way. And a fifth one appeared behind them. Maybe by the time Anna got here there'd only be five vampires left.

Gemellus spun away from one and then pinned him against the wall, reaching in with both his hands underneath his rib cage to pop it out and open like a reluctant DVD case.

"Yes!" I shouted at him before he could ask, and I watched him bury his face into the screaming vampire's heart. "You can kill everyone in the hallway but me!"

As he worked it was harder to see him move and react. I knelt down to pull a pair of pants off a dusted corpse for him to wear, but he was doing just fine nakedly. I got flashes of the new vampires coming at him. Club clothes, brown or blond hair, tanning-salon skin—and hungry hissing teeth. Each of them burst like an ash-filled balloon as Gemellus struck out with his hands and feet, broke and twisted them, crushed them against the wall, and in one inspired move used one's torn-off arm to impale another before both fell to dust.

Gemellus had missed out on centuries of bloodlust, and now he seemed to be trying to catch up, all the while biting, feeding, filling up, getting stronger. I found myself becoming profoundly glad he was on my side—and worried that I hadn't made him swear enough. The carnage was mesmerizing, and the dark part of me wanted to join in. I looked away to ignore it just when I saw a familiar face in the throng.

"Not him!" I raced up, dragging pants along. "Not him!"

Gemellus paused, a few seconds away from killing Jackson—and Jackson was there holding a lighter out.

Gritty dust fell in lazy circles from all the vampires Gemellus had just killed. Ten or eleven—I'd lost count. My eyes wept and I'd inhaled enough vampire dust to practically count as one. The still-naked Gemellus was slicked with the stuff; he looked like a golem.

"Who is he to you?" Gemellus asked.

I looked at Jackson, his hand still out, thumb upon the lighter's striker. Gemellus didn't know what it was that Jackson held, but I did.

And if he knew just who Jackson was to him, he'd probably kill him.

Jackson looked from Gemellus to me and grunted. "Where's Lars?"

"Gone."

"I didn't think you were like that," he said, still holding the lighter up.

"And I didn't think you were like that. With Natasha." There was a backpack across his back, I had no doubt the computer was in it.

"Just because I don't know how it works doesn't mean I don't know what's valuable."

"May I?" Gemellus asked, leaning in.

There was a chance Jackson didn't know what he'd done. Raven had ordered Wolf to order Jackson, and it'd been a change from killing people, drilling bone out of a vampire's dusty daytime corpse. But I could see him putting two and two together as fear lifted his face.

I shook my head, begging him not to say anything—

"It's you," Jackson whispered.

"We've met before?" Gemellus said, taking two impossibly fast steps closer, while Jackson held the lighter out like a cross. "You . . . ," he said in recognition, his voice sinking.

"Gemellus, stop!" I shouted, and he did so.

Jackson's eyes flickered from Gemellus to me. "Don't let him kill me, Edie. I was just following orders—I didn't know—she never told me what they were doing—I needed proof to take back to House Grey—"

I swallowed, throat suddenly dry.

He stopped talking and his jaw clenched. "You're not like this. I know you."

"You should ask Lars what I'm like." Cold black tar welled up inside. It would be so easy to sic Gemellus on him now; I wouldn't even have to bloody my own hands.

Gemellus lifted his lips in anticipation, showing fangs that had taken thousands of lives. The tip of my tongue went to my newly sharp canines involuntarily, and I tried to imagine drinking blood, hot, salty, sweet.

Never, baby. Not if I can help it. "The computer for your life."

Jackson made a strangled noise. "I have to have something to show for all this—"

"You'll be alive. That'll have to be enough." There was enough dust in the hallway that if Jackson turned the lighter on we'd all go up. He had to see that.

"Then what happens to me?" he shouted. "If I can't give this to House Grey, and Wolf dies—the past forty years I've put into this have been for nothing? I'm just cast back out into the world again? I don't know what it's like out there anymore—I can't just walk back out into it and be human, pretend like none of this ever happened to me."

"I'm sorry, Jackson. It's the computer, or your life," I said. Gemellus growled and leaned in. Jackson's eyes flickered over Gemellus's shoulder at me.

"I mean it. I swear. Give me the computer—and the lighter—and I won't let him kill you."

Gemellus howled something obscene in a language I didn't know.

"Hold!" I shouted back at him, and he held. Jackson watched our exchange, and he swallowed.

"You swear it on the life of your child?" Jackson said.

"I do."

Jackson hesitated, then slunk to the far side of the hallway, coming around Gemellus—who turned as he did so to keep him always in sight.

"Lighter. Then computer. Then you go and take the fastest car you can and get the hell away from here."

Jackson moved so that he could see both of us. The hallway was still clouded with dust from all the new-borns Gemellus had slaughtered.

"No tricks?" he demanded.

"You know me. I've never been the liar."

Jackson nodded, then unshouldered his backpack, setting it on the ground at the same time he pitched the lighter forward in a low arc over my head. Gemellus caught it without taking his eyes off him.

In an instant Gemellus was behind me. "No one was here to see your honor but me, and I will not tell your child of this," Gemellus said, his breath hot on my neck. Jackson was backing, wide-eyed, down the hall.

"No."

"But you have no idea what he did to me!"

"He only did what he was told, which is what you're

going to do," I said, turning on him, my voice flat. "Put on these pants." I handed them over to him, ignoring the hatred burning in his eyes.

"I still get to kill Raven," he said.

And as if to answer him, there came an explosion from up above.

CHAPTER THIRTY-THREE

"What was that?" Gemellus asked as I ducked down.

"I think if you want the chance to kill Raven, you're going to have to hurry."

"Artillery?" Gemellus guessed, sounding impressed. "I'm looking forward to meeting this guardian of yours."

The building rumbled again. When I looked back, Jackson was gone.

"I'm sure she'll be happy to meet you too."

He held out Jackson's lighter. "This is a weapon?"

I nodded.

"Show me."

"Not here. We'll light ourselves on fire." We needed to get out of here—Jackson wasn't the only person with a lighter in the building. Plus if there were more explosions and we were trapped below—

"He's above us. I can feel it!" Gemellus shouted. "Tell me the layout of this building."

"Destroy this utterly, and I'll talk." I handed the backpack to him, and with his hands he set to turning it and everything in it into atoms.

I knew enough to make sure Gemellus had crumbled

the hard drive before I'd let him stop, and I explained the different floors of the club and the one-way glass as we moved. Each time we turned a corner I expected to find another wave of newborns, but apparently Raven had bigger problems upstairs. Gemellus let me lead, but only barely, maybe worried I'd let my conscience get the better of me again.

We reached Hell in record time—and Anna's bomb had blown open the entrance to the Garden of Eden, leaving a wide hole in the back of the room. This explained why we'd felt the rumble below: It'd been right on top of us. The thick structural beams holding up the next two floors were in place, but everything else in the room had been blown ten feet to the right, including new vampires—the air here was heavy with dust, too. There was fighting on the deck—a wall of newborns, shrieking hunger and surprise. I thought I saw the swish of a scythe and I both hoped and couldn't imagine that Dren was here, fighting for me. I saw Jorgen's head pop up over the crowd—standing, he was taller than any of them. He spotted me and let out a baleful howl. I wanted to howl back at him.

I expected us to go join that throng—I knew Anna was outside there, fighting her way in—but Gemellus grabbed my arm and shook his head. "He's higher." He strode out into the center of the room. "Is this the strange glass you told me about?" he asked, pointing up. I nodded as Gemellus looked up at the ceiling.

"Corvus! I come for you!" he yelled with wild abandon. One of the newborns at the back of the garden turned and ran for him. He caught the man and flung him back into the group, bowling three other vampires down, attracting the attention of the outliers. Hungry faces turned toward us—but not as hungry as Gemellus. He looked back at me. "Take me up to him."

I nodded again. Up seemed safer than staying here.

We ran up the stairs to Purgatory. A fresh wave of newborns had been held in reserve, or just woken up. They surged mindlessly forward, and Gemellus picked up a nearby table and sent it spinning across the room at chest height. It cleaved through the three nearest and pinned a figure I couldn't quite see to the back wall. Other newborns crowded in, all looking like they had at the beginning of their night out, dressed to impress—and now dressed to die.

"May I?" he asked again, crouched to run at them.

"Yes. Please!"

"Wait, wait! You owe me!" said a familiar voice. As Gemellus mowed his way through the newborns I circled warily to see Estrella, pinned beneath the table. I hadn't realized Gemellus had flung it with such force—it'd ground into her like a buzz saw, nearly lopping off her chest and arm, embedding itself into the wall behind her. One of her arms hung limp, and the other couldn't get ahold of the table's smooth surface to free herself with.

She looked relived to see me. "Save me," she commanded, and her voice rumbled with the tone of command. But I wasn't hers, and Celine was nowhere in sight.

Save her to what, heal and fight more?

"You owe me," she said. "You promised me a favor."

"Under duress."

I'd seen her tuck into test subject sixty-four's neck. She'd lived long, and she was no stranger to blood.

"A promise is a promise," she hissed.

I looked back over my shoulder, to where Gemellus was glorying in the violence of his kills, laughing as he went through the newborns like a rabid dog among hens.

"I did." I grabbed hold of the table's edge, and her face lit up before I went on. "I'll kill you. Instead of letting Gemellus do it." I closed the table on her like I was slamming a door. Darkness swam in my vision, and a horrible part of me was pleased with myself.

Dust spurted over the top edge of the table and spilled like hourglass sand down by my feet. I watched it flow with the angle of the floor, tilting now toward the far side of the room, sliding across the one-way glass.

A snarl behind me warned me just in time, and I leapt away with strange instinct, barely missing a newborn's attack.

Gemellus was two-deep in newborns, which left this other one free to tangle with me. I held my chain-covered arm up as he led in for a second time with his teeth. Enamel grated on metal so hard a tooth popped off. He was stunned by this—I was too. I needed a weapon, fast—I reached back to rip one of the legs off the table I'd used to smash Estrella. The newborn was twice my size, more wary now, and a full vampire where I was not. I waved him back with the stake, chain-shielded arm out, and felt like a gladiator in a Roman arena given far too little cover. Not engaging wasn't an option: He was between me and the door, and Gemellus still had his hands full at the other end of the club. I shouldn't have let myself get separated from him.

He took three steps and pressed me back against the wall. The leg-stake was still in front of me, but I'd just lost the room to use it. The newborn loomed, licking the space where his missing fang should be, and roared before leaning in.

"Gemellus! Save me!" I shouted—just as a scythed blade appeared out of nowhere over the newborn's shoulder, drawing from his shoulder to his hip, cutting him in two like a tear in reality.

"I hope I'll do," Dren said, appearing out of the cloud of newborn dust. He was wearing his trench coat, his hat, and his crookedly evil grin.

"Dren." I sagged and coughed and grinned. "You almost cut my nose off."

He waved his scythe at me casually. "You should have stopped sticking your nose in other people's business a long time ago."

"Are we winning?" I asked with hope.

"Won't know until we're through."

I saw Gemellus's attention turn, and he launched himself at Dren. "No!" I shouted at him, as if he were a bad dog, and he drew up short. He was still covered in the dust of others, with a disconcerting concentration of it on his mouth and at his throat.

"I take it we're on the same side?" Dren asked of me.

"For now," Gemellus said, as if that might not last long.

I looked through the glass below at the fighting inside Hell. I couldn't tell who was winning; there was too much chaos.

"He's higher," Gemellus prodded.

I looked from Gemellus to Dren. "He's Raven's Sire," I explained. Dren gave me a slightly alarmed look. "If we can get up there, we can make this whole thing stop—"

"It's not safe—" Dren started just as another wave of newborns came up the stairs, following a baying Jorgen.

"This isn't either." Gemellus looked to me.

With the older vampire, there was still a chance.

Dren made a sound of either agreement or disgust, then wiped his scythe blade off on his thigh. "We'll hold them off here. Do what you will, but hurry."

I nodded and raced for the stairs.

CHAPTER THIRTY-FOUR

Gemellus mounted the steps two at a time, and together we emerged into Heaven. Raven was nowhere to be seen, but Wolf was waiting for us, and Gemellus growled.

"Corvus!" he shouted.

Wolf leapt for Gemellus, and Gemellus for him.

They ran at each other at full strength and quickly went down to the ground. The sound of bones breaking and reknitting filled the air, along with the grunts of impact, the sound of flesh hitting flesh. They fought like titans, trading blows that would have broken lesser men—or lesser vampires.

I didn't know what kind of fight Gemellus was anticipating, but I doubted this was it.

"Corvus! Appear! I command it!" Gemellus said after throwing Wolf back fifteen feet. It felt like the room thundered, even though the words weren't meant for me. Raven was nowhere to be seen—and Wolf didn't have to listen. I started to get worried Gemellus would die, and then who would stop Raven? Maybe Dren was right, and I would've been safer downstairs with him.

"Call off your dog!" Gemellus shouted when Wolf next let him catch his breath.

Raven finally emerged from the back of Heaven, walking as slowly as he could—Gemellus hadn't told him to move quickly, and so he hadn't.

"Wolf, stop," he said quietly, obeying his old Master to the letter of the law. But Wolf didn't relent—he had Gemellus on the ground now and was clawing at his throat.

This contradicted the way I thought vampires had to act—I thought the entire system was built on blind obedience. Then Wolf and Gemellus traded places quickly in the way fighting dogs sometimes will, and I caught a glimpse of dull metal at the sides of Wolf's head, as if the younger vampire had gray headphones on.

"Silver?" I whispered as I realized just what Raven had done. Wolf still had his ears, but Raven had poured silver into them. He couldn't hear Raven anymore to obey—if his ears scarred the way my arm had, he wouldn't be able to hear anything ever again. He'd be following his last order forever, presumably to kill Gemellus.

They twisted and fell against the floor again; I heard it groan with their weight as they landed. Wolf had his hands latched in a death grip around Gemellus's throat. Raven looked over their tangling bodies to me.

"So you decided to become a vampire after all?" he said, his voice still low. His face looked strange, pained, eyes red, with smears of scarlet on both of his cheeks.

"Have you been crying?" I asked, scared of him and for him both at once.

He didn't just sit down on the dais at the far side of

Heaven, he collapsed, as if something had hit him. "Natasha's gone. I felt her go."

"No—"

"He ate her. The monster of my Master that you freed ate her—" Raven reached into his coat, pulling out his silver knife.

"No! I saw her! She's fine!"

"Don't lie to me, Edie," he commanded. I felt it wash over me and through me and couldn't have disobeyed him if I'd tried.

"She was worried you would need help. She dosed herself with stem cells, like the others."

Raven's face fell anew. "Then my own monster gnaws her now."

"But she's alive—sort of." I looked from him to Gemellus and Wolf's evenly matched wrestling.

"Not with the life I wanted for her."

"If you wanted to play Romeo and Juliet you should have gotten her the hell out of here!"

"Where to? Tell me where it would have been safe for us from your Beast?"

"She's not like that!" I fell to my knees pleading with him as his face went dark.

"All Masters are eventually. I should know." He watched Gemellus and Wolf's fight with bleak satisfaction. "Come here, Edie. I'll show you what she's like."

I got up off my knees and crossed the room to him, just as Dren raced up the stairs. Seeing him, I shouted, "Dren, help Gemellus!"

Dren started forward, then stopped. "When our kind fights like that, only cowards want other people to get involved. Is your new friend a coward?"

"Wise words from the Beast's lapdog," Raven said. I was walking as slowly as I could, and I could still speak—

"Dren, kill him then. Please." I didn't know what Raven was going to do to me—*to us, baby*—but the implacable look on his white face smeared with red was frightening.

I could see Dren calculate his chances of reaching me before Raven did.

"Wolf and I are well fed on others of our kind. You would have a hard time defeating us." Raven stood and almost instantly crossed the room to where I was. He placed himself behind me, silver blade drawn and at my neck. "Summon the Beast."

"It's still not too late."

"Tell that to Lars," he said, setting the blade down on my skin, and I gasped in pain.

"I can make her listen, Master. I swear it."

"Only because you don't know how we are. Meant to kill from the moment we are born. We cannot think of others before ourselves, and it is a joke to pretend there's ever been another way. My Natasha wanted to cure humans, and instead the darkness made her able to kill for me. My blood perverted even her sweet heart. Your Beast cannot back down from this challenge any more than I can rescind it now."

"I am not a monster," I whispered, hoping it was true.

"Yes, you are. Just like me, just like I was made." His hand caught under my jaw and he tilted my head forward, I thought for a horrible second to kiss me. Then his mouth opened and his teeth caught into my hair and tore raggedly against my scalp and I screamed as I felt his fangs grate against my skull. Blood poured out from the wound, covering my eyes as the wound took its time to heal.

"Summon your Beast," he told Dren with bloody lips, "or next I will suck out her eyes."

Dren had been trapped at the far side of the room, scythe up, unsure what to do next. He incrementally lowered the scythe. "Anna!" he bellowed. "Get up here!"

There was a sound at the stair and Jorgen emerged with a swollen belly, like a mockery of the child I carried inside, and Anna came up after him.

"Good boy," she said, petting his massive disfigured furry head. Then she looked over to all of us.

She was a sight. A horrific yet beautiful sight. Her blond hair was tinted gray from all the newborn vampire dust. Her clothing was torn. But she was intact, and there was a sad smile on her face.

"In the tales of the Beast that I've heard, the Beast does not have friends. So imagine my surprise when you requested that we save her," Raven said from behind me.

"Your storytellers are wrong then. I have many friends—and also many enemies. Which are you? Choose carefully."

"Like you would give me a choice." What had Gemellus done to turn him into this? There was a wheezing gasp from the wrestling vampires as Wolf gained on Gemellus. I could see where Wolf's fingers were straining into the meat of Gemellus's windpipe; if Gemellus gave him even one more half inch of leverage, he would twist it free.

"Just because you were raised without honor does not mean there is none."

"And all of this?" He twisted us both to look through the glass at the carnage below. "Ignored? Erased?"

"We have ways of making you forget."

I could feel him weighing his options as he held me. Trust someone he'd never met, who'd just destroyed his livelihood, love, and house, or play his final awful card? The blade hovered, burning me as he considered, and I knew the moment he'd made up his mind. Poor Natasha; Raven never was going to be able to outrun his past.

This is it, baby. I'm sorry. I loved you and your father.

Then he released me. I fell to the ground in limp surprise. The knife clattered beside me, dropped.

Had he—were we?—I twisted to look up at him, but nothing had changed. "Edie, pick it up."

My hand reached for the knife like it was told.

"Kill her, or kill yourself. You choose."

The silver blade was a living thing in my hand, twisting in the air like a snake. Either I pointed it at me, or it had to be pointed at Anna.

CHAPTER THIRTY-FIVE

I looked hopelessly at Anna, and at Dren, and at Gemellus, fighting myself. I didn't want to die. But I didn't want to kill her. The blade wavered as I tried to make up my mind, picking between two horrible options.

"Help me. Please," I begged anyone who could listen. I took a staggering step toward Anna, as if pulled by the knife.

If I did try to kill her, would she kill me? What if she somehow changed me now? That would be a way out, but it wouldn't save the baby. I needed to live—but could I live with myself knowing that I had killed a friend?

"My people have your land surrounded and we've already killed everything in this building," Anna said. "End this, and I swear I'll let you live until dawn."

"You heard her. Go to her, Edie."

I took another stumbling step forward. "I don't want this. Make it stop. Gemellus—"

"Don't talk to him," Raven commanded. Dren stepped forward to intercept me, but Anna put her hand out, denying him.

"It's going to be okay, Edie," she said, taking a step toward me. "I promise you it's going to be okay."

"No. It's not. This is the least okay thing in the history of forever." My resolve flagged, and the weapon spun in my hand, blade aimed straight at my stomach.

I'd been stabbed once by vampires before. Perhaps it was fitting that I stab myself as they had now.

"Don't do that," Anna warned.

"I don't want to—I don't want any of this!"

"I know." She took another step toward me. What if she took the knife away? Would I use something else, bound to fulfill Raven's last terrible command? I had visions of me going at my radial pulses with my own teeth, or trying to bare-handedly twist off Anna's head.

"Make it stop. Please. Think of something. Fast," I begged, knife inching closer toward my belly.

I can't do this to you, baby.

"Don't," Anna said, reaching out for me. She was so close now, only three steps away. As my attention went to her, so did the knife. Her arms were still open, so close she could hug me.

"Come here, Edie," she said, and leaned in—and I did as I was told.

Three things happened at almost the same time:

Anna and I cleared the line of sight between Dren and Raven. Dren raised his scythe and threw it at him.

Wolf spotted the spinning weapon heading for his Master and let go of Gemellus to leap up for it like an eager dog, meeting it halfway, and the scythe spun across his neck like a guillotine blade. Wolf died instantly, midair, spilling ash on the floor like a burst of sudden rain, followed by the sound of two dull silver pieces falling.

And I found myself covered in my best friend's blood.

"Oh, God, no," I whispered as we sank together, me holding her, the knife in my right hand piercing through her back, up into her heart. I looked up into her dying eyes—there was no surprise there, just a magnificent sorrow. Raven's compulsion was gone now, I was in full control again, but it was too late. Blood poured out, as if without end, as her body desperately made more to re-place what her silver-pierced heart couldn't pump, as if she were a fountain and we were both drowning. Then her head sagged back and she went limp in my arms.

"I'm so sorry, Anna, oh my God—"

She didn't say anything. And she'd lied to me. It wasn't okay.

I dropped the knife, kneeling in a pool of her blood, put my hands to my face, and wept.

CHAPTER THIRTY-SIX

"I invoke!" Raven shouted the second Gemellus was free.

"Accepted," I heard Gemellus say, but I wasn't looking. All I could see was Anna's face, lying in an ever-growing pool of blood.

The sounds of their fight began behind me, as footsteps neared. I looked up and saw Dren.

"I didn't mean to—"

"I know. It's okay."

"No, it's not!" I screamed up at him. He sank down on his heels beside me, the retrieved scythe across his knees. How was I going to explain this to my child? We got free because your mother killed her friend?

"She'll only be dead for three days. Assuming all the mythology's right about living vampires and that sort of thing. Nobody mentioned silver, but we won't tell anyone else about that. It'll be our secret, okay?" He reached behind Anna, pulled the knife free, and slid it across the room. I was conscious of Gemellus and Raven behind us, whirling in the dust and bloodstains, but I was too blinded by tears and sorrow to tell who was ahead.

I nodded, willing to clutch desperately to any belief that would undo what I'd just done.

"She had to die, Edie. This is her change. If you think about it, you were the only one she could trust to do it," he went on.

"Not even you?"

"Oh, no. Especially not me. I'm inherently untrustworthy." He stood up again. "Jorgen," he said, and whistled, and the Hound trotted over. "Go tell the others we're on our way." Jorgen disappeared down the stairs. "You're strong enough to carry her, aren't you?" Dren asked. "There might be a few left. I'd rather be free to fight."

I nodded again. She hadn't turned into dust, and we weren't leaving her behind. Those things were good, right?

Oh, please, baby, please.

I swiped a bloodstained piece of hair away from my face, making an even bigger mess of things. "What about them?" I asked, leaning forward to pick Anna up.

"Not our problem. We need to be on the road by dawn."

I looked back. Gemellus was still my concern. As much as I wanted to leave him, I didn't dare set him free. And he had gotten me this far.

"Raven will either die here or be punished in other ways. There's blood in the water now, and Los Angeles isn't a very deep pool. Besides, if we're not here, then Gemellus can start giving Raven commands—if he is who he claims to be."

No time to ask Dren what he meant by that now, but it gave me an idea—along with Anna's limp body pressing the contents of my pockets against my thighs. I'd been through so much in the past week. I didn't go through all this not to be free.

I carefully put Anna back down on the floor and turned to the scene behind us. "I command you to uninvoke him," I demanded, not knowing if it would work.

Gemellus seemed to momentarily have the upper hand. He tried to finish Raven off, and Raven only barely managed to push him back in time.

"You can't kill him. I change my mind, I forbid it. So uninvoke him now."

"It doesn't work like that," Dren began.

"It does now."

Gemellus shoved Raven back. "I forsake your rights and you are mine again to command."

"But I invoke!" Raven shouted, trapped, wildly looking for someone to help him.

"Tell him to be still. Tell him he can't move, or say a thing."

Gemellus looked at me, breathing heavy. "Revenge on him should be mine."

"I know, and it will be. But I need something from him first. Tell him to stick his arm out."

Gemellus reached out and punched Raven before commanding him. "Stick out your arm."

"And clench your fist," I said.

"You heard her," Gemellus threatened.

Dren looked torn between guarding Anna's body and coming over to see what we were up to. "Edie, what the hell are you doing? Dawn comes—"

"Dawn's always coming. She's quite the whore," Gemellus said with a grin. "Do as you're told." Raven, as trapped as I had been, obeyed.

Gemellus stepped away, and there was that pull between Raven and me again. If he'd ordered me, I would have had to listen. I could read what he wanted me to do in his eyes, how he begged. But my hands were covered in blood, and that made it easy to look away.

I tore needles out of packages and thought about missing, and a hundred more painful places to poke him than his arm sprang to my mind, but I concentrated on the task at hand. Blood flowed up into the butterfly needle's hub, and I shoved a test tube onto the tubing's free end. Raven's blood twirled down the tubing like it was a straw, then filled the vacuum of the test tube.

I'd grabbed six test tubes earlier, and now I filled them all. Blood was power—hopefully if I ever needed it, these would be enough.

Gemellus chuckled darkly as he returned, realizing what was going on. "I thought you wanted to go back to human."

"I do. But I also never want to have to rely on anyone else," I said, still not meeting Raven's eyes.

"If you drink that without him, you'll be a rogue without a House."

"That's fine."

"Edie—" Dren said, encouraging us to hurry up. I disengaged the needle, letting the last drops flow into the final test tube. Not even a pint. I wasn't sure what good they'd do me, but I'd rather have them from a vampire who was going to be dead soon than one who was still alive. I looked over at Gemellus. He'd retrieved the silver-bladed knife.

"I assume you're done with this?" he asked, turning

it in his hand to offer the hilt back to me. His tone and his gesture were sarcastic.

"Very done." I slid the last slightly warm tube into my pocket. "Kill him fast. We'll be waiting outside." I ran for Anna and picked her up.

CHAPTER THIRTY-SEVEN

Dren made a growling sound as I threaded the stairs holding Anna behind him. "No one likes rogues."

"Do you have a Master?" He didn't seem like the type who did. And he snorted, but he didn't answer me.

Purgatory was covered in dust, which, oddly, matched the décor. We were halfway down the stairs to Hell when it felt like I'd just been kicked in the chest by a donkey. "Whoa—" I stumbled down a stair, and Dren whirled to catch me. The squeezing feeling in my chest didn't stop.

"That's what it feels like when your Master dies."

I didn't ask him how he knew. I put my back against the wall and breathed—my heart was beating wildly, and I didn't know if it was in freedom or in fear.

"Can you continue?" he asked.

I waited another moment, to see if another attack would hit me. When it didn't I nodded. "Yeah. Just stay near."

Hell looked like it. Whereas before, Raven's club version of Hell had been cheesy pointed-tail devils and flames, the version we walked out into looked like it'd come from another dimension. There were holes punched in walls, support columns were diagonal, the bar looked like someone had taken a bite out of it, and the stench from broken liquor bottles was strong.

Jorgen was waiting for us there, eager to lead us outside. We went together into the entry hall. I'd never gotten to see what was past the Catacombs's front door.

"Wait—" If I'd felt Raven dying—

Gemellus thundered down the stairs after us, triumphant. Dren's eyes narrowed.

"He's coming with us," I said.

"So I feared," Dren said drily.

Gemellus pulled up. "Do you want to know if I killed him with or without honor, first?"

"No. It's just that we didn't bring any extra boxes to carry freeloaders back home in."

"He's not a freeloader. He's the only reason I lived this long—he killed at least twenty newborns by himself before you all arrived."

Dren's mood changed, ever so slightly, in Gemellus's favor, and Gemellus looked to me, burdened with Anna. "Would you like me to carry her for you?"

I pulled back. "No." She was mine. With her in my arms, I stepped outside.

It was damp out, and the air tasted like wet cement, as it sometimes does in cities when it's humid but not quite enough to rain. The asphalt was covered in a thin layer of sweat, just like I was.

"Rain," Dren said, and started cursing loudly.

There was one black trailer truck, the only vehicle in

the street, and it was parked in front of the Catacombs, engine idling. A female daytimer I didn't recognize hopped out of the back of it.

"Don't worry about it—it's dry inside, and I've got the whole thing rigged to blow. There's enough dust in there to take this whole block into the ground." Then she blinked and looked at me, and Anna, and then turned back to Dren. "You let her die?" Her voice arched, and I thought she might slap him.

"Keep your voice down. Vish—may I introduce you to the Beastkiller, also known as Edie. For what it's worth, Anna went willingly. I suspect she knew."

The daytimer named Vish gawked at me. "You killed her. Why?"

My mouth opened like a gasping fish. Because I'd been commanded? Because I'd desperately wanted to save my child?

"There'll be time for stories later—we need to get on the road," Dren said.

She kept staring at me, but picked up a radio at her waist. "Containment unit, we're loading up."

Dren gestured into the belly of the truck that Vish had just dropped from. "The boxes are in there. Hers is the central one."

"Thanks."

Despite being a daytimer, I couldn't leap up into the back of a truck while holding Anna gracefully. Gemellus did it first, and then reached down to help me.

There were three boxes end-to-end. They looked like human-sized oil drums, made out of sturdy metal with overlapping seals—and I could see that they locked from the inside.

I set Anna down inside hers carefully, arranging her as I had Lars not that long ago. And, like number sixty-four, she looked like a sleeping fairy-tale princess, if you ignored the blood. Had she really known what she was doing all along? I hoped one of us had.

I closed the lid, and found Gemellus frowning. He looked horrified at the idea of going back into any sort of confinement. "Where will you sleep?"

"Not in one of those things. On the ground here is fine."

"I should warn you it won't be safe." Dren mounted up in the back. "If we get run off the road and crash, you could be exposed to light."

Gemellus nodded. "Better that than to sleep in a cell again."

"Try to at least fight a few of them off before you fry." Dren walked over and ratcheted the lid on Anna's box down with ties. She'd be secure but not trapped—once she woke up, she'd be able to break through canvas ties with no problem.

"You think we'll be attacked?"

"The greatest killer of our kind is helplessly dead for three days until she becomes reborn. You tell me." He hopped into the foremost box and started to lie down. I reached for the lid before he could close it.

"Will we at least have a head start?"

He looked to the woman whom I assumed was his daytimer, and she shrugged. "Depends. Were there any survivors? Did anyone escape? Did they have cell phones?"

"I'm not sure. I was a little busy." I didn't know what had happened to Jackson—if he'd been killed by someone else, or gotten free. And Natasha—and the Shadows—shit. "What did you all do with bystanders?"

"We did our best to minimalize casualties," Dren said, growing irritated with me. I wouldn't let go of his lid, so Vish stepped in.

"This block is industrialized. Mostly we just kept homeless people from sleeping in their stoops—and we'll blow the building before anyone else can get in in the morning. I'm going to get on that." She turned and strode toward the back of the truck.

"Wait!" I ran after her.

"For what? You have someone else you need to kill?" she asked, sounding peeved.

"No—just wait. Please." Anna hadn't come all this way for Dren to let me die now. I hopped off the truck and went back to the Catacombs's doors. The building was dark now, the power down.

"Shadows!" They'd said they were fast—and if everything inside was truly dark—"Shadows! We're leaving! Get up here now!"

I crouched, listening, one hand out into the darkness on the floor. Feeling nothing, I started snapping my fingers. Despite the fact that they would have gladly left me behind—and some of them had, taking their chances with Celine—I'd made a promise.

"Hurry it up, Shadows!" I shouted, hearing the words echo, and feeling the weight of all the wounded building above me as it creaked. I didn't dare run back downstairs for them now.

"We're hurrying!"

A chill took my hand, as if I were shaking hands with Death, and then the Shadows forced their way inside to hide against my palm. "We're here!" they said, muffled. "When she stopped being dead we tried to kill her too. We think we only made her mad."

"Who?" Then I heard a sound like a raging bull from the depths of the hall.

"Oh, no—" I spun and ran out of the building like it was already on fire.

I leapt into the back of the truck where Dren's box lid was already closed, and I beat on it like a drum. Gemellus lay down in the corner like a life-sized statue, closing his eyes. "Dren—there's one vampire left—"

"Old, or new?" he asked without opening up.

"New—but she's important. We have to kill her—"

"She'll go when the building does—" Vish said.

"She's smarter than that." What was it Jackson had told me about earthquakes? The vampires would survive and just crawl through the rubble until they extracted themselves? Even if her lab wasn't intact anymore, if she was—

"We're running out of time—" Vish pulled me away as Dren opened his own lid.

"We can kill her later," he said. "That's the nice thing about vampires, we keep coming back."

"But—" What if Natasha went underground with what she knew? And built her own army up?

"The sun for her will be just like the sun for us. We have bigger things to worry about—unless she can hurt us in the next three days, we need to go." Dren closed the lid of his box again with a resounding thud.

"The containment unit's packed and ready to roll," said a voice over the radio on Vish's hip.

"Is she alive?" asked a familiar voice on the radio.

"Asher?"

Vish jerked her chin up at me. "Do you want to stay back here all day or not?"

"No." I wanted to see the sun. I didn't want to be in the dark ever again in my life.

"Then go get in the containment unit's cabin. He's waiting for you there."

I went to run out, then thought better of it and reached for Gemellus. He'd tucked the silver knife into his belt. I didn't want to use it, but I put it into one of the pockets of my pants and ran for the back of the truck bed, my hand still clenched around the Shadows.

CHAPTER THIRTY-EIGHT

Dren was right: The sun was on its way. A second truck was idling right behind ours now, the cab so high I couldn't see in. Vish closed the back of the first truck up behind me with herself inside. I wondered what Gemellus would think of being guarded by a woman come dusk.

I jumped for the door of the second truck, found it locked, and beat at it with my free hand. "Let me in!"

The cabin door didn't open—but one behind it, to the trailer, did. Four daytimers I didn't know stood inside, all armed to the teeth.

"Gonna light it up, let's go let's go let's go—" came Vish's voice on the radio from all of their shoulders—and a familiar arm reached out of the pack and grabbed me.

"Edie." Asher pulled me inside as the door slammed shut and the truck we were in was rolling. He squeezed all the air out of me, and there were no words between us, just the physicality of making sure that someone else you loved and thought lost was not a ghost.

"I'm just going to assume all that blood is someone else's," he whispered hoarsely.

"Mostly." I pulled back, breathing hard. I'd only left him a week ago but I could read the passage of that time around his eyes. My exploits were aging my shapeshifter.

"I know you can survive anything you put your mind to, but—" he pulled me to him again and kissed my forehead and stroked his fingers through my hair, catching on all the tangles and scabs.

There was the sound of a very large explosion from behind us. It rattled the truck and I could hear crashing glass—and then came a second softer sound, that of the Catacombs collapsing, tons of concrete and lumber falling into the caverns beneath.

All that mattered to me was that it was behind us, and that I was here, safe with Asher again. "I made it." I wasn't okay, but I was here. It counted for now.

"So you killed that other girl for nothing, eh?" one of the daytimers I didn't know asked Asher. I felt him stiffen under my arms. Old Edie didn't generally approve of killing people, and Asher knew that. New Edie couldn't throw any stones.

"She was wearing your necklace," Asher explained, pulling my chain out of his pocket. Celine.

"When you were supposed to be holding the line," the other daytimer pressed.

"The line was fine." Asher held me roughly. "I needed to know. I saw her racing by with your necklace on and I thought the worst—"

"It's all right." I didn't need to hear the blow-by-blow. No one would be crying for Celine, least of all me.

The female daytimer leaned in to give me a smile. "I wish I had a man that willing to throw down for me. It was stupid—but sort of sexy, in a murderous way."

"Thanks, I think," I said. She put her hand out.

"Lilah," she said.

I couldn't shake her hand because I was still holding a thimbleful of Shadows. I inhaled to explain this, when they decided to speak.

"Did you kill them too?" Their voices were high and small.

Asher frowned, and the other daytimers stared.

"Shadows," I explained. "Long story. Some of them were with Celine, the necklace-lady. The rest stayed with me."

"Not that I know of," Asher told my hand.

The Shadows didn't respond again. The door between the RV-like living quarters we were crowding and the driver's cabin was open. We were headed west, away from the sun, but it was almost light everywhere now.

"Holy fuck," said the driver. I recognized him, Mr. Galeman. He'd once been a patient of mine.

"What?" Lilah started forward, gun in hand.

He pointed at his sideview mirror. She ducked in, and I could see her disbelieving expression reflected in the windshield. "What the hell is that thing?"

I had a feeling I knew who it was.

CHAPTER THIRTY-NINE

"Kill it," Lilah commanded.

Two of the other daytimers started pulling a panel off the ceiling of the cabin. Asher started pulling me back into the rest of the trailer. It was half living quarters for daytimers during the day; two boxes with unknown occupants were strapped down in back.

"This isn't your fight anymore, Edie."

"No—I need to see." I had to know. The second ladders were pulled down and the daytimers mounted them, I smashed the Shadows to my chest and felt them dive underneath my left breast, chill against my heart. Then I squeezed in beside the daytimers, grabbing hold of the roof to pull myself up.

Racing up the street behind us was something utterly unreal.

"What is it?"

I grabbed someone else's binoculars to look. "It's Natasha."

She was five times the size she'd been when I saw her last—she must have dosed herself hard, hoping to wake up in time to help Raven fight, but instead the vampire cells had made a monster out of her. She looked like a mutant, bigger in all directions, bubbled with tumors and dotted with spots of ash from where the fabric she'd found to cover herself with hadn't done a good enough job and light had seeped in. I'd seen vampires manage to be awake during the day. They just didn't function as well—but Natasha didn't need to be functioning to kill us, charging down the street at us like a pissed-off water buffalo.

I turned toward the daytimer nearest me. "You have to kill her. And make sure she's dead. All the way."

"With pleasure," he said, setting a sniper rifle into a mount on the roof. It locked into place and he aimed as carefully as he could and shot at her. It looked like he hit her head, but she didn't stop.

"More," I encouraged him.

"It's daylight," he muttered, re-aiming. I knew what he meant—the vampires weren't up to divert attention from us. If anyone saw us out on a highway doing this, we'd be pulled over by cops and the coffins would be broken into for sure.

He shot again. This time, it looked like it hit her chest. Still nothing. She was gaining.

"Use silver!" I shouted.

He spared a dark look at me. We were in a caravan of vampires. Of course no silver weapons were allowed—except for the one in my pocket.

With a giant leap forward, Natasha grabbed hold of the back of the truck, making the entire trailer shake. Asher pulled me down as the frequency of the gun reports increased.

"I'm not losing you again—and I'm not letting you

go anywhere unarmed." He pressed a gun at me. I had never shot a gun before—but I could see myself doing it as I felt Natasha come closer, hearing her weight thunk against the trailer's ceiling as she came for us. The daytimer didn't care about being seen anymore, it was life or death—gunshots echoed through the cabin and hot casings flew out and ricocheted down. Asher pushed me behind him, toward the cabin, to where we could both sight out the window.

A ballooned hand swatted the gun away, tearing it free from its mounting, as the daytimer dropped inside, barely missing decapitation. "Shoot, shoot!"

Guns rang out in the small space and the hand yanked back.

"Did we get it?" Lilah asked.

"Do you want to go up and find out?" another daytimer asked.

"Natasha!" I shouted up. "Natasha, you felt him die, didn't you?"

There was no sound except the whistling of the air as the truck picked up speed. I could only pray that the trailer was high enough that no one else could see Natasha clinging to the top of it.

"I was there! He thought you'd died—he was distraught—he told me to tell you something!" I shouted at the top of my lungs. "I'll tell you what it is. Just let me come up."

The noises on the top of the trailer ceased, and all the daytimers looked at me.

"Edie, no," Asher said.

I looked back at him. We weren't the only ones who knew what being in love was like.

I hauled myself up before he could stop me.

Natasha was crouched there, panting with the effort of staying awake. Her face wasn't her own; it was too small for her head, hiding behind a curtain of bangs. She looked like she'd had too many steroids and then been hit with radiation like the Hulk. Half of her skin was sloughing away, blisters forming and breaking open with tiny puffs of ash. I realized she'd doped herself so hard that she was healing almost as fast as she burned. Her cells had, for a brief moment in time, actually made her immortal. She'd become the cancer that she once feared.

My hand was over my pocket with the silver knife, like I was a gunslinger—but I had something I wanted to tell her first.

"He said if I ever saw you alive again to tell you that he loved you. And he wished everything had gone differently. You were the only thing that ever mattered to him, and all he wanted in this world was to protect you."

Natasha hunched forward—I thought, to come for me. If she did, she was so close, there was no point in running; she'd catch me before I fell back down the hole. But her whole body was racked by sobs, and the blisters of skin were rising and popping more frequently, like miniature volcanoes, leaving a smoke trail in the wind.

The exhaustion, the sorrow, the bloodlust, and too much vampire blood—everything swirled, and she set a mighty hand down. Her charm bracelet was cutting into it like a string through dough.

"I'm so sorry, Natasha. He's gone, and there will never be anyone like him again."

She threw her arms back and her head up and faced the sun. It eroded her faster as the wind of our speed blew her hair back. And she made a mournful sound. I recognized it for what it was, the sound of true love lost.

The sunlight, now that it had its teeth in her, wouldn't let go. She was disintegrating before my very eyes. She sobbed and she howled and then she lowered her voice and spoke with her misshapen jaw.

"Tell my dad I love him," she said.

"I will," I lied. And the sun finished her off. She exploded into a cloud of dust. Her charm bracelet fell onto the roof of the trailer as the scraps of her clothing did, and I watched it bounce once then fall, glittering to the asphalt below.

I fell to my knees and felt a profound sense of sadness at the waste of her life. Then I crawled back up to the opening of the trailer, and looked down at four separate guns. The daytimers there moved back, let me in, and resealed the hatch.

"What did you say to her?" Lilah asked as my feet touched the ground.

"What any fourteen-year-old girl wants to hear."

"How did you know?" she pressed.

"Because I was one, once." I refastened the button over my pocket with the knife. Like Dren had said, silver would be our secret for now. Same for my six test tubes of Raven's blood.

I'd tell Asher when we were alone, but no one else here needed to know. Raven had said that he'd had spies on Anna, and I knew all I wanted to know about

House Grey. No guarantees these other people here were safe.

But for the moment, I was. And Asher was—and our baby. I'd done it.

"Beastkiller indeed," said the man who'd been manning the sniper rifle.

"Any casualties?" asked Vish on the radio.

"No. We're fine," Mr. Galeman answered.

I put a hand across my stomach—and Asher's met me there. I looked up at him, and he was furious, but he shook his head instead of fighting with me. "I knew what I was getting into when I started dating you."

He held my necklace up, a question on his face. He had taken it off Celine, which was a little disgusting, but it'd been mine before she'd stolen it—and I wanted it to be mine again. I turned inside his arms and he knotted the chain at the back of my neck.

"Good," Vish responded. "Keep your wits about you. It isn't over yet."

I realized what she meant. Just because Natasha was finished didn't mean others wouldn't try. And attacks would be much more likely in daylight, when our trusty team of vampires was asleep—what with us having the added hassle of keeping away from humans who didn't know what was going on, and the law. Port Cavell was at least two days away, driving straight through—and Anna would be dead for one day after that.

Plenty of time on the road for anyone with a grudge to start a fight. Or a war.

The shorter chain on the necklace made the stone hit at the V of my throat. I had Asher's strong hands around me still—and now I was strong, too. I knew what I was capable of. I didn't have to like it, but I was still alive, and so were the people I loved—and hopefully Anna was going to come back to life.

I wasn't going to let anyone or anything change that. No matter what.